MIGNON G. EBERHART is unexcelled in America as a writer of books which are at once mystery stories and superb novels of character. And in this book, more than in any other she has yet written, she has produced an exciting and baffling story in a full-bodied novel of undeniable literary merit.

DANGER IN THE DARK is the story of Daphne Haviland—a girl who fled from a prenuptial party given in her honor to keep a tryst with a former lover—a girl who fled from a man she didn't love, but was going to marry, to a final meeting with a man she loved but was never going to see again— a girl who ran through the wind and snow to meet love and found murder.

The strange events that followed Daphne's discovery of her fiancé's body move with mounting excitement and at a rapid pace to an astounding climax.

Sinister brilliance has always marked the work of Mignon G. Eberhart. She has the macabre quality of a Poe, yet through her terror-filled pages move warm, living people, caught up in a thrilling web of murder. Now, in DANGER IN THE DARK, she has written a masterpiece of crime and detection and a truly great story in its plot, its setting and its characters.

DANGER
IN THE DARK

Mignon G. Eberhart

DANGER
IN THE DARK

Doubleday, Doran & Company, Inc.
Garden City, New York   1937

PRINTED AT THE *Country Life Press*, GARDEN CITY, N. Y., U. S. A.

DANGER
IN THE DARK

CHAPTER 1

THE day before the wedding Dennis Haviland
returned.

No one expected him. The letter, written in
Amelia's spidery handwriting, in which she made
brief and rather bitter mention of the wedding, was
gathering dust in an unclaimed-letters file in the
Buenos Aires post office. He knew nothing of the
wedding until he landed in New York, bought a
Chicago *Tribune* and looked at it—hungrily, after
his year's absence, and hunting for familiar names.

He found them in plenty.

But it was the picture he saw first.

It looked out of the page straight at him. Daphne
in a fashionably simple tailored suit, with a hat below which her eyes were level and remote. She wore
gloves, so he couldn't see the huge sapphire on her
left hand, and a sable skin crossed softly under her
uplifted chin. And she didn't look at all like Daphne.

He stopped abruptly, letting people jostle past
him.

No, it wasn't like Daphne. Of course, it was a
posed photograph, made for that purpose. And she
looked very handsome, very poised, and a little un-

friendly. There was no hint of gaiety in her eyes, no faint tremor of a smile about her closed lips. Her chin was lifted a little, the fine bones of her face a bit more clearly defined than he remembered. Fine bones, he thought absently; family, though she isn't really a Haviland. Good God, how like Amelia that sounded! And it was queer how a man could think in two layers; one on the top of his mind, superficial and articulate—one deep down and wordless.

It was her mouth that looked natural and like Daphne, and that was all. It was so—so resolute. That was it. He could remember her in her childhood, holding her mouth just in that unsmiling, resolute line when she was determined to undertake some feat of derring-do which the boys—himself and Rowley—had themselves accomplished, boastfully and with swaggers. She was younger than they, and they teased her and ordered her about, but they were proud of her, too.

A baggage truck trundled by; a porter shouted, and somebody jostled his elbow, said, "What the hell, did you rent this space?" and Dennis looked up, lifted his slender, peaked black eyebrows and moved good-naturedly to one side and returned to the paper.

It was then that he read the paragraph below the picture.

It was a brief paragraph. It said that Daphne Haviland was being married the next day. At Miss Amelia Haviland's place in St Germain. The immediate family and a few of their closest friends would be present. Rowley Shore was to be best man. The immediate family were Mrs Archie Shore, her son, Rowley Haviland Shore and Miss Amelia Haviland; John Haviland would give his daughter in marriage. And she was to be married to Benjamin Brewer.

That was as far as Dennis read.

There were some additional notes. A Bermuda honeymoon, an apartment at a good address; a reference to the late Rowley Haviland, the bride's grandfather, and to the fact that Benjamin Brewer was president of the Haviland Bridge Company; a mention of schools, clubs, the Haviland name—all of it words that were like threads making a background. Dennis, however, saw nothing of it, for he was hailing his porter.

He took the eleven-o'clock plane for Chicago.

Later, when the weather was important, he remembered that trip above and through opaque gray-white clouds, the glimpses of snow-covered hills and ribbons of black that were paved roads; the lights of Gary twinkling through the curtain of falling snow, and the red blast furnaces. Somewhere below there were the Haviland furnaces. The Haviland plant where steel was made for Haviland girders and Haviland rails and sent out over the world.

He thought of it briefly: the Haviland Bridge Company. Once a small business: owned and controlled by one man. Now a great steel-fabricating company whose products went all over the world. In Shanghai, in Rio, in Cape Town, he had seen that well-known, poignantly familiar mark: "The Haviland Bridge Company." They had built, long ago, only bridges; small jobs with old Rowley Haviland himself acting as construction superintendent. He wasn't old then, and he was a great engineer and a great opportunist. The small jobs leaped to big jobs. It was a period of expansion and building, and the Haviland Bridge Company grew overnight. And in 1914 it became actually the Haviland Steel Company, although it was incorporated as the Haviland Bridge Company and the name was never changed. Steel was needed: steel was needed perhaps more than anything else in a war-mad world. So Rowley Haviland made his own steel: made it and sold it: undertook and delivered huge contracts. By the time the war was over he had established a great steel-fabricating company and had founded a private fortune for himself and his family.

Had, in fact, not only accumulated a private fortune but had provided—thoughtfully, after long and anxious consideration—for its preservation. His entire fortune was invested in the bridge company, and he willed all that stock, justly and fairly, to his children, with the exception of various small cash bequests. And he provided, as fully as he was able to do, for the future and safety of the company.

Or, at any rate, felt he had done so.

A phrase from the famous will floated into Dennis' memory: ". . . with the knowledge that in case of future . . ." *Need,* was it, that came next? *Economic pressure?* The exact wording of it escaped him, but the intent was clear enough. In case of future need the Haviland Bridge Company (and thus the Haviland fortune) was amply provided for and safeguarded. Well founded. Well provisioned.

The self-satisfaction, the more than tinge of complacence about it, was justified.

It was a great, far-reaching business.

But it seemed to Dennis just then as unreal, as remote as that changing red glow of furnaces had been. For Daphne's picture came before him again, and he could think of nothing else.

The plane circled into the wind and dropped downward into lights which streamed sharply into the early December twilight. Later, too, he remembered the cold, wet air on his face as he stepped from the plane. But at the time he kept thinking of the look about Daphne's mouth.

A lot would depend, of course, upon Daphne. But he could tell when he saw her. He was sure of that.

He reached St Germain an hour later, and since there was no one to meet him, walked through the snow in the chill, purple twilight, with thickets of firs and shrubs black and still along the road. He knew every foot of the way. Away below as he turned was the river; frozen over and white with the new snow. How often they'd skated there; Daphne with her cheeks as red as her cap and her eyes like stars. And Rowley and he. Here was the corner of the high limestone wall.

Yes, a lot would depend upon Daphne.

He turned into the winding drive. As the lights from the low, sprawled bulk that was the house began to glimmer through the bare trees, he had his first qualm. After all, it took something to face down the combined resistance of the Havilands.

He paused, staring through the heavy dusk at those lights. In the pause a light car suddenly turned from the public road into the drive, and as its bright lights fell upon him he moved out of its path. It chugged briskly past him; it was the station truck, laden with his own luggage and with a multitude of packages and boxes which loomed up dimly above him. Packages and boxes that had to do with the wedding, he supposed.

Daphne's wedding.

It would take some thinking over, this thing he was going to do. But he was going to do it. There was no other possible way.

He turned aside from the drive and plunged upward on a little path through shrubs that raked and stung his face. He looked at that moment remarkably like ruthless old Rowley Haviland—nose and chin jutting out and eyes that seemed to withdraw and consider, under the sweep of those black eyebrows. At the end of the path was the little old springhouse, hideous in the daytime for its fancy peaked roof and its encircling windows of many-colored glass, in the twilight a black shape that again, and in the top of his mind, aroused memories of childhood.

It was unlocked; it was cold and dark and musty inside, but there was a bench and a place to sit. He lit a match or two, discovered an old steamer chair and sat down and lighted a cigarette.

It would take some thinking.

Calm and deliberate thinking, as he hadn't been able to do in the plane. He must make no mistakes;

it must be swift and certain and well planned, not impulsive.

He turned his coat collar up and pulled his hat lower, and in the little recurrent glow from his cigarette his brown face looked lean and grim.

The cigarette spent itself in ashes and a small charred end, and he lighted another. But he made the greatest mistake when, because it pressed against the chair and thus rather sharply into his ribs, he took a small, cold steel thing from his pocket and sat there turning it absently in his hands, watching the reflections of the tiny red circle which was his cigarette.

Almost exactly six hours later, Daphne Haviland let herself quietly out the front door of the dark and silent house and paused for an instant on the step. It was very dark and snowing again and very still. It was cold, too, and she pulled the collar of the fur coat she'd hastily flung around her up about her ears, and the coat itself tighter around her body. She thought vaguely that she ought to have changed; she hadn't realized it was snowing again or that it was so cold. She hadn't, in fact, thought of anything but the thing she had to do. Gold kid slippers and the thinnest of hose and a yellow velvet train. How still it was, she thought suddenly. How very black except for the faintly luminous look of the snow nearest her.

Dennis would be waiting. Had been waiting, probably, for some time.

She listened and tried to look about her. But the

snow struck against her face and made a moving, obscuring veil, and she could see nothing beyond it.

Well, she knew the path to the springhouse.

She went on down the steps, conscious of the coldness of the snow through those thin gold slippers. But the snow wasn't heavy on the drive; it had been cleaned late that evening. Where was the path? Gradually black firs and shrubs began to show themselves dimly. She still heard no sound, and the driveway was fairly open.

She found the path, a shadowy break in that veil of snow-laden firs, and turned upward into it. It was steep in places, and the snow was heavier there, and she slipped a time or two; again she thought vaguely of her yellow velvet train. It was a Jacques gown, one of her trousseau, and the snow would stain it forever; she wondered if, when all of that terrifically complete trousseau was worn out, used up, gone and out of her sight, the pain in her heart would be gone, too.

Well, that was hysterical.

And it was no good letting herself go, when she still had to tell Dennis. Tell him that those mad moments in his arms, there in the hot little library, were truly mad. Tell him it was too late. Tell him that, after all, there was no escape.

Tell him that, in only a few hours now, she was to be Ben Brewer's wife.

Snow clung to her eyelashes and mingled with tears, but she was not crying. She wished Dennis had not come home; she wished the events of those six crowded hours had never taken place. Her heart was sore already with the memory of them.

It had been difficult enough before he came back. And she hadn't known until that short, ugly interview with Ben after dinner how she hated the man whose wife she was so soon to be.

She caught herself again as she slipped, catching hold of a branch of some shrub, which shook little showers of snow on her cold bare hands. Around this turn——

She stopped abruptly, panting a little, to listen. It had sounded very like a movement—a footstep, or someone brushing against shrubs somewhere near her. Dennis?

But there was no further sound, and the darkness in the little path was deep.

It was confusing, too—it and the snow against her face—and she reached the springhouse before she expected to. It loomed only a little darker than the surrounding gloom, only half visible through the obscuring, bewildering veils of snow.

Contrary to her expectations Dennis was not waiting for her. And after she'd waited a moment or two and her breathing, quickened by that climb along the twisting, difficult path, quieted and with it her pulses, she thought of entering the springhouse. It would afford shelter from the snow, and she was very cold.

She heard no movement at all now anywhere about her in that confusing darkness. If Dennis had been on the path or anywhere near, she was sure she would have heard.

She turned toward the door of the springhouse—fumbling a little for it, finding suddenly the latch.

She was faintly surprised to find the door was slightly ajar. She pushed it farther open; it was damp and cold and musty inside and very dark. But it would be dry. She entered.

Built before the days of electricity, and in the days when there had been great faith in the physical benefits derived from artesian wells and sun rays falling through stained glass, the place had never been wired for lights. But she knew every inch of it and had, upon entering, no sense of unfamiliarity.

Except that it began to seem, as she waited, listening for Dennis, very dark. And very still.

But why not? Besides, a heavy night fall of snow has its own peculiar silence—a silence that holds secret motion. Dennis should come soon.

She was very cold, and her slippers were damp with snow.

No sense in getting pneumonia, plus a broken heart. A broken heart—odd how apt some of those silly phrases were. It was exactly the way it felt—as if something very deep and vital had been shattered —and the shattering of it hurt. Terribly.

Someone was in the springhouse.

The thought leaped suddenly and unexpectedly into her mind and was oddly sharp and clear, as if someone had spoken it.

Someone—but there was no one. It was completely dark—utterly still. If anyone in that small dark space had so much as breathed, she would have heard it. No one was there.

No one was there. It was cold and dark and empty and—and, queerly, there was a rose.

She rejected the thought at once and with it the small fragrance that seemed to creep out of the darkness around her.

Her thoughts shifted back again to the dinner just past. The bridal dinner. Herself in the handsome yellow gown, sitting beside Ben, conscious of his heavy presence, his possessive look, and once his hand on her own beneath the lace cloth. Of the candles, wavering so that the whole overheated room, the long table, the flash of silver and crystal, the faces began to seem unreal and nightmarish. So that only Dennis' brown, lean face watching her from the end of the table, over that lake of crimson roses, with the candles wavering between, was real.

Those roses—it was as if one were there, too, in the chill, unfathomable darkness surrounding her so closely.

Following her—accusing her. That was fanciful, too; hysterical. She must be cool and very convincing. She must make Dennis understand.

But there was certainly someone in the spring-house.

Again the sharp, queer conviction thrust its way into her thoughts. Made itself keen and predominant, so that, quite suddenly, she was uneasy and listening. It was as if the tangible, instinctive knowledge of a presence near her persisted so strongly that at last it forced her to recognize it.

She moved uneasily, trying to search the darkness

around her. She said a little unevenly, "Is—is anyone here?"

No one answered, of course. There could be no
one there.

But somewhere in the darkness there was certainly a rose.

Well, there was nothing about a rose to frighten
anyone. Nothing wrong in that still, familiar little
springhouse.

But it wasn't familiar. Not any more. And there
was something, somewhere that was wrong.

It was strange and dark and—she was fumbling
into the blackness for the open door when she heard
Dennis on the path.

Heard him, and immediately he came, a dark, tall
figure in the gloom, carrying something—oh, his
bag, of course; his face above her became a white,
faintly discernible oval, and he cried, "Daphne!"
and entered the springhouse, pushing the door wide.

"Dennis—I——"

"What's wrong?"

"There's—someone here, Dennis."

"Someone—— Nonsense, Daphne."

But he had a flashlight, and suddenly there was a
diffuse circle of light which glimmered against an
opposite window and darted to the floor.

Darted to the floor and jerked, and Dennis said,
"God!"

Daphne didn't scream. She didn't move or speak.
She knew though that Dennis was kneeling beside
the black huddle on the floor, and his body shielded
her for a moment from that sight.

Then he was standing again. And Daphne still didn't move or speak.

She knew that Dennis had turned to her, she knew he was about to say something. But he didn't say it, because all at once there were sounds outside and someone else at the door, and it was Rowley. Rowley who blinked in the sudden light, looked at them, looked at the floor, started to say something which sounded like "What are you——" and then just mumbled and stopped, as if hands had clutched his throat.

Then he, too, was down beside that huddle, looking grotesquely thin and tall in the evening clothes he still wore. He said in a strangled way, "It's Ben," and rose.

"It—it's Ben," he said again into that immense silence. "He's—dead, isn't he?"

No one replied. They stood there, looking at the thing at their feet.

CHAPTER 2

THE flashlight in Dennis' hand made a bright fan of light which touched the tips of Daphne's wet gold slippers and centered on the crumpled, gleaming white patch which was a shirt front. In the shadow above the fan of light each could see the others' faces, white and strange. Rowley had left the door open a few inches, so there was a slit of blackness behind him through which cold and snow sifted. Daphne was trembling violently. Dennis shot a swift glance at her over the flashlight and said:

"Shut the door, Rowley."

Still without taking his eyes from the thing at their feet, Rowley put out his hand and closed the door. Then he knelt again beside the sodden hump of blackness. In the middle of that white, shining shirt front was a spreading red patch. Neither Daphne nor Dennis moved or seemed to breathe as Rowley's thin hands hovered above it, somehow avoiding the wet redness while he searched for a heartbeat. Rowley wore no topcoat and no hat, and his black hair was like a tight satin cap outlining his narrow head; his sallow, sharply aquiline face was pasty white. He groped along a thick outflung arm,

14

pushed up the white edge of a cuff and hunted on that strong wrist for a pulse.

Dennis suddenly shifted the flashlight so it centered now upon the face of the thing at their feet. Its eyes were half open. At the edge of the light lay a large, red rosebud, a little withered now, with its petals showing a purple tinge. A rose from the bridal dinner.

Daphne felt herself swaying. Dennis noted it and said sharply, "There's a chair over there." But she couldn't move and, indeed, did not hear it, for Rowley was rising.

He dusted his knees and looked at Dennis.

"Well, there's nothing we can do for him."

"A—doctor——" Daphne thought she was speaking aloud, but the words came out in a stifled whisper.

"No use," said Rowley. "He's dead. Why did you kill him, Dennis?"

Dennis started to speak and stopped, with a suddenly rigid look about his mouth. He did not look at Rowley but still, fixedly, at the dead man. His brown face was less brown in that light, his eyes dark and shining. He still wore evening clothes, too, but he had on a topcoat and had had a hat. It was somewhere in the shadows behind him. It and—*and the bag*. Rowley would see the bag, thought Daphne, only half aware of the thought. He would inquire about it—or make his own conclusion. But it didn't matter now. It didn't matter because Ben Brewer was dead.

It was only then that she comprehended the thing

Rowley had said. Ben Brewer was dead—and Rowley had said, "Why did you kill him, Dennis?"

But Ben couldn't be dead. Not in that short time —not anyone so strong. Not anyone with so furious and powerful a hold on life and on things. And on people. Not Ben. She must have made some sound, for Dennis said, "Take the flash, Rowley" and handed it to him and put his arm around Daphne.

"You'd better sit down over here. Don't look at it. We'll get you back into the house in a moment."

She let Dennis put her in a chair and wrap his coat around her, tucking it under her slippered feet to keep them from the cold dampness of the cement floor.

"Now don't look at him. Don't think." He put his hand under her chin and turned her face up so he could look compellingly into her eyes.

"We'll fix things somehow. Don't—don't go to pieces, darling."

"Dennis!"

He bent over her, taking her wholly into his arms and putting his cheeks against hers.

"Daphne, Daphne, trust me."

"She's all right," said Rowley. "She's got more guts than either of us. Why did you kill him, Dennis?"

"He didn't!" cried Daphne. "He didn't! He was— here. Ben—like that." The first moment of shocked stillness that was like a dreadful kind of paralysis had passed, and she was beginning to feel again. She made herself look at the well—at the colored glass, dim and gray now, in the window that faced her.

They'd had stories about every window in the little springhouse when they were children. She and Dennis and Rowley. And the springhouse itself had assumed many roles. Swiss Family Robinson's home in the trees. A beleaguered castle—herself alternately the maiden in distress and the army to be ordered about by the two generals. There, just before her, was the concrete shelf around the spring, and the corner against which Dennis had fallen the day he and Rowley had climbed to the little ledge that ran around the conelike roof of the tiny house. The scar was still there probably, hidden by his dark hair. And now they were there again—she and Dennis and Rowley. Only this time it was no game.

She forced herself to stop trembling; Dennis' coat over her own fur coat was warm, and she could hold herself steadier. But she wouldn't look at Ben—Ben Brewer. It couldn't be Ben Brewer—she was going to marry him the next day—that day, for it was after midnight. It couldn't be Ben Brewer.

"I didn't kill Ben," Dennis was saying coolly. He fumbled in his pocket and took out cigarettes. "Cigarette? Daphne?"

Rowley had matches. He wasn't as calm as he'd pretended, for his hand was unsteady when he held a light for Daphne.

It gave them a moment of recovery.

Rowley said through smoke, "I suppose we could cover him—but there's nothing here. Yes, he's dead all right. Not a chance to do anything for him. If you didn't kill him, Dennis, who——"

He was going to believe Dennis, then. Rowley

was sometimes curiously like his mother in disposition, though so unlike her in looks, slow to perceive and convince, tenacious about inquiries.

"I don't know who killed him," said Dennis. "We found him like this." He was quicker than Rowley always; and Daphne could tell by a kind of certainty in his voice that he had made up his mind about something. If he had hesitated before, it had been due to perplexity or to the shock of the thing.

"God!" said Rowley suddenly. "He looks awful. I can't—old Ben——" He took a long breath of smoke, exhaled slowly and said again in a collected way, "We've got to do something about it. We—— What do you mean, you found him like this?"

"Just that. Daphne and I found him here. Like that. Just before you came. We hadn't had time to call anyone—had just realized that he was dead when we heard your steps on the path and——"

She looked away from the window and at Rowley, and she saw the question coming.

"How did you happen to be here?"

Dennis, too, had seen the question coming. Would he tell Rowley?

"We had a crazy notion for a walk in the snow. Sort of a farewell—you know. Daph getting married tomorrow—leaving, all that. A sentimental journey. Isn't that right, Daphne?"

It was a demand. What? Agree, of course. She said quickly, "Yes—yes."

He went on, "We thought we'd take a look at the springhouse—scene of old times. We came to the

door, and it was open. We came in and"—he didn't
look now at the thing at his feet, but it was as if all
of them were staring fixedly at it—"and there he
was. Just like that. I had this flashlight and——"
He put his cigarette to his mouth; it made a bright
little glow of crimson, and he went on, "He was
dead. I felt for a pulse. Wasn't any. Then you
came."

"Oh," said Rowley slowly, watching Dennis.

Dennis exhaled smoke and added, "We hadn't
got over the shock of it. We were stunned. I don't
think we'd even said anything."

Rowley turned the flashlight suddenly so it swept
in glancing rays about the springhouse, the eight
colored windows, garish and old-fashioned in day-
light, dull and meaningless at night; the peaked roof,
the bench running around it; the spring at one side
edged in concrete, with a wooden railing and, now,
frozen. There were a few cobwebs from the previous summer; several steamer chairs folded flat. A
damp cement floor. Obviously no one was concealed
there.

"No one here?" he said.

"No one. And we didn't hear the shot. It must
have occurred before we left the house."

Dennis' voice was less strained. He was relieved
because Rowley had accepted that explanation. Had
Rowley failed to see the bag? She turned to look
for it, and it wasn't there. Where was it? He had
had it in his hand—he'd left it outside, then. Had
dropped it at the door of the springhouse. Instinc-

tively she felt that Rowley must not know of it; must not be permitted to see it. Instinctively, and because of Dennis' swift, false explanation of their presence there and his unspoken demand that she subscribe to it.

Later she wondered what they would have done had there been more time. More time to comprehend it, to realize that Ben Brewer was dead and what that death would mean. Rowley had come too soon.

"Where's the weapon?" said Rowley suddenly. "He's been shot, I suppose—no knife could make a wound like that."

"I don't know. I tell you we found him just like this."

"There's no gun anywhere. Unless it's under him."

There was a small silence. Then Dennis said in a flat voice, "We'd better look, I suppose."

"Yes." Rowley cleared his throat. "If it's suicide——"

They looked, and there was no gun. No knife. Nothing but that purplish rosebud.

"He could have tossed the gun outside in the snow," said Dennis.

"With a wound like that?"

"No, I suppose not. Well, we'd better call somebody. Rouse the house—get doctors, police. God, what a mess!"

Quite suddenly Daphne could see headlines: Dead Following Bridal Dinner. Benjamin Brewer, president of Haviland Bridge Company . . . The account of the wedding had already gone to the papers; a photograph of herself in her wedding gown and the veil that hung, ready, in her room. Horrible. Could they stop that account of it? she wondered crazily.

"But, good God," said Rowley suddenly, "he couldn't be murdered. There's no one who would murder him. I mean, he—— Well, after all. Murder," said Rowley and stopped abruptly, so the word hung there in the chill silence of the little spring-house and echoed against its walls and seemed to pick itself up and repeat itself, whispering, in the shadows above their heads. Murder. Murder of a man. Murder of Ben Brewer. Murder and a black sodden bulk lay at their feet which had been—two hours, an hour, a few moments ago, perhaps—a man.

Daphne was trembling. Curious how gradual was the comprehension of anything so ugly—you saw the thing and recognized it but were not altogether conscious of it. Of all its significance. You grasped at this or that coherent thought, but everything was distorted. Murder there—where they'd played those years ago.

She stood suddenly. Dennis' coat fell with a muffled little thud to the floor. She said unsteadily, looking from Dennis to Rowley and back again:

"It can't be murder. There's no one to kill him. No one who—— It must be suicide. There's no one but the family here—Aunt Amelia—your mother, Rowley. My father. We three. It isn't murder."

Again the word was left in the silence, hovering, repeating itself.

Then Dennis said slowly:

"Look here, Daph. This is going to be bad either way. I mean—I mean, with the wedding tomorrow. There 'll be an awful lot of publicity—talk—whether it's murder or suicide or——"

"Good God," said Rowley suddenly and violently again, "it can't be suicide—we're forgetting——" Again he stopped and stared at that bulk on the floor as if mesmerized by it, lost in some dark speculation.

"You mean Ben's suicide the night before his marriage to me," said Daphne. "You mean it would be—would be——"

That was horrible, too. That was incredible, really, in its potential ugliness. Newspapers, stories, talk—whispers at last, to follow her all her life. Suicide—the night before he was to be married to her. The questions: Why did he do it? Why?

Dennis' hand was on her arm.

"Don't look like that, honey. We'll fix it. We'll——"

"Hell," said Rowley, "I wasn't thinking of Daph. It's the company. The business. Oh, my God!"

He tossed his cigarette into the little hollow around the frozen spring and turned vehemently toward them.

"We'll have to—to do something. Murder's bad. But suicide is worse—it 'll wreck things. Everybody knows about the famous will. Everybody knows about the rows; stockholders are all onto it and watching and scary. Some siding with him, some with us—oh, you know what it's been. Well, you don't, Dennis, because you've been away all year. But it's been hell for everybody concerned. Now if he is a suicide they'll say it's on account of business."

"That might let Daph out, anyway," said Dennis slowly.

Rowley gave him a quick, dark look.

"Let Daph out, yes—only there 'll still be plenty of talk. But it ruins us all financially. Wrecks the business as surely as a—a bomb." He looked again at the thing there on the floor and added, with a kind of thin anger, "I never liked Ben Brewer. I don't give a good goddam what really happened to him. Johnny thought he was smart, but I could never see it. Mother figures he was going to ruin us anyway, given time. But no matter what other people say there's just one explanation the stockholders will jump at, and that's failure. Ben was first and foremost a business man, and they know it. The Haviland Bridge Company will vanish like a—a—— Anyway, it's murder," he said conclusively. "No weapon."

"So you'd prefer murder to suicide," said Dennis, watching his cousin. "I suppose you have an idea about what murder brings with it? Inquiry, publicity, all of us grilled mercilessly, the worst possible motives attributed to everything we admit, and at the last somebody——"

Rowley glanced at him sharply and said, "Somebody a scapegoat, you mean?"

"I mean if he's murdered somebody did it," said Dennis. "That's not a pleasant thought, either."

Rowley's sallow face looked faintly green.

"Give me another cigarette, Dennis."

If only it weren't so cold, thought Daphne; it was partly the cold that made her shiver so. She wrapped her coat more tightly around her. Below it the yellow folds of velvet dragged upon the floor.

"But—but we ought to do something," she said. "We—— There's no use in standing here talking of it—I mean, well, it's nothing we can change. We can't make it suicide—or—or murder or anything. No matter how much we talk of it we can't make it any different."

"Here's a light," said Rowley and held it for Dennis' cigarette. The little point of light wavered, and above it Dennis and Rowley looked at each other—a brief look, understanding.

Daphne recognized it.

"You can't——" she cried again jerkily. "There's no way—you can't change it, hide it—make it any different. There's no use in talking like this as if we could. He's dead. He—he's there. We've got to do something about it." Her voice was high and unsteady, and Dennis said quickly:

"Now, Daphne—don't, dear. Look—I'm going to take you to the house. Then Rowley and I will decide——"

"You can't decide anything. It's done. He's dead. Nothing that you say will make any difference. Call the—the police."

"Yes, yes, we'll do all that. But give us a little time. After all, there are ways and ways—I mean, well, we ought to—to prepare the family. Perhaps we can figure some way out of it. That is, some way which won't be so bad for us all. Rowley's quite right about the business, Daphne. I've known something of what this year since Grandfather's death has been. I know how nervous the stockholders have been with this grand quarrel going on in our midst. After all, we can't exactly toss away the family fortune. Our only source of income. The thing Grandad spent his life building up."

"I wonder," said Rowley in a whisper, as if he did not want to hear his own voice making the monstrous proposal, "if we couldn't just dispose of him somewhere. After all—if there's no body, there's neither murder nor suicide."

"*No. No!*" cried Daphne with sharp terror and vehemence. But Rowley and Dennis were both looking again at that black heap. The red had spread further on the gleaming white shirt front—or had it? And the three of them were in that springhouse again together, plotting—wrangling—but this time it wasn't a game. It was truth and terror and death. Murder.

For, of course, it *was* murder. Otherwise there would have been a weapon. Murder—and someone had murdered him.

And there would be no wedding tomorrow.

There would be, instead, police, inquiry, unspeakable and hideous things through which they would be dragged.

Why were you in the springhouse? they would say. Oh, to meet Dennis Haviland. Why?

It was a suddenly lucid thought springing out of all that chaos of disaster.

It was the first time that, consciously, she saw their danger.

With a start she realized that Dennis was speaking. Speaking very thoughtfully and in a whisper, too.

"It might be done," he said, looking downward.

CHAPTER 3

A<small>ND</small> in that packed moment of sheer horror Daphne considered it, too.

It would mean that Ben Brewer would simply disappear. There would be questions, comment, inquiry—perhaps they would say he'd been called away—he'd gone on a trip. And then didn't come back. Perhaps they could fix up some explanation for it.

Dennis was resourceful and quick; Rowley slow but ingenious. Together they plotted well. They always had. And they always had made her agree; agree and even defend them later to the aunts. For in those days she could always stand up to the aunts, because they knew her father would side with Daphne; too indulgent, they called him—too fond of her because of her likeness to her young, dead mother. She felt a swift, frightened conviction that they were drawing her with them into a dark and hideous path; as if they were making her plan, too, how it could be done. She had always been helpless against their combined strength; they had always managed to win her over in the end. They were going to do so now.

Oh, it was fantastic—nightmarish—impossible.

But there was that mute and awful presence in the springhouse.

And Dennis and Rowley were going to do something with it. She knew it; she could tell by the way they looked at each other.

But she wouldn't be drawn into it; not only that, she wouldn't let them do it. After all, such a thing demanded secrecy, and she would tell the truth. She would tell her father and the aunts what really happened. And she would tell the police.

They were men now, Rowley and Dennis. And she a woman. Those childhood days were long past. This old springhouse was just an outdated and outmoded heap of wood and concrete and glass. Its feeling of continuity, of the immutability of time, had no truth and value. It belonged to the time of a slim little girl with yellow pigtails and wide blue eyes. It belonged to two boys—one of them brown and hard and unafraid; the other one a little sallow and thin and, always, prudent.

And those children were far away and distant. Lost.

In their places were three adults with the same names but with thoughts and motives and secret lives of their own. Drawn together again in that place by murder—sharing that horrible dilemma, shocked and terrified by the thing Rowley had suggested. Hideously impressed by the doubtful solution it offered. But it was wrong: it was gruesomely askew.

No, she wouldn't be drawn into it. And she wouldn't let them do it.

"I'm going to cover him," said Rowley abruptly. "I can't stand looking at him and—and thinking about it. He's—so damn big. Where's your coat, Dennis?"

He turned toward the open steamer chair where Daphne had sat, but Dennis said something quickly and forestalled him and himself took up the coat and fumbled with it for a moment and then placed it across Ben Brewer's body. It was a relief. A fold of the coat covered the flashlight for an instant before Rowley stooped and pulled it out with a quick, nervous gesture so there was again a fan of garish, diffuse light spreading upon them, leaving the springhouse half in light and half in shadow.

"So long as nobody sees this light," said Dennis. "The windows must be visible through the trees, and there's nothing but windows."

"Everybody's gone to bed hours ago," said Rowley. "Anyway, it's snowing so hard that no one can see——"

"But you saw, Rowley; you saw the light. Didn't you?"

"Yes, I—that is—— Don't look at me like that, Dennis."

"Rowley, why did you come here? What were you doing?"

It didn't sound like Dennis. And all at once it was as if the door had blown silently open and a chill, strange draft were whispering about them. Rowley was ghastly pale in the half-light. He glanced from Dennis to Daphne nervously and said quickly:

"I—I wasn't sleeping. I happened to look down—my window's on this side—and saw the light——"

"You're lying, Rowley. I know your tone when you lie. Besides there wasn't time. You couldn't have seen this light and dressed and come down through the house——"

"I was already dressed. I tell you, I couldn't sleep, and I hadn't——"

"Hadn't tried very hard, had you?"

"Don't take that tone, Dennis. I didn't kill him."

"Do you know who did?"

"No. No, I tell you. Oh, good God, Dennis, if we start quarreling——"

"Why did you come down here? You'd better explain, Rowley."

"I came because I saw the light. I—I was downstairs already. I happened to look out a window. Saw a—gleam of light through the trees and came up to see what it was."

Dennis' brown hand reached for the flash and snapped out the light.

"You are still lying," he said, his voice hard and cold in the black void that instantly surrounded them. "Did you see anybody anywhere?"

"No. Nobody," cried Rowley thinly. "Turn that thing on again, Dennis. It—it's bad enough in here without—— Turn it on, I say. Look, you can put it under something. Hide it a little. But we can't stay here in the dark with—with—— And we can't move it—decide what to do——"

He was moving, taking a cautious step or two along the concrete floor. It was pitch dark and terri-

bly still. So still they could hear each other's breathing and those cautious, sliding steps. He was trying
to reach the flashlight in Dennis' hand. Dennis said:

"It's all right. I'll fix it so we can see. I'll—fix
it——" Curious how voices rebounded in the darkness, against those eight walls. It sounded as if Dennis were speaking from somewhere near the door,
quite the opposite direction from which he stood.
Rowley was moving—no, Dennis was moving.

"Dennis," said Rowley's voice sharply out of the
blackness, "what are you doing?"

"Nothing." This time there was no rebound of his
voice, and almost instantly the light was turned on
again, only now it was under something, so only a thin
ray showed.

"I put my hat over it," said Dennis. He didn't
question Rowley further, but stood there looking
thoughtfully downward.

"I'm going to the house," said Daphne. "I'm going to call the police."

It was as if she had not spoken.

For Rowley and Dennis continued to stare at that
long hump under the coat, both of them lost in
thought. The thin light brightly illumined a patch of
damp cement floor and a fold of Dennis' coat which
did not quite cover an outstretched hand, so the tips
of the fingers showed—thick and powerful-looking
even then, with broad, handsomely manicured nails.
Again Daphne felt a sick wave of incredulity. And
again she remembered that hand on her own for a
hot, still moment at dinner—touching her fingers
under the lace cloth, reminding her that in only a few

hours she would be his wife. Herself only half hearing the things Ben said, because she was looking and trying not to look at Dennis beyond that expanse of lace and silver and Amelia's best Coalport; and in spite of herself she had caught his eyes and had known somehow that he knew. Instantly and sharply she had pulled her hand away, and Ben had turned and given her a long, watchful look. Ben always saw everything; and he was always wary, always guarded. *How, then, had he been murdered?*

"He's so damn big," said Rowley again out of the gloom above that small patch of light. He spoke with a touch of peevish resentment, as if blaming Ben.

Dennis was a tall black shadow beside her. Except for the patch of light on the floor, the springhouse was in almost complete darkness; she could see the blacker shadows of the two men—the dim white patches of their shirt fronts and the paler ovals of their faces. It added to the nightmarish aspect of things, yet at the same time gave it a kind of truth and poignancy, as if it permitted the fact of murder to stand there, too, beside them in the shadow.

She pulled her coat more tightly about her. Through her thin slippers she could feel the damp chill of the floor. It was so horribly cold and still— with the snow blowing against the door behind Rowley so that it trembled and sighed as if it wished to open itself. Or as if something outside in that snow-muffled blackness were trying to push itself against the door.

"Yes, he's big," said Dennis. "He—— Odd I

never thought of how difficult it would be to—to get away with a body. I mean, it's sort of imperishable, isn't it? Of course, there's the river." He spoke in a low voice, tentatively.

Rowley's voice was hushed and tentative, too.

"I thought of that, too. It's frozen. But we could —break some ice. It would soon freeze over again."

"And be covered by the snow. It's lucky it's snowing. Otherwise there 'd not be a chance. Our footprints would show. But with the river——"

"Oh, stop, stop!" cried Daphne in a choked way. "You must not——"

"The trouble with the river," went on Dennis without looking at her, "is that sometime the body will come up again. Soon as it thaws. I think they could tell even then from the wound and state of— of *it*—what happened. It would only put off the inquiry. But the river, of course, would be the——" He stopped, as if to arrange words, and finished: "The easiest way."

"Dennis, Rowley!" cried Daphne, flinging out her hands violently toward them into the twilight. "You are both mad."

Rowley was shaken, too; she could see the tremor of his cigarette as he held it to his lips. There was a tremor in his voice, too. He said, "Yes, it would be easiest. In fact, I——" He stopped, and Dennis said:

"Yes, I know. I couldn't, either."

Daphne cried in short, jerky whispers, "I can't stand it. You are both mad to think of such a thing. You can't seriously consider it. Don't you realize that it's impossible? That we've got to face this—tell

everybody the truth about it? You can't possibly do
anything else. Please, Dennis." Her hands were on
his arm now, feeling the smooth texture of broadcloth, finding his hand. It clasped her own, but he
said nothing. "Dennis, I can't let you. It is too dreadful. Too—— Why, it's dangerous, too! Don't you
see how dangerous it is?"

"Not as dangerous," said Dennis in a stiff, remote
voice—"not as dangerous as—as some other things,
Daphne."

She was beginning to sob now—with terror and
with shock; with a horrible nostalgia for things to be
as they had been before she had opened that springhouse door and had plunged upon disaster.

Rowley stirred impatiently.

"Oh, for God's sake, Daph, you'll have the whole
house out here. All you have to do is keep still about
what really happened. I mean—I mean about his
being here. Dennis and I will see to the rest. We'll
plan it so no one ever knows. I—— Look here, Daph,
we've got to do this. You don't realize how things
are with the company. You don't understand what
Ben's murder or suicide would mean just now. Dennis does. You don't know, and you are going to wreck
us all for a whim——"

"Whim!" cried Daphne in furious, choked repudiation.

"Yes, whim. If it would help Ben, or bring him
back to life, or anything, it would be different. But
he's dead. There's not one thing we can do for him.
If he were here he would be the first to——" He
checked himself, suddenly aware of the ugly aptness

of his words, and Dennis took Daphne's cold hands.

"He's right, Daphne, dear," he said. "I'm going to take you to the house. It 'll take just a moment or two, Rowley. I'll be back."

He put his arm around Daphne's waist, turning her toward the door.

"No, no!" she cried again. "Don't you care for— for truth and justice and——"

"I care for something else very much more," said Dennis grimly and opened the door. Snow struck lightly upon their faces. Rowley spoke beside them, and his voice was thin and frightened:

"I say, Dennis—you *will* be back, I suppose? It wouldn't be a good idea, you know, simply to call the police and let them find me—with it."

"Good God, Rowley," said Dennis, "you can think of the damnedest things!"

"I'll stay in the doorway," said Rowley, unperturbed. "If anybody comes but you, I get out."

"That's like Rowley," said Dennis, leading Daphne around snow-laden shrubs. "Look out— here's a step somewhere here. He would suspect his own mother—and as to that, I can't say I blame him. He'll be in a state of jitters by the time I get back. Still he was cooler about the whole thing than I would have thought Rowley could be."

It was dark in that chaos of snow and blackness and cold, but still there was a faint luminousness about it, and white shapes loomed out here and there. It was good to feel the clean snow on her face. Fresh air to breathe. Back there . . .

Yet somehow, strangely, there was a quality of

furtiveness in their cautious steps. Of flight, of
escape.

She fell to shivering again, violently.

"Dennis—who killed him?"

"I don't know, Daphne. I don't know."

"Why?"

"Why was he killed?" He considered it, guiding
her down that slippery little path and below the thick,
crowding shadows of the firs through snow that went
between the straps of her slippers and was icy and
cold around her silk ankles. "How can I tell?" he
said finally, wearily. "Wait here a second." They
waited, listening. There was no sound at all. The
snow muffled the sound of their steps as they emerged
cautiously from the path onto the driveway, with the
black shadow of the house ahead and its many unseen windows.

"Walk lightly," Dennis whispered so close to her
ear she could feel his lips and his warm breath.

And the caution roused her suddenly to a new and
disquieting thought, and that was the thought of immediate, unseen danger. Danger because murder had
walked in that night of blackness and of swirling
snow that muffled all sounds and made them secret.
And murder has its own secret terror.

The firs were thick along the drive, and there were
tall clumps of shrubs all about—any of them tall
enough and thick enough to conceal a man. And if
the snow muffled her light footsteps and Dennis', it
would also muffle another's footsteps.

They reached the deeper shadow of the entrance.
Directly above was the great window, dark now and

almost invisible, which commanded a view of the entrance. There were steps, and Dennis' hand was on the cold latch of the door. Her face was wet with snow: all around them were those flying, bewildered veils.

"Where's your key, Daph?" he whispered.

It was a wrench to go back to that time when she had left that door.

"Key? But I had no key, Dennis. I unlocked the door. It's a night latch. The door is heavy, you know. Push harder."

He pushed harder. Swore and worked the latch. Turned finally and put his hand on her shoulder with a queerly desperate grip.

"You must have the key, Daph. You must have it. Good God, I've got to get you back into the house. You don't understand—you are so stunned by this that you haven't had—all along while Rowley and I were talking—the faintest notion of the things we are, all of us, going to be plunged into. Daph—oh, my darling, you must have the key."

But she hadn't it.

And the door was locked now and would not open.

CHAPTER 4

It was Dennis who found the open window. A drawing-room window it was; one that was actually one of the two french windows, reaching to the floor. The altar for the wedding was to be there; before the windows ferns and tall jars of chrysanthemums were already arranged. The pungent odor of the flowers crept through the well of darkness beyond the open window.

"It was unlatched," whispered Dennis. "Florists forgot it, I suppose. In you go, Daph—wait!"

In the cold darkness he took her suddenly in his arms.

"My dear, I love you so," he said. "Somehow, someway we'll come through it all right. Don't forget that." He kissed her, too—not as he had kissed her earlier that night in the hot little library, while that table laden with wedding presents winked and glistened and made an accusing witness, but soberly, gravely. "Go to your room at once," he said. "You'll be all right. Try to sleep—if you have any sleeping powder, take it. I'll manage to see you before anybody comes to question you. Don't wait, Daph—for the love of God, do as I say."

She was inside, out of the snow, and Dennis on the outside was carefully, very cautiously closing the window again. He was gone suddenly into the snow, so she could no longer see the dim outline of his figure.

But he had to go back to Rowley, of course. Rowley waiting beside that in the springhouse.

Don't try to think—don't stand here in the darkness, listening. There is danger in waiting; danger in thinking.

"Go to your room," Dennis had said, "at once."

She groped in the darkness. Something brushed her hand lightly and seemed to move away and returned. A fern—one of the flowers—she was standing in the little alcove made by the french windows; after dinner they'd all gone into the drawing room to look at the flowers. How were they arranged? She couldn't remember the arrangement, for she'd been thinking of that mad scene with Dennis. Of the thing she was to say to Ben. And they had insisted on her coming with them to look at the floral arrangement; three weary-looking men in wrinkled white smocks, boxes and burlap-wrapped ferns and green raffia trailing around. Gertrude in the middle of it in her ruby velvet with her pale eyes glittering. Amelia talking to Ben about the huge white chrysanthemums. Ben . . .

No one had thought of this—of murder.

And she mustn't think of it now. This was to have been the altar—where she was to stand in her white satin gown.

She groped among the flowers, which swayed into blackness, and she had to remind herself that they

were really ferns and great white chrysanthemums.
Good, she was through them now; only their scent
remained in the thick, moveless blackness. Opposite
the improvised altar was a sort of aisle through small
gilt chairs which were already arranged in ranks
across the wide room. "Family and intimate friends
were present . . ." She touched the smooth round
back of a chair and, fumbling a little, found the aisle.
That was simple, to go from one chair to another
directly to the door. And the door opened easily, with
only the faintest creak of its old hinges.

There was, as usual at night, no light in the hall,
but once there she was more certain. Nothing had
been changed there, no furniture moved aside and
rearranged for the wedding. She crossed it, her feet
making furtive little taps on the thin old rugs, her
yellow gown swishing, whispering a little along the
floor. In spite of the familiarity and certainty she
felt, she became confused in crossing that blank space
of complete blackness and brought up against the
newel post unexpectedly. Her whole body seemed to
leap, and her heart rocked her with its beating. But
it was only the newel post. Now up those narrow old
stairs and along the hall. Dennis had told her to go
to her room at once.

It was a goal; vaguely she felt that when she
reached it and turned on the lights something would
shift and things would become natural and real again.

It was the first time she had thought of turning on
lights; but light would be dangerous; better not.

The banister was smooth and cool to her touch;
she clutched her skirt in her other hand, pulling it

high over her wet, silk ankles so she would not trip.
She knew the house as she knew her own small hand.
She knew that stairway and the creak on the third
step from the bottom. The small, stealthy creak of
weight on the dry old step.

She avoided it, not quite sure she'd counted the
steps right, relieved when the next step and the next
did not, either of them, utter that small sharp rasp,
clear and distinct in the midnight silence of the hall.

That step and the next; she was near the top really
when the third step creaked.

Creaked once and stopped.

Even her heart stopped beating to listen. It was
the step near the bottom of the stairs, the third step.
No doubt about that; she knew it too well.

But there was no further sound from the cavernous blackness below her. Ceilings were high in the
old house; the stairway beautiful and old but very
narrow. So narrow two people could barely pass
upon it.

Two people!

It was Dennis!

She was so certain of it, and the certainty came
with such a rush of relief, that she turned and
clutched the banister and whispered into the darkness below:

"Dennis—Dennis. Here I am."

He did not answer.

"Dennis——" she started to whisper again and
stopped.

For it was not Dennis.

It was as if something inside her had screamed it.

She turned blindly in the darkness and ran up those remaining steps, found the wall, turned, running along that hall whose every twist and turn she knew so well, clutching her skirt, following the wall with a groping hand—so narrow it was that anywhere along it, if the doors were closed, she could have touched wall with both hands. She found her own door; always her room since she was a child. She flung herself inside it; found the lock and the heavy old key and turned it and reached for the light switch.

She gasped for breath and leaned against the door and blinked in the sudden light that spread over the little, bright room with its chintz and brass fenders and old mahogany.

The first thing she saw was her wedding veil—a white cloud of net with an old rose-point border, hanging there from the chandelier. Ghostly. Accusing, as if she had killed Ben Brewer. As if she had been the cause of his death.

"I can't let you marry him," Dennis had said. "You are never to be his wife."

But he hadn't meant *that*.

He hadn't meant murder. But the thought of it added a last touch of horror and despair. She stumbled to the chaise longue and sat there before the dead fire, her face in her hands, her coat dragging from her shoulders, stained yellow folds of velvet around her wet, gold slippers.

There were in the house, that cold winter night of December ninth when Benjamin Brewer was murdered, only members of the family. They had

assembled for the wedding, and in spite of its pre-
tensions and the aroma of tradition and wide-flung
connections with which the Havilands had managed
to surround themselves it was not, now, a large family. And it was one in which a curious little pattern
seemed to repeat itself but did not in actuality. For
Dennis, brought up under Amelia's care though he
had been, was actually the son of a distant cousin.
Daphne was the daughter of Johnny Haviland's
young wife, and very like her, everyone said. Of the
three Haviland children—children that is, of old
Rowley Haviland dead, now, a year—Gertrude was
the one who had given old Rowley a grandson. She
had promptly named her son Rowley and had even,
after her divorce, considered dropping her married
name, which was Shore. But she was a conventional
woman and did not like resorting to her maiden name,
with the complication, always having to be explained,
she thought, of a son growing up. Besides, if she re-
sumed the name of Haviland it would put her on an
equal footing again with Amelia, who had never
married. So she called herself Mrs Haviland Shore
and strove to forget the brief advent of Archibald
Shore who had been definitely a mistake—which in
itself rather astonished Gertrude, for she felt she
had inherited something of her father's acumen and
force, and he did not make mistakes.

Also she kept a separate residence, living in the
ugly, massive house on Bench Street near the lake
and the Loop and coming to Amelia's house in St
Germain only for holidays. But she spoke of her
house as the Family Residence and Amelia's house

as the Country Place—where Amelia said, neatly
and definitely, "my house" and "your house." And
she'd felt that the family residence was the place for
any family event of importance such as a wedding.

But Amelia had felt so, too, about her own house
and had won in the little conflict. Mainly because, in
the first days after that engagement had been an-
nounced, Gertrude had declared that, wedding or no
wedding, Ben Brewer would never darken her doors,
and she was obliged to stick to it even when the marriage became, as it was from the first, inevitable.

So Amelia won, and Gertrude assuaged her feelings by recalling the already well-known and oft-
referred-to fact that old Rowley Haviland had died
in her house. It had been a definite feather in her cap.
It was due actually to the fact that he was stricken
suddenly one day of cerebral thrombosis and there
was time only to be rushed from the Loop office to
her home in Bench Street, where he died, speaking
no word and looking to the last remarkably able and
fierce. But still he did die there and was buried from
there.

And after the funeral the famous will was read.
That, too, in Gertrude's house, and obscurely Amelia
blamed her for it, as if, had the thing taken place in
her house, the will would have proved more suitable.

But still in effect there was an odd mother-son,
father-daughter, mother-son pattern. Gertrude Haviland Shore and her son, Rowley Shore. John Haviland and his stepdaughter, Daphne. Miss Amelia
Haviland and Dennis Haviland.

Not that Amelia was in any possible sense mothcrly. But she had in a remote, detached way done her duty by this son of a distant Haviland; had given him a home and cod-liver oil, schooling and dancing lessons and braces on his teeth, sundry effective disciplining. Had seen to it that Dennis had everything in the way of good schools, travel, and social background that Gertrude had given her own son.

From almost the first, too—after the death of that other Daphne—Daphne had been, but more remotely, in their charge. The aunts saw to clothes and dentists; and later, chaperoning. But after all, Daphne was a girl; the other two were boys. They brought them all up as cousins and Havilands. But Daphne would grow up and marry out of the family.

She would marry out of the family and, which was more important, out of any possible connection with the Haviland Bridge Company.

For this family had a center, a spring, a tenacious, sturdy core, and that was the business. The plant. The Haviland Bridge Company. They lived by it; it usurped their greatest and deepest interests; it was not only a source of income, it was a well of pride; and it was deeply personal, blood of their blood and bone of their bone.

It had been that from the first to old Rowley Haviland. He was domineering, shrewd, fiercely possessive as he grew older, and notional; he had had to incorporate, and he had hated that and had hated the men who invested money in Haviland Bridge stock, though he used them and the money they brought. He kept to the last the control of the thing in his own hands.

But he came to the end of his furious, engrossed career in perplexity. His daughters were not men. And his son, Johnny Haviland, was not the man, he felt, to undertake the management of the company. There had been rocky times in the not far distant past. There were more rocky times to come. Johnny had his uses and his values; there was no one who could keep the stockholders in good temper when dividends were low better than Johnny; nobody who could better soothe and manipulate a delicate situation. Johnny was handsome, charming, social—all those things had their uses, as Rowley Haviland knew. But he needed a man with force and drive and, when necessary, ruthlessness. He needed, too, he realized sadly, a man with brains.

So he looked about for such a man and found him. It was not easy—neither the decision nor the training and advice he had to give—for Rowley Haviland was jealous of his own power to the last. But his love for his company—the thing he had made through years of sweating labor and anxiety, sleepless nights, grueling days when he'd learned hard lessons of self-preservation—years of wariness, of selfishness, of grim and determined fighting for his own existence and devil take the hindmost—his love for the thing he'd built out of those years was greater than his hatred for the man who would eventually take his place. So he selected Benjamin Brewer, a man of about thirty-five; young enough to give the company years of vigor and usefulness, old enough to have business judgment and acumen. But then Ben Brewer had been born with all that, and it matured under Rowley Haviland's teaching. Force and drive and hardness; no sentiment when it cost you something; no wavering: Ben Brewer, said Rowley Haviland in his will, was to succeed him; was to have a block of stock which he had enabled the younger man to buy; was to manage the affairs of the Haviland Bridge Company with all the autocracy and power which old Rowley Haviland had possessed. For the stockholders' vote alone was not a majority. And while the blocks of stock which the old man left to his three children were in themselves a large share, still he left the stock with strings on it. They could not sell. They could not dispose of it. They could not borrow on it. They were to live on the income of that stock; they could will it as they pleased, although he preferred it to be kept, as it had always been, a family business. But he tried, so far as he could see, to guard against any rashness, any costly mistakes, any possible contingency which might endanger the fabric of the thing he had built. And since he could see very far the will was as tight and explicit as a will could be. There was no possible chance of breaking it. They had to accept it.

And with it, Ben Brewer.

It was a shock to Gertrude and Amelia. They were as fiercely jealous of possession as their father had been; and as jealous of the company. This outsider, this upstart, this stranger put in over their heads to manage the Haviland Bridge Company—to exercise, even, control over their own fortunes. It was an outrage; old Rowley Haviland had not been responsible when he died. No one should have permitted him to make, or have the power to make, so unfair a will.

So they fought it. Or, rather, tried to fight it. For their father had foreseen even that. And had made the provisions of the will so tight that no lawyer would undertake that fight. Their only possible argument, they were told, was to prove Ben Brewer incompetent, and this, in spite of the fact that they believed him incompetent, and believed that under his management the company would soon cease to exist, they had been unable to do. And it was true that things had not been going too well; that certain innovations had been not too successful. But still they had to accept Ben Brewer.

Gertrude seethed and talked. Amelia kept her thoughts, whatever they were, to herself and quietly put what money she could into annuities.

Johnny through it all took neither side, unless passively, by retaining his own position as a vice-president, he sided with Ben. All of them—Johnny, and Rowley Shore, and even Dennis—were engineers. It was a foregone conclusion. For there was the company. Johnny had long been a part of it. Rowley had an office and a title in the design department and was reasonably efficient. Dennis, more distantly related, and standing no chance of inheriting (unless from Amelia), would still have been given a place in the company if he had wanted it. He chose a three-year contract with a Russian firm; he emerged with a considerably deeper understanding of the exigencies of the profession he had chosen, a curious, reluctant love for it, and enough money to bring him home at the time of his grandfather's death. There was also in the famous will a five-thousand-dollar cash bequest to each of the three children, Daphne, Rowley and Dennis. Daphne bought Haviland Bridge shares with her money, scarcely conscious of the transaction. Rowley took his and said nothing. Dennis bought traveler's checks and went around the world.

Slight as the transaction was, it was Daphne's only definite connection with the company up till then.

It was only after Rowley Haviland died that the aunts began to perceive her possible importance in the close-knit scheme of their lives. Eight months after old Rowley Haviland died and the management of the Haviland Bridge Company passed out of his hard, ruthless old hands, Daphne became engaged to Benjamin Brewer.

And the wedding was to take place in Amelia's house.

It lay sprawled and rambling and old, on a hilltop just out of St Germain and overlooking the river. It was always an old house; it could never have had a youth. Amelia had managed to retain the charm of high ceilings and spacious drawing rooms belowstairs and such minor beauties—paneled old doors, small fireplaces, a handsome fanlight or two—as the house provided. There were many added wings and irregularities of structure; unexpected steps up or down; narrow passages and narrow stairs; floors that creaked and doors that hung unevenly. They needed the fireplaces, for in the winter cold drafts crept between window and door casings and found their way through the house. Amelia had also retained, but certainly without intending to, the spirit, the curious secret personality that an old house, much and long lived in, possessed. Especially a house with many closed rooms.

The servants lived in rooms over the rebuilt garage. Usually Amelia was alone at night in the house. She had a complicated system of locks and bolts and, during the years since Dennis had been away, preferred it that way and flouted Gertrude's protests. Her locks were efficient, she said.

Not a flea could get in—or out—of the house after she had locked up for the night. She often said it.

Daphne was thinking of that—dully, with dreadful, blank weariness, when Dennis came.

She heard the low tap of his fingers, and she knew it was Dennis and went to the door. His face was gray. Rowley was not with him.

He said, whispering:

"It's done, Daph. I've got to talk to you. Before the police come."

It was then three o'clock.

CHAPTER 5

He gave a quick look down the dark little passage and came into the room, closing the door.

"No one is about," he said in a half-whisper. "At least, the house is quiet—everybody's asleep. God, what a business!"

"What have you done, Dennis?"

"Everything's all right. At least, I think it is. We've fixed it to look all right." He hesitated. "I'd rather not tell you exactly how, in case—— Look here, Daph. We couldn't talk with Rowley there. I told him anything I could think of to explain our presence in the springhouse. Tell me now—what did happen?"

"Did Rowley find out why we were there?"

He shook his head. "No, I don't think so. I got the bag back to my room. Look here, Daph—how long had you been in the springhouse when I came?"

She began to tremble again, and he saw it.

"I've got to know, my dear. I can't do anything to help you unless I know."

"Yes. Yes." She sat down on the end of the chaise longue again, looking at the man opposite her but

seeing that dark twilight in the springhouse and a
black huddle on the floor.

He watched her for a moment, then sat down himself on the little green slipper chair near her and took
her hands in his own.

"It's like this, Daphne. We've only got a few moments—every second I stay here is a danger to you.
For anything that is done this night, anything at all
that anybody has seen or heard, will have tomorrow
a—oh, a horrible significance. But we've got to see
exactly where we stand. There'll be police, inquiry.
You don't know what it means. I want you to know
exactly what to say, to be prepared."

"Will they say I did it?"

He looked deeply into her eyes for a long moment.

"Not if I can help it," he said then. "You see, you
are bound to be one of the prime objects of police inquiry. If, that is, if—anything goes wrong. If they
aren't satisfied. You were to be married to him. You
didn't love him——"

"But no one knew."

He looked away at that, frowning.

"There'll be—well, listen, Daphne. When we
were in the library tonight—when I—when I had
you in my arms and was trying to make you promise
to go away with me—and I—I kissed you, remember?"

"Yes."

"Well—someone closed the door."

"*Dennis!*"

"Yes. I—I hated it, of course. But there was no
use telling you about it. I just saw the door move and

close. I had closed it myself before we began to talk. I didn't want anyone coming in, interrupting. I was —I was determined you were not to marry him. I would have killed him first."

"Yes, you said——" She stopped abruptly and caught her breath and cried in horror, "Dennis, you said that! You *said*——"

"Did I? I suppose so. Well, then that was overheard, too. And I'd just kissed you and said, 'We'll meet at the springhouse, then, at midnight or as soon as the house is quiet'—and I looked up and over your little head and the door was closing. Slowly and without a sound."

"*Who*——"

"I don't know. I don't know who it was or how long someone had been there. I didn't go to see, because I didn't think it mattered. I'd won. I was—I was dizzy with triumph. And with loving you, Daphne. All I could think of was that you were going away with me. You'd promised. I'd have you, in spite of them all." He dropped her hands and rose suddenly and walked to the little mantel and stood there looking down at her again.

"This is the thing, Daphne: Somebody knew about us. Knew I'd persuaded you to go away with me. The night before your wedding to Ben Brewer. Do you see? And to meet me at the springhouse. Now then, Ben is found murdered at the springhouse—murdered at the very time we were to meet. Murdered. Well, you see, Daphne?"

She nodded, too sunk in horror and—now—something like terror, to speak.

"So you see, falling in with Rowley's plan was the only thing to do. It offered escape—and besides, there was good sense in what he said. He's rotten selfish and remarkably cold-blooded." He paused, thinking of Rowley's cold-bloodedness. He, Dennis, could do a thing if he had to—but Rowley'd been so extraordinarily calm. He felt dimly that he had underrated this cousin of his. "Now then, my dear—won't you tell me what actually happened?"

"I didn't kill him," she whispered. "Oh no, Dennis—I didn't. I didn't want to marry him. I'd never wanted to, but I hadn't realized what it would be. Not till last night, when it was too late. But I didn't kill him. Oh, believe me!"

"Don't shake like that, honey." He started toward her as if to take her in his arms, checked himself abruptly, said, "Begin at the beginning, Daph. I mean when you left me there in the library tonight. After I'd won and you'd promised to leave with me. Tell me just what happened."

His dark eyes went swiftly to the clock on the mantel. It emphasized that unspoken, urgent need for haste—for swiftness; for something to be done before an approaching storm.

She was twisting her hands together, looking up at him with a face so white, so set in horror, that Dennis deliberately looked away from her again, making himself listen only, remembering that a life he loved with every breath he drew and every beat of his heart lay actually in his hands that night. Give me wisdom; show me how to save her; what to do—it was like an unuttered prayer; he fumbled for a cigarette, got

it out, remembered he'd better not smoke. So small a
thing as the scent of tobacco, floating along the corridor of the old house at that time of night, might betray them.

"First, I take it you told Ben you couldn't marry
him?" he said.

Daphne moistened her lips.

"Yes. That is, I—I tried to tell him. He wouldn't
listen."

"What did he say?"

"He said all brides felt like that. He—he
laughed." She tried to shut out that swift memory of
Ben's face, easy, smiling, flushed a little from the
formal parade of wines at dinner, confident of his
power. "I insisted, said I didn't—didn't love him—
that I was sorry——"

"What did he say to that?"

"He said he'd always known I didn't love him.
That it didn't matter, because he—he'd make me."

Dennis looked away from her again and thought,
The man is dead. No use wanting to kill a dead man,
because he's already dead. Crazy. He subdued that
hot, ugly anger and managed to say coolly enough
and quietly, remembering that they mustn't be heard
through the thin old door across the room:

"And then?"

Her voice was unsteady. Her eyes tragic and blue
as a midnight sky. And he daren't go and take her in
his arms and promise her to take care of her. To
love her. To . . .

"Then he—he held me so I couldn't move. He'd
had enough to drink, so he wasn't guarded and

watchful, as he usually was. And he told me that I'd
have to marry him. That I couldn't get out of it. He
knew it was you, Dennis. He—he always knew things.
That was why he had such—such strength, power."

"Did he threaten to get at me?"

"Only—only through me, Dennis. And I don't
know how. But he—he won after all. I could feel myself giving away—it was as if you were farther and
farther away from me. As if I could see your face
from—some place far distant. Too far to help me. I
knew I'd have to go through with the wedding. That
I was mad to promise you to go away. That I was
carried away—out of my head. That it couldn't really
be done. And then Ben said—he said very slowly, as
if he meant it, that I must never try in any way to
influence him when I was his wife. He said, 'I can
crush you all. And I will if I choose to do so.' "

She looked up at him, trying to make him understand, trying to control her voice as she told him,
mindful, through it all, of a pressing need for secrecy.
Not to be overheard.

"And then I knew I was caught again. That there
was no use trying to get away. That I must marry
him."

Dennis got out a cigarette again and was turning
it around and around with hands that shook. He
didn't dare look at her, and at that moment he hated
the dead man as he had never known he could hate
anything.

"That was what you came to the springhouse to
tell me," he said.

"Yes. I—I told myself I owed that to you. I

wanted to—to say good-by forever to you, Dennis."

"Now, then—you came directly to the spring-house?"

"Yes. I waited till the house was quiet. Then I slipped downstairs and out the front door. I turned the night latch, as I told you, so I could get into the house again."

"Did you see anybody on the way?"

"No. Not a soul. I was already outside when I realized that I'd not changed my slippers. But it was too late to go back, for I didn't want Ben to see me, and I——"

"You felt he would be watching?"

"I don't know, Dennis. I don't know. And I didn't see him or have any sense—then—of being followed. I was desperate. I was coming to see you for the last time. Perhaps he was there, perhaps he was watching and following me—I don't know."

"When you reached the springhouse what did you do?"

She shut her eyes, trying to remember exactly.

"I stood there for a moment and—and listened, I think. I wondered if you were already there. I couldn't see anything. Once I thought I heard you—a sort of motion off away from the path, though. As if something had brushed against the shrubs. No, that was when I was on the path. But it was nothing. It was snowing so hard, I thought I'd go into the springhouse——" It was horribly difficult. He knew it and said very gently, "Go on, my dear."

Her throat ached and hurt. She said, forcing out the words, "So I went into the springhouse. I couldn't

see anything at all: I didn't have any matches. I
didn't—didn't like it. It seemed—all at once—as if
something were there with me. And I kept smelling
a—a rose. That rose."

"Did you speak—move about?"

"I think I said, 'Is anyone here?' There wasn't any
sound, of course. It was just then that—you came,
Dennis. That's all."

"Then you didn't know it was Ben?"

"No."

"Is there any possibility that your talk with Ben
was overheard—or that he told anyone of it?"

"I don't think so. I don't know."

"Well, then," said Dennis slowly, "I suppose he
came to be sure—came because he knew we were to
meet there—and someone else——"

"Who?"

"I don't know, Daphne. But whoever it was—left
no clue at all." If he had left a clue, it was gone, now,
thought Dennis. He turned the cigarette in his fingers, thinking furiously. How to save her—how to
keep the sordid, hideous thing from getting her in its
slimy tentacles. She hadn't wanted to marry the dead
man; she had been another sacrifice to the Haviland
company, and an unwilling sacrifice; she'd been seen
in the arms of another man; she'd been heard promising to meet the other man, to go away with him. To
meet him at midnight, to meet him at the springhouse
in the snow.

The wedding day only a few hours away. And at
midnight, in the springhouse, the prospective husband murdered.

And Rowley finding them there. Well, Rowley couldn't talk now. They were together in it. So long as Gertrude didn't get the story out of Rowley. Gertrude—that was a danger point. Gertrude hated him, Dennis. Well, he'd have to face that when it came. Just now . . .

"Look, Daph. This is what you must do. Don't question it. I'm—— I'll take it on my shoulders, and I'm doing, God knows, the best I can do. You've got to pull yourself together, my dear, and—and have a story ready. Understand? If it doesn't seem right to you now, later it will. You are—— You've had a hideous experience, you can't think or—or plan for yourself. Will you do as I tell you, Daphne, my darling?"

"I—— What, Dennis? Why?"

"Because you are in danger, Daphne. You know you are. I believe your story; I know you couldn't have killed Ben. But—but I want to keep you out of it altogether; it's the only safe way. You never know what detectives and inquiries and—well, juries—"

"*Juries!*"

"—will do," finished Dennis hurriedly. "Don't be frightened. Oh, my dear!" He took a long breath and went to bend over her, taking her hands again in his own. "First, you were not out of this house tonight. Understand? No matter what they say, you were not out of your room after twelve."

But someone knew.

"There was somebody on the stairway," said Daphne with stiff lips. "Just now. When I came upstairs. And I thought it was you."

It gave him a really ugly shock. She could see the fright leap into his eyes. He paused as if to steady himself against it.

"What do you mean, Daphne? For God's sake, what——"

She told him; briefly. "Was it the murderer, Dennis?"

"I don't know. I can't—— Oh, good God, why did I leave you! But in the house—it seemed so safe—the danger out in the snow and——" He stopped. It was worse, then, than he'd thought. Daphne herself . . .

"So whoever it was knows I was downstairs," said Daphne.

"Yes. Yes, I see." He mustn't let her know how it frightened him. The old house with all its narrow corridors, hidden closets, sharp and sudden turns when you couldn't be sure what was waiting for you. Yes, it was worse then he'd thought. He said, "Well —it's—it's all right now, Daph."

The clock on the mantel struck a thin, hoarse little note.

"I must get out of here. Even your light burning so late—if anyone sees it—— Now remember, Daphne. When the police come, you know nothing at all of all this. You were not out of your room during the night."

"But whoever was on the stairway——"

He said grimly, "We'll have to risk it. No matter what the police say, stick to your story. I've tried to fix it so they won't suspect—if it works, they'll be decent—won't hound you to try to trap you."

"What have you done?"

"Fixed it to look like——— Oh, it's all right, Daph. You'd better act surprised—anyway, remember that. Don't let anyone know you were out of your room during the night. Don't let anyone know you quarreled with Ben."

A sudden thought struck her, and she rose, stumbling on that draggled little yellow train, so he caught her in his arms to steady her and held her, then, tightly.

"Dennis—will they blame you?"

"No," he said with quick assurance. "At least, I'll take good care that they won't. Trust me. I'll look out for myself."

"Dennis, you—you didn't kill him," she said. "I mean—if you did it would be me—it would be because of me—I would love you no matter———"

"Well, I didn't kill him, Daphne," he said and laughed. A queer, cold little laugh that didn't sound like Dennis. "I didn't kill him," he said. "Someone else had that pleasure."

She clung to him suddenly and put her head against him, and he looked down at her shining soft hair. After a moment he put both hands around her face and lifted it and kissed her.

"I know, darling," he said gently. "I know."

He released her and went to the door.

"I'm going now. Remember, dear, and keep your chin up. Lock the door."

He was gone, then, making no sound. She crossed the room and locked the door, listening for his footsteps. She heard nothing.

Presently she realized that she must move; must do as Dennis had said to do. Let no one know what that night had been. What was first? Why, to take off that dress, of course. Turn out the light. Pretend to sleep.

There was still no sound in the corridor, and she did not know till afterward that he went to the window seat at the turn of the passage and sat there the rest of the night.

The narrow branching corridor was dark—Amelia had never held with night lights—but it was so narrow that no one could approach and pass by him in the direction of Daphne's room without his knowing it.

He shouldn't have left her to go through the house alone. The thought of it now appalled him. Yes, it was going to be bad.

He wondered about them all, there in the chill, waiting darkness, thinking of them intimately as he knew them. Gertrude with her slow, blank eyes and those recurrent, violent, nervous headaches and those fits of rage. Amelia with her amazing hidden obstinacy below that fragile, gentle exterior. Amelia should have been a man. And Johnny with his affability, his handsomeness, his bland evasion of the sisters so at last they accepted him as neutral—as property belonging to neither of them. Rowley. . . . He frowned. He wished that Rowley had not come upon them there in the springhouse. He must watch Rowley; even as a child you could never count on him. Especially when Gertrude got hold of him.

Who *had* killed Ben Brewer?

And how would that death affect the Haviland
Bridge Company? How would it affect that family to
whom the company was more than meat and bread,
for their very being was woven into it?

He sat there till the first, cold gray light of dawn.
He didn't dare smoke, and every small sound the
house made during those hours brought him to sharp
attention, every nerve alert.

They had, he decided, done everything possible to
turn in another direction that floodlight of inquiry
which so soon would be upon them. He hoped they
had made no mistakes. He went over and over again
every step in that grisly process. He was desperately
tired. And mainly he wanted to wash his hands, scrub
them with clean, hot soapsuds. It wasn't till the wal-
nut bookshelf in the corner of the hall beside him began to show its outlines clearly, and the flat little
cushion on the window seat took on a bluish green
color, that he remembered with horrible abruptness
one mistake.

He sat upright—his skin prickling a little with the
shock of it. How could they have done that? In all
their plan and talk and sweating efforts, when they
thought they had covered every possible loophole
for suspicion, how could they have forgotten such an
important thing! He got up—no one seemed to be
stirring; there was no sound in the sleeping house,
and with the coming of light it had stopped its creaking. He went through the narrow, silent passages
toward the stairway, a tall, grim shadow in disheveled evening clothes. He forgot the third step
from the bottom and how it creaked, and cursed him-

self as he trod on it. That was the sound Daphne had heard. Thank God, she'd run away.

He went on across the wide hall, gray now with sparse cold light, and reached the drawing room. He paused there to listen and to open the door with extreme caution. The drawing room was gray, too— the piano a blunt dark bulk in one corner, the odor from the flowers bitter and strong. He could barely see the outline of the little gilt chair nearest him and, at the far end of the long room, the door that entered the small, oak-paneled library. There was a door from that room, too, into the passage leading, at last, past a closed and useless music room, to the central hall again. The strategic importance of that door and that passage had been a part of their plan. He did not intend to look toward the door leading into the library, but he did so for a very short moment. It was still, however, too dark to see objects clearly at that distance. That was lucky, he thought, and went to the french windows, thrusting his way through the massed ferns and flowers. One jar he sought with his hand, as if to steady it as he passed, and remembered with something like a physical wrench that instant during the night when something had thrust unexpectedly against the jar and it had rocked on its pedestal and threatened to crash to the floor. He had caught it—Rowley had cursed under his breath; his face had been damp and his hands shaking when the heavy vase was upright and steady again.

It was better not to think of that hour or two. The windows—his hands felt along the bolts. The win-

dow was closed as, inconceivably, they had left it.
How could they have done it! That which was the
keystone, the kernel of that plan. They'd closed the
window and had turned the venetian shade so that
the small light they were obliged to use—carefully
shaded, an instant or two at a time—would not show,
in case anyone were in the snow outside, watching
them. There was no one there; there could be no one
there, and both of them knew it. But nevertheless
there was that feeling that they were under observation. Odd. He thought now with sharp recollection
of the taxi fellow—but he wouldn't . . . Probably
he hadn't even come. There was an automatic bolt
on the long french window; when it closed it bolted
itself. Part of Amelia's amazing and thorough system of locking herself in.

He turned and pulled up the venetian blinds, hating the little sucking whisper they made in that horribly silent room. He found the bolt, released it and
opened the window. Hating, too, the sound it made
as he pushed it slowly open.

There. That was better. But it had been a near
thing, and his hands shook with the sense of catastrophe, narrowly averted.

Was there anything else?

Every instinct urged him to leave that room
quickly, without a backward look. He forced himself
to remain and to go over every step in that process,
every small joint in the edifice they had built up.
There was no other mistake—nothing, at least, that
he could find. He even went near the window and
looked down into the snow. Lucky it had snowed so

hard. There were, of course, traces of footsteps—
not the outlines of the steps themselves but small,
broken depressions, covered now with snow; the outline was there, but nothing that would show, say, a
heelprint or the size and outline of a shoe. He
wondered about the path leading through shrubs and
thickets of firs up to the springhouse. That was a
danger—one of the weak points. Something they
could not help. But it would be fatal to go and look.
He could only hope the snow had done its work and
that the police cars and the doctor's car coming hurriedly along the drive would destroy any evidence
the snow had not covered. When had it stopped
snowing—— But it had not stopped, although the
fall was lighter. That was good. Well, there was
nothing more he could do here. And the household
would be abroad early that morning—servants letting themselves into the house, starting preparations
for a wedding that was not to occur. For the life of
him, as he reached the door again, he could not help
glancing toward the library. But chairs and piano in-
tervened, and he could see nothing.

Again with extreme caution he let himself out the
door. No one was in the hall, and it was perceptibly
lighter. There were as yet no sounds from the south
L where the kitchen and dining room were. He
thought again of Daphne and the stairway in the
darkness. He must remember this time about the
third step.

Oh, God, the latch on the drawing-room door!
He'd forgotten about fingerprints. They'd used
handkerchiefs continually, hadn't they? They'd been

very careful about fingerprints. Now he'd smeared his own all over that old latch and the broad iron handle of it. He hesitated and went back. Better wipe it clean; no fingerprints would be bad, but his own found there would be worse. Besides, other people entering the room—as many other people would shortly be entering it—would leave diverse and blurring marks upon it. The police would not find it suspiciously free of fingerprints. He took out his handkerchief and wiped the latch on both sides and closed the door. As he did so a swift, devastating thought flashed over him.

What a grim irony it would be if, in destroying clues to the murderer of Ben Brewer, he managed to leave clues involving himself! A fine net of evidence hopelessly entangling him, so that no explanation, no final truth could possibly extricate him.

There was no way to gauge the potential power of the police; they did things, found things, reasoned from bits of evidence which the layman did not even know existed. Suppose, without knowing it, he had left evidence against himself; evidence that they would link, if they discovered it, with his love for Daphne, her promise to go away with him; with her final decision that she could not go, which would furnish so strong and urgent a motive for the murder of the man who stood between them. Whom she was to marry in so short a time.

It was not a pleasant thought. Neither was the recollection of that other evidence, that ugly, mysterious bit of direct evidence which he had so far concealed.

Well, his only insurance against it was to have made no mistakes. He had thought there was none. But the closed window had shaken him.

He hesitated, wanting to go back again into that room, to look again carefully at every smallest link in that false chain. He fought down the impulse and turned toward the stairway.

But he realized the seriousness of the thing they had done; had realized it from the beginning. It made them technically—didn't it?—accessories after the fact. That was at the best. At the worst—well, he wouldn't think of that. At the best they had hindered the police; had obstructed the cause of justice; had completely destroyed any evidence left by the real murderer.

Yet there had been no choice in the matter. He had realized that, too, almost the instant when Rowley had stepped into the springhouse. If Rowley had been only a few moments later! If Rowley hadn't come at all!

It was unfortunate that Rowley had turned up just at that point. And that he, Dennis, had lied fluently but not too well. But then he had had to lie—tell the only thing he could think of at the moment which would explain his presence there with Daphne and in a small measure protect Daphne.

And Rowley's tale of finding them there bending over the murdered man would carry a far greater weight of suspicion with the police than their own tale of Rowley's coming so aptly on the scene.

Who *had* killed Ben Brewer?

Well, that would come later. Just now there was

so much to think of, so much to be prepared for. In only an hour or two now the police would be there. Himself, Daphne, all of them facing inquiry.

Oh yes, the third step.

He checked himself on the very verge of putting his weight upon it and grasped the banister so as not to lose his balance.

The hall was lighter, too; thus it was that he saw the reddish smudge on the ivory spindle just below his hand.

He saw and bent to look at it, and every nerve in his body tightened.

It was certainly blood.

Blood, now dried, and faintly smudged. But still —he measured with his own hand—still it was just about the place that someone, grasping the banister —arrested by the creaking of that step as he, Dennis, had been arrested at the recollection of that creaking—would have placed his thumb.

Someone, arrested in his stealthy advance up those steps by the creak of the third step—by Daphne's pausing ahead of him and her whisper in the darkness, "Dennis—Dennis. Here I am."

He stood there, staring at that small reddish smudge as if it epitomized—as in a rather horrible way it did—all the ugliness and horror of the night. As if it set a grisly seal upon the thing.

And at the same time it crystallized in the most dreadful way something that had been formless, a nebulous kind of shadow which had not, till then, taken definite shape and form. And that was, of course, that whoever had left that bloody thumb-

print on the spindle had been someone in and of the
house, familiar with its ways.

He steadied himself; he'd known that all along—
at least it had been there in the back of his mind.

There was a sound of some kind from the kitchen
wing, and he lifted his head sharply to listen. Laing
would be coming into the house soon; if he hadn't
just then. He must not be seen there—still dressed
and in that dangerous vicinity.

Well, then—there was a bloody thumbprint probably belonging to the real murderer. What to do
with it? Probably belonging to the real murderer.
For there was also another possibility, and that was
that Rowley or he himself had left that thumbprint
on the old ivory spindle.

If it was Rowley's the whole truth of the thing
would immediately come out and would be far more
damaging to himself and to Daphne than it could
possibly be to Rowley. And if it was his own, added
at last to all that other evidence that existed, it
would be horribly convincing. Convictions had been
made by twelve good men and true on less evidence.

And there was no way to tell certainly which it
was. No way to tell even the size of the thing, for it
was smudged. Yet there were clear enough lines, too.
The police could tell—could identify it swiftly and
with dreadful certainty.

There was another faraway sound from the
kitchen wing—as if a door had closed and someone
had spoken. He must hurry.

Again that devastating thought flashed through
his mind.

Suppose he had left somewhere and somehow evidence that would enclose upon him like a net—suppose he had left such evidence, and this bloody thumbprint was the only real clue that existed. That he and Rowley between them had not destroyed. Their only testimony to the truth.

The only clue leading to the real murderer. What irony, again, it would be if he had destroyed that one saving clue with his own hands!

CHAPTER 6

THE trouble was that someone was moving about in the kitchen or somewhere in the back part of the house.

There was not time to think, to follow the several possibilities involved to their logical and several ends.

Dennis himself had never been adverse to risks, although he had, too, a solid strain of shrewd common sense, so he was not really a gambler.

But it wasn't Rowley, it wasn't himself; it was Daphne who made it important. Daphne who made it impossible for him to take the risk.

And he must hurry.

So he took out his handkerchief and was about to rub out that smudged thumbprint when he thought of the thing to do. It would be noticed, of course, but no one could say when or how it happened. And there would be no possible way, Dennis thought, of tracing it to him.

His knife was in his pocket and the wood was soft below successive layers of paint. The noise it made seemed horribly loud, but it was not a difficult thing to do except that his hands shook a little with the need for haste. But in a moment he had it; a small slice of the wood with the bloody thumbprint intact. It left, to be sure, a jagged, unpainted scar on the soft ivory spindle just below the banister. But he assured himself that, although they would be certain to notice it at once, still there was no way at all to trace it to him. And he had the fingerprint.

It was with a strong sense of again having averted a catastrophe that he put the thing in his pocket. If it was his own or Rowley's thumbprint, then the truth that so horribly involved Daphne would not be brought out by its discovery.

But if it was a clue leading to the murderer, then he had it. Preserved; intact; at hand in case of later need.

He saw no one and heard nothing on the way through the twisting upper hall to his room. He undressed, disarranged the bed to look as if it had been slept in and flung himself down upon it. The possession of that one bit of real and material evidence—always providing it was evidence, and he thought it was—gave him an increasing sense of safety. Of holdings in reserve.

But it held its own significance, too.

It was rather horrible to realize that those small reddish lines could be translated into—good God, into a murderer. Suppose, eventually, they looked at it and said, "This is Gertrude's thumbprint," or "This is Johnny's," or "This is Amelia's."

He had again a wave of incredulity and of revulsion. And again a wish to destroy it.

But he didn't, although he didn't know exactly what he would do with it.

And he didn't, then, give full thought to the extreme and dangerous importance that thumbmark might possess.

He was groggy with fatigue. Well, in an hour or two now, it would begin. He went to sleep and dreamed that the thumbprint turned out to be Daphne's and Rowley was telling someone about it.

At seven, as it came out later during the inquiry, Laing, and Mrs Laing, the cook, and Maggie, the middle-aged housemaid who was Mrs Laing's niece, crossed from the garage to the house through unbroken snow, opened the back door with Laing's key, entered the house and went direct to the kitchen.

Breakfast was to be at eight, and because the wedding was set for twelve and there was not much time for all that was to be done before the caterers arrived at ten, a family breakfast was to be served in the dining room. This was contrary to Amelia's usual custom, for she was a sensible woman and a firm believer in breakfast trays as contributing to family amenity. But that morning only Daphne was permitted a tray and Maggie, a stolid soul, preoccupied with an obscure liver complaint, brought it to Daphne, lighted a fire and opened the curtains and did not give the white-faced girl a second look.

It was a family breakfast, but it was not promptly attended. In fact, only Gertrude, Amelia herself and Johnny Haviland turned up.

At eight-thirty Laing and Maggie went to dust

the small library which had been left to the last. All the other rooms were in a state of incredible neatness and shininess and—even to the flowers which had been arranged just after dinner the previous night—ready for the wedding. But the library had been used all along as an informal sitting room and workroom, and in it all the confusion of last-minute arrangements had accumulated. Belated wedding gifts, boxes, tissue paper, lists—a long table littered with odds and ends. On it, among other things, three long boxes of thick white envelopes, already addressed and stamped and ready to be put in the mail that day.

Laing opened the door. The curtains were still drawn, and there was a lingering odor of stale smoke from the night before and on one small table a forgotten and sticky liqueur glass. Maggie went to open the curtains; Laing himself approached the long table where wedding presents stood and winked and glittered. First he saw that, curiously, some silver candlesticks, a silver tray or two, and several other objects he could not remember but which impressed him even then as being the most valuable of the lot, were heaped together on the floor. Then curtains rattled lightly on their rings, and a path of light went across the floor and struck upon a sort of huddle that lay half in the doorway that led into the drawing room and half in the drawing room.

Laing didn't know exactly what happened next, or when he recognized it as being the body of a man. But all at once he was bending over it, and it was Benjamin Brewer, and Maggie was screaming.

It was that scream that brought them in from the dining room. It was that scream that brought Dennis Haviland awake and to his senses and hurrying down the stairs in a bathrobe. It brought Rowley at last out of his own room—fully clothed, precise, remarkably cool in the face of the almost unbelievable confusion downstairs.

Daphne, desperately drinking black coffee upstairs, seeing herself in the mirror opposite—white and taut, with black marks under altogether sleepless eyes—did not hear Maggie's scream because her room was at the very end of the south L.

All night, in that ceaseless, stabbing whirl of questions there had been one that was immediate, that was something to be faced. It was: When would they tell her? When would they discover that there was to be no wedding? All those other seething questions were to have their hours of urgency, too. But just then, forcing herself to drink hot black coffee, it was, When?

And she must face it so they would not guess. Dennis had had his way; he'd made the decision for her. She knew of no better course than to follow the one he had laid out for her. She didn't know exactly what Dennis and Rowley had done except that Dennis seemed assured and satisfied that it was right and best. But during those night hours she had seen the force of Rowley's argument. And she had seen other things.

Ben had been murdered. There was no weapon. Then who had murdered him?

She poured more coffee, spilling it.

And they sent, at last, Johnny Haviland to tell her.

At first view of his face she knew why he had come. He stood in the doorway hesitating, looking at her with his light blue eyes anything but jolly, his fair, handsome face no longer pink, his wavy, light hair disheveled—looking, for the first time in his life, perhaps, his full fifty-five years. He did not seem to see that there was already something amiss. He closed the door and walked toward her heavily —not gracefully and youthfully as usual. He sat down on the bed and looked at her and jingled keys in his pocket nervously.

"Daph," he said, "there's something—something very bad. I mean—it's about Ben."

Seeing his distress, she had a quick impulse to tell him she already knew—to put her head on his shoulder and sob out the story of the night. Last night, as he had dealt out cocktails and jokes and compliments, Rowley had looked at him and smiled and said, "Johnny was born to be the father of the bride."

The father of the bride. Escorting her on his sleekly tailored arm to that altar of flowers.

"Daph," he said, his mouth trembling a little below that small trim blond mustache. "Daph—did you love Ben? Because he—well, there was a robbery last night. That is, an attempted one. It—well, it seems that Ben heard the noise or something and— and went downstairs and they——"

"Ben!" said Daphne.

"He's hurt," said her father, watching her. "He's dead, Daphne. They've sent for the police."

She couldn't look into his eyes. He knew her too well: he would see too much. Her gaze fixed itself on a corner of the yellow satin eiderdown; a round braid binding turned itself in an S curve, and she was always to remember it. It and the sharp little ticks of the old Seth Thomas clock with the yellow face that stood on the mantel. Outside, the snow had stopped falling at last. On the little slipper chair was the yellow dress, its train draggled and still damp. She must hide the dress, she thought suddenly: Dennis had said there must be nothing to show that she had been out in the snow during the night. A night when, he had also said, every single event would have a significance.

Johnny looked at her, cleared his throat huskily and rose and went to the window, where he stood staring out upon the dreary, gray morning and jingling the keys in his pocket.

"The police are on the way now," he said. "They will be here any time. Gertrude thinks there is likely to be quite a lot of inquiry. Though the thing seems clear enough—I mean, the robbery. All that. But she thinks the police will question us all."

"Yes," said Daphne, tracing the yellow curve of braid with her finger.

"It's hell downstairs," said Johnny worriedly. "You'd better stay up here, Daph. Maybe the police won't ask for you at all. We'll tell them it's been a shock to you." He stopped and mused and said, "Gertrude's wild. Telephoning—she said to tell you she'd stopped the account of the wedding in everything but one edition of the papers. She got hold of Mrs Beely in town and gave her the list of guests, and she's doing all the telephoning she can. God, what a mess!" He checked himself abruptly, said, "You're taking it well, my dear. I'm proud of you," but didn't look at her.

He knew, though; he must have known in his heart that she'd never loved Ben. But he hadn't known any more than that; and she must talk, say something, ask questions. "What happened?" she said. "I mean, when did they discover it—how . . ."

He told her. ". . . And do you know what Gertrude said when she heard Ben was dead?" he finished. "Well, she just stood there and looked at Laing, with her eyes popping out and her face sort of purple, and she said, 'Thank God.' Just like that. 'Thank God.' I was pretty upset myself; couldn't believe Laing—shock, you know. And then Gertrude said, 'Thank God.' Meant it, too—in spite of all the complications of the wedding. Well, he's out of the company now."

He got out a cigarette and lighted it, his perfectly tailored shoulders a graceful silhouette against the window. "It's hell downstairs," he repeated. "Nobody knows what to do. Dennis phoned for the police finally. Funny," said Johnny reflectively, looking out the window. "Funny nobody else heard anything. Not even the shot."

Someone knocked purposefully. Johnny gave a convulsive little start and said "Gertrude" under his breath, and Gertrude entered.

"My dear!" she said. "So Johnny's told you. Well, there's nothing I can say, I'm sure. You know how I felt about Ben—although heaven knows I wouldn't have had this happen. Today of all days," said Gertrude, wheezing; and closed the door sharply behind her. She was a thick, robust, authoritative woman, younger than Johnny by perhaps two years and with his blond hair and light blue eyes, but altogether without his grace and vivacity. She wore a bright blue knitted dress, and the excitement had brought on her asthma, so her large, tightly restrained bosom heaved and she pressed both wide hands upon it. Her fine light hair was askew under its net, and her eyes, usually slow and blank, were shining like glass.

Daphne shrunk a little as she advanced briskly.

"Now, Johnny," she went on, decisively, "I hope you broke it to Daphne as gently as possible. Don't be troubled about any of the arrangements, Daphne. I've seen to everything. Even to calling Dr Lonergan to tell him there would be no wedding." She paused and said in an absent way, "He was very shocked. Really quite upset. Well, of course, it's a most unusual thing—three hours before the ceremony. But there, I came to see about you, Daphne. I'm afraid the police will want to see you; I think you'd better get up and dress."

Johnny turned from the window and said. "But we——"

Gertrude interrupted instantly: "No, Johnny, I'm afraid we can't. They'll want to see her, I'm sure— and after all it isn't as if—well, I mean to say——

'Well, anyway, don't you think you'd better see them if they ask for you, Daphne?"

Gertrude's glittering eyes were traveling about the room. In another second she would note the stain on the yellow dress. Daphne sat up quickly.

"I'll get dressed at once," she said, clutching the yellow eiderdown around her rumpled little nightgown. "I'll hurry."

Gertrude's eyes leaped to her at once. She'd spoken too hastily, too eagerly, thought Daphne. But Gertrude was never very quick in perception, although her slow suspicions, once roused, were extraordinarily stubborn.

Johnny, however, turned quickly from the window.

"That's a good girl," he said rapidly and in a relieved way. "That's my girl. Keep a—er—stiff upper lip. She'll be all right, Gertrude." He came over to Daphne, still rattling the keys in his pocket, and kissed her lightly. "Come along, Gertrude. We'd better get back downstairs again. Be there when they arrive." He took Gertrude's firm arm and turned her toward the door.

And as Gertrude, always reluctant under pressure, disappeared, Johnny looked back at Daphne.

"You—you are all right, aren't you, honey?"

"Yes."

It didn't satisfy him. He started to speak, stopped, and finally put up his hand in a gesture meant to be, vaguely, encouraging. The onyx ring on it flashed, and he was gone, and Daphne got up and closed the door and locked it and looked at the yellow gown.

She must do something with it. Call Maggie and ask her to sponge it? But Maggie would be curious. Would remember. Besides, velvet didn't clean readily. Send it to the cleaners? But that would be difficult that morning; impossible, really, with the telephones in constant use, with people everywhere, with police and inquiry and—— No, that was no good. She went to more drastic remedies. Suppose she burned the dress in that little fireplace. It would be very easy to do—except, of course, for the fur bands on the shoulders. But would not Gertrude and Amelia discover its absence—question it? Not necessarily. For in the back hall downstairs were two trunks already closed and locked and labeled. She could suddenly see those labels: "Mrs Benj. Brewer, S.S. Conte Grande, 1st class"—all of it written by Amelia. In a corner of her room was another trunk, still open and unlocked, waiting for the last-minute things. Of course, they all knew she'd worn the yellow gown at dinner. But there would be confusion about it; it might be days—weeks even—before either of the aunts noticed its absence.

And she could remove the bands of fur and hide them somewhere.

She took the dress in her hands, and again someone came to the door and it was Maggie. Daphne had time only to hang the dress, hurriedly, far back under the sloping roof of the little closet.

It was a different Maggie, electric with excitement, her cap on one ear and her apron disheveled.

"They've come, Miss Daphne," she said. "And Miss Gertrude sent me to help you dress. Oh, Miss

Daphne," cried the woman. "Ain't it horrid! Him dead and all, right on your wedding day." She looked at the wedding veil, shuddered, crossed herself and said excitedly, "There's reporters here already. What 'll you be wearing?"

There was, even there, a perceptible sense of the tremor and confusion that filled the house; of distant doors closing: of movement and people and voices. Of cars suddenly in the driveway.

CHAPTER 7

I<small>T WAS</small>, however, a good hour later that they sent for Daphne. Johnny, biting his small mustache, adjured her not to be nervous.

"It's only a matter of form," he said. "Only a matter of form. But think before you speak, my dear. Think before . . ." They were at the head of the stairs, and he waited for her to precede him down that narrow stairway. Past the place where she'd stood for a terrified moment during the night. Down into the wide, familiar hall that was all at once different, for there were people there, crowds of people—and sudden, blinding flashes of light.

She shut her eyes involuntarily and put her hands upward to shield her face and knew that Dennis had come from somewhere and was standing just below her on the stairs.

"No pictures," he was saying pleasantly and very firmly. "Not just now—please."

Gertrude's voice, strident and protesting, came from somewhere, too; then Johnny was leading her across the hall and into the little passage leading to the library.

Reporters. Reporters, police, inquiry—and they

were plunged in the middle of the confusing, terrifying maelstrom. And it was, of course, the wedding,
the romance that would give the thing extra news
value.

The door to the library opened.

There were two men standing at the table, which
was still laden with a confusion of wedding gifts and
wrappings. As she entered, both of them looked up
sharply. One, the small one with the somber dark
eyes, nodded briefly, and the other, looking at her
curiously, came at once to the door and went out.
Johnny fidgeted and resorted to a social manner.

"You'd better sit down, my dear," he said. "This
is the man from the county police headquarters. Mr
Wait—my daughter, I hope you won't need to ask
her many questions just now, Mr Wait. This—this
dreadful business has been, naturally, a very
great——"

"I'll talk to Miss Haviland alone," said Jacob
Wait briefly, looking as if, quite suddenly, he had
conceived a brooding hatred for her. As indeed was
not far from the truth. For he had just looked again
at the dead man, and he felt sick with the sight and
smell of murder.

He turned toward Daphne, and the light fell more
strongly upon him. He was a bored-looking little
man, dark, with large, morose dark eyes in which
there was a new kind of glow. So there was a pretty
woman in the thing, he was thinking. Burglary, huh?
A pretty woman—more than pretty, he decided
swiftly; she had the cleanness of line, the restraint
and sensitive delicacy of feature that the Anglo-

Saxon races breed. She had also, probably, temperament; looked it, anyway.

Burglary.

The glow that entered his eyes was actually one of hatred. He hated murder because, always, it got under his skin. Because he was acutely sensitive to it, as if he were inconceivably equipped with tentacles which, in spite of himself, reached out and absorbed the horror and sick reality of the thing. So, besides hating murder, he also hated the people involved in the thing.

But more than anything he hated it when there was a woman. A beautiful woman. There was a small, warm strain of Jewish blood in him; thus he was deeply imaginative and perceptive; thus also he was direct, so that he recognized certain fundamental principles of behavior. When a woman entered the thing there were likely to be any number of emotions involved in it. He hated emotions, too, because he understood their importance.

So he looked at Daphne with a morose, ruby glow away back in his dark eyes. There she was. And there was murder.

Burglary, huh? Another word linked itself with "burglary" and "murder" in Jacob Wait's mobile consciousness. That word was "phony."

It was a word that changed his course entirely and immediately. He stood there for a moment looking down at Daphne while she braced herself to look back at him. To answer the questions he would ask her. To avoid traps; to evade. To lie, if necessary, without flinching.

So it was a queer kind of shock when, abruptly,
he didn't ask anything. He turned instead, walked
to the door, spoke to someone beyond it and came
back and stood again behind the tall chair, resting his
arms upon its high back and looking thoughtfully
at the floor.

And suddenly Gertrude came into the room, with
a queer startled look in her blank blue eyes, and was
followed by Rowley and Dennis and Johnny and
someone else—a man Daphne had never seen before,
but who, she knew at once, was attached to Jacob
Wait and the police. All at once another man, in uniform this time, was in the room, too, and was seated
at a small table and bending over a shorthand tablet.
And Dennis was looking at her.

She met his eyes for only a brief, guarded instant.
He turned abruptly and sat down in one corner of
the divan opposite, so his back was to the light.
Johnny hovered in the background; Rowley, his
opaque dark eyes sullen in his sallow face, sat on the
arm of his mother's chair, and she put one strong
hand on his knee.

"Everybody here but Miss Amelia Haviland,"
said Jacob Wait with a rather startling knowledge
of names and faces. "Close the door, Schmidt. Did
you send for Miss Haviland, too?"

Schmidt, the plain-clothes man, a weary, thin man
with a lined face, signified that he had and closed
the door.

"Let her in when she comes," said Jacob Wait and
looked at them thoughtfully. "I asked you to come
in here," he said briefly, "because there are some

things we aren't quite sure about. It occurred to me
it would save a little time, perhaps, to have you all
together. It is painful, I know. I'll be brief." He
said it neatly and smoothly but with no particular
conviction. He added without a pause, "Did you
hear the shot, Mrs Shore?"

Gertrude was taken aback by the abruptness. She
looked at him, blinked slowly and said, "Uh——"

"Did you hear the shot, Mrs Shore? Your room
is nearest this end of the house, I believe. At least
it seemed to me it was directly above the drawing
room."

"Oh," said Gertrude. "I didn't know you'd been
upstairs. Why, yes. I mean that is, my room. No, I
didn't hear the shot."

"Did anyone hear the shot?"

No one had; at least no one admitted it.

"You understand," said Jacob Wait, "that we'd
like to fix the time of the murder. It is of considerable importance."

"I don't see," said Gertrude, recovering, "that is
makes any difference whether we heard the shot or
not. It seems to me you should be getting out—police
and—and cars and try to catch the murderer. He's
likely miles away by this time. I should think you
would be watching the roads and getting in touch
with towns around here and——"

"That," said Jacob Wait, managing to check Gertrude and still speak without emphasis, which was
rather a feat, "has been attended to. All that," he
said, his eyes smoldering. "What time did you go to
your room last night, Mrs Shore?"

Gertrude wheezed and turned a soft mauve. "About eleven, I think. We all came upstairs at the same time."

"When did you last see Mr Brewer?"

"Why, I don't——" She stopped, thought, blinked and said forcefully, "We were all in this room together. I think Daphne was the first to go —that is my niece. I went upstairs a moment or so later; I stopped in the lower hall to speak to my sister, who was looking at the lock of the front door. I think the men—that is, my brother and Mr Brewer and the boys"—her wide hand indicated Rowley and Dennis—"stayed here awhile. But it was only for a few moments, for I heard them on the stairs and in the upper hall shortly after I'd reached my own room."

"Is that right, Mr Haviland?" said Jacob Wait, looking at Johnny.

Johnny, also startled, blinked, too, and pushed his hands in his pockets and said, "Yes. We had a high-ball," he said, explaining. "Ben was just ahead of me, going upstairs. We stopped a moment in the upper hall, and he said good night and turned and went down the hall to his room. At least, I suppose he did. I didn't wait."

"His room is beside your room, Mrs Shore, isn't it?"

"Yes," said Gertrude. "Just above this room. Which explains why he heard the burglars when no one else heard them. And then, of course, Ben Brewer always heard things. He was——" She

stopped abruptly, looked at her hands and concluded, "He was extremely alert," and left it
there.

"Did no one else hear any sound during the
night?"

Again no one had. Rowley was looking at the
floor, so his narrow eyes were shadowed, but there
was a kind of tight look around his thin mouth.
Daphne wondered, suddenly, how Rowley felt about
it; Rowley had been, except when he was obliged to
side with his mother, rather neutral in that year-old
battle. Yet he had felt, certainly, no faith in and no
liking for Ben Brewer.

She didn't dare look at Dennis; she was afraid
that in spite of herself her look would reveal something. But she was acutely conscious of his presence
there on the divan; his tall, tweed-clad figure; his
brown face and the queer kind of tenseness, of readi-
ness about him which she sensed rather than saw.
Jacob Wait said suddenly:

"How was Mr Brewer dressed last night?"

He had not addressed anyone in particular. Someone—Gertrude, was it?—started to speak and
stopped, and Johnny said uncertainly, "Do you mean
at dinner? Why, he wore ordinary evening clothes.
Tails. White tie. Why?"

"I take it you had touched nothing about the body
when you called us?" said Jacob Wait. "Is that
right, Mr Haviland?"

"Why, yes. Yes, of course," said Johnny, looking
anxious. "We saw at once what had happened. Oh,
I believe we—we felt for a pulse. That kind of thing.

But he was dead. There was nothing we could do, and someone said we mustn't move the body. Then Dennis talked to county police headquarters, and they told us not to touch anything. So we didn't."

"When we arrived, then, the body was exactly as it was found?"

"Why, I——" Johnny's light, worried blue eyes went around the room and returned to Jacob Wait. "Why, I think so. Yes. He had on that bathrobe—and still had on the trousers of his evening clothes—I noticed that. And no shoes. He'd probably taken them off so as not to make any sound."

"Then he was probably undressing when he heard the burglars?"

Johnny blinked again, jingled things in his pockets and said explosively, "Good God, I don't know. Looks that way. He had no coat on—no shirt or vest—still he might 've been asleep or in bed, and just pulled on trousers and bathrobe——"

"First removing his pajamas," said Jacob Wait, "and putting on his underclothing."

Johnny frowned.

"Well, I don't know what he did," he said. "Maybe he was just undressing when he heard them. How do I know?"

"If he was undressing when he heard sounds in this room and came downstairs, then the affair must have taken place very shortly after eleven. That is, very shortly after you had all gone to your rooms. Thus it seems that someone else ought to have heard the sound of the shot at least. If Mr Brewer was only undressing to go to bed, it doesn't seem as if everyone would be already and very soundly sleeping."

He still addressed Johnny, who frowned again and chewed his trim little mustache and said rather pettishly that it didn't seem so.

"But perhaps," said Johnny, brightening, "he didn't undress at once. Maybe he sat and—and smoked awhile. Something like that."

"Perhaps," said Jacob Wait. "But there was only one cigarette end in the tray in his room. However, you are perfectly right, Mr Haviland. He might not have undressed at once. Indeed, our only possible conclusion is that he didn't. Yet he must have been killed about midnight or shortly after."

Gertrude's eyes snapped.

"Midnight!" she said suddenly. "Oh no. He couldn't have been killed then. I——" She stopped so abruptly, it was as if the momentum of her speech carried her on: "I heard——" she mumbled and sat there with her wide face flushed and her eyes like glass, staring at the detective. Rowley had put his long thin hand over his mother's hand but otherwise had not moved.

"You heard what?"

"Nothing," said Gertrude, staring. "Nothing."

"Come, come, Mrs Shore. You were about to say you heard something to indicate he was not killed at midnight. What?"

"I——"

"You heard——"

"I heard—sounds," said Gertrude reluctantly.

"Sounds? Where? What kind of sounds?"

"In his room," she said slowly, as if the detective dragged out the words one after another. "As if— he were walking about."

"What time was that?"

"About—I think about two o'clock," said Gertrude. "However, I—I'm not at all sure of it. In fact, I think I'm entirely mistaken. And I know nothing at all about it—nothing at all."

"Thank you, Mrs Shore. Did you hear anything else?"

"Anything—— No! Certainly not! Sounds at night are very confusing; very——"

"Thank you."

It stopped her. She opened her mouth, closed it, gave Daphne a queer glassy look which had something perplexed and troubled and at the same time stubborn about it and then stared at the floor.

Who had been in Ben's room, walking about? Dennis, probably, or Rowley. Getting that bathrobe; doing what they could do bolster up the burglar theory. How much in that moment of perplexity had Gertrude's slow but tenacious reasoning grasped? Rowley probably had thought of all those details: he was innately ingenious.

And—and something had gone wrong.

There was too much the detective wanted to know.

They all felt it. As if it were a chill little wind creeping through the room which tinged the most inconsequent inquiries with significance.

Inconsequent, apparently tangential inquiries, such as the next one. "When," said Jacob Wait, "were the flowers arranged for the wedding?"

He looked at Gertrude, who considered it suspiciously, decided she could safely reply and did so:
"Last night. The men came as we were finishing dinner."

"When did they leave?"

"About ten, I think."

"The windows were closed then?"

The windows. Gertrude's voice was immediately
less wary.

"Yes, of course. That is, I think so. It seems that
one of them must have been left open. Without our
noticing it. It was wide open this morning when we
found him. Wide open and snow blowing in."

"All the other windows were locked?"

"You asked that before," said Gertrude. "Of
course they were locked. Amelia—my sister—always
saw to that herself."

"But last night apparently she missed the drawing-
room window?"

"Well, it seems so," said Gertrude. "But after all
—in the excitement of the wedding and all———"
She stopped again, her eyes very blank and light
above her bright blue bosom. Rowley rose from the
arm of her chair, walked over to the table and
lighted a cigarette.

Daphne thought: There's something under this.
There's something he knows. We all feel it. Everybody is on the defensive. Everybody. Even Gertrude
feels something hidden in this detective's questions
—feels that they have direction, force, a kind of
thrust against us. What was it, then? Where was
their mistake? But it was all a mistake. They had

been terribly wrong to undertake that ugly deception.

Yet, if they hadn't, it would have been worse. She mustn't look at Dennis: her very look might seek reassurance. She sat perfectly still, her hands clutched together on the lap of her old brown tweed skirt, the brave green scarf at her throat making her eyes darker blue and her face paler. Her soft, short brown hair caught gold highlights. It was impossible, she thought suddenly, that all this could have happened in only a few hours. It was, however, extremely real: the lights, the dark day; the wedding presents on the table (they would have to be sent back, all of them; with a note dictated by Amelia; horrible!).

The policeman at the shorthand table looked at Jacob Wait and straightened his back with a little sigh. The small table was too low for him; the straight chair too little and stiff. And by the looks of things, there was going to be a lot more notes to take. He wished he could smoke and glanced enviously at Rowley's cigarette. The plain-clothes man by the door looked at Jacob Wait, too, and became, if possible, more impassive. So that was the way the wind was blowing, was it? Well, this time Wait was wrong. It was an open-and-shut case of burglary.

It was cold in the little library. Cold and gray and, for a moment, very still. So still that they all heard the knock on the door, and Johnny's neat shoulders jerked toward it and Gertrude put both hands on her bosom.

"Well," said Jacob Wait.

It was the door from the drawing room that opened. There were men with muffled voices in the drawing room. Johnny of them all was the only one who could see into the room, and he stiffened suddenly, staring, his eyes round and fixed in his white face. What were they doing in there? thought Daphne; and then knew.

A man stood in the doorway and said shortly, "We've got the bullet. Want to take a look?"

Jacob Wait walked into the drawing room and closed the door behind him. Johnny looked white and sat down. Rowley puffed smoke and said, "Well, if that's all, let's get out of here."

But the policeman was strolling toward the other door, hovering exactly before it.

"I don't think Mr Wait's quite finished questioning," he said wearily but very politely.

And he wasn't. Though it was perhaps five minutes before he returned. A queer, silent five minutes, during which Johnny sat, still and white, and stared at the floor; Rowley smoked rapidly; Dennis refused to look at Daphne; and the policeman drummed on the table with his pencil. Daphne loked at the stubby brown toes of the oxfords she'd put on and thought of the walk over snowy fields she'd taken yesterday. It was then that she'd said good-by to all her former life; said good-by to Dennis. And had been glad that he was not there. And then she'd returned to sit in that deep chair in front of the fire and Dennis had come—out of the twilight and her own thoughts, and he was real. He was real, and he told her he loved her. Had always loved her. Had come home because he loved her. And she must not marry anyone else.

He'd knelt down with the firelight gleaming on his dark hair and making points of light in his eyes; he'd taken her in his arms and put his cheek against hers.

And from that moment nothing had been as it was intended to be. It was as if his coming had swung things off a carefully balanced axis; had knocked them from their prescribed course so events and emotions and desires went careening about crazily.

And among those things, murder had been loosed.

Well, that was horrible. And Dennis' return hadn't caused it.

She looked at the deep brown chair on the other side of the fireplace. Gertrude was sitting there now, a stiff, strong blue column, her eyes fixed on the door into the drawing room and her wide hands twisting and worrying a little lace handkerchief. Johnny, too, was watching the door now—his usual sartorial perfection indefinably disturbed, his wavy light hair tousled, as if he'd run his hands through it; his handsome face stiff and old-looking with small swollen pouches under his eyes. Rowley was standing at the window with his back to the room and wreaths of smoke floating around his narrow, shining black head.

And Dennis.

Dennis was looking at her. Had been quietly watching her, she knew at once, for some time, sharing perhaps her thoughts. It was a kind of shock to meet his eyes, to let herself receive one long, deep look.

It was a look that warned; that reminded her of all the things he had told her; and that, yet, encouraged her. Keep your chin up, Daph. It was as if he said it across that still, waiting room.

Oddly, in that moment, she felt again a little current of warmth and excitement because he was there. Because during that year she'd been so desperately lonely for him; because there had been moments when she couldn't remember his face clearly at all— and there had been other moments when she remembered it so clearly her heart ached with the memory. Times on a crowded street when someone, walking along ahead of her, moved or turned or carried his shoulders so that for a fleeting instant it was like Dennis and the image remained to haunt her. Because at last she had needed him and had not dared to let him know, and now he was there; across that little space.

And now, thought Daphne suddenly, she was not to marry Ben Brewer. But she couldn't more than glimpse that thought, as through an opened gate one may glimpse sunny meadows and blue sky and a dappled road beyond.

Jacob Wait came suddenly back into the room. And with him all the ugliness and horror of the thing that, inconceivably, had happened, and the briefly opened gate closed again.

He stood there, a small, dark man, looking at them as if he hated them.

Phony, he was thinking. Well, he'd better get the thing over.

"Schmidt."

"Yes, Mr Wait."

"Take a detailed statement from each of 'em. Beginning—oh, yesterday noon."

"Yes, Mr Wait."

"Look here," said Johnny suddenly. "What do you mean, detailed statement? You act as if—as if you suspected some of us. Nobody here had anything to do with it. It was an attempted burglary. None of us knows anything about——"

"A few windows left open, a heap of wedding gifts on the floor don't make a burglary," said the detective in a bored way. "Of course, if we could fix the time a little more accurately it would help. You see, the murder occurred, according to the doctor, near midnight. But the window in there has been open only an hour or two."

CHAPTER 8

A T THE little table the policeman's pencil jerked. He gave the detective one quick, sharp look and went back to writing. After a moment Gertrude said in a loud voice:

"*Window?*"

Rowley turned slowly toward the others and put his cigarette end neatly into an ash tray.

"How do you know? What do you mean?" he said coolly, facing the detective.

But Jacob Wait looked back at him with those morose dark eyes, said suddenly, "Flowers" and turned and walked out of the room again.

It was unexpected.

"Well!" said Gertrude, staring after him and then around the room. "Well, I must say——"

"What does he mean, flowers?" said Johnny anxiously. "Those flowers in there?"

"I don't know what he means," said Gertrude, twisting her handkerchief. "I know, I think he's a fool. A plain case of burglary and——"

Rowley approached her and put his hand on her arm.

"I suppose he means something about the changing temperature in the room," said Rowley calmly. "I mean if the window was open all night the flowers would have been exposed to the cold over quite a long period of time. Naturally, then, when the window was closed and the room warmed—if it is warm now—the flowers would droop—turn brown or something. I don't know exactly what, but I suppose it's that." He was speaking to Gertrude and to Johnny, but he was speaking very distinctly, and Dennis was listening. Over Gertrude's head he and Rowley glanced at each other. What was it? thought Daphne. What had they done—or failed to do? There was a curious white look around Dennis' mouth. A voice at her elbow said, "Your statement, please, miss." It was the man called Schmidt.

"Statement?" said Daphne in a small voice.

"Just tell me what you did, beginning yesterday about noon—where you went and all that. Particularly anything at all about the murdered—that is, this Mr Brewer."

"Yesterday—noon?"

"Yes, Miss Haviland."

"Well, I—I—— We had lunch about one-thirty. Just my aunts and I. My father came out from town later in the afternoon. I went for a walk—a long walk. I got home——"

"Did you see anybody you knew on that walk?"

"Why, I—— No."

"What time did you get home?"

"About—five, I think."

"Who'd you see when you got home?"

"No one. That is, until later. Then the others arrived."

"The others?"

"My father. My cousins, Rowley Shore. Dennis Haviland. Ben——"

"Ben? That's Mr Brewer?"

"Yes."

"Then what?"

"Why, we—we talked and then dressed for dinner. Then there was dinner, and afterward we all went to watch the flowers being arranged. Then we came back in here and had coffee and went upstairs about eleven."

"When did you last see Mr Brewer?"

"At—— Why, in the hall I think, as I started upstairs. He spoke to me. He——" She stopped, and the policeman looked up from his tablet.

"Oh," he said. "You was—it's you he was to marry. Oh—I'm sorry, Miss Haviland. I didn't realize. Well, that's all, except did you see him again before you—that is, before he was killed?"

"No," she said, thankful for the phrasing of his question. "No."

"Thank you."

"May I—may I go now?" said Daphne.

"Oh yes," said the policeman. "That is, don't leave the house, of course. Mr Wait will want to see you again. Now then——" He turned toward Gertrude. Daphne rose. It was with a sense of escape that she turned toward the hall. Behind her she could hear Gertrude's voice, strident, protesting, but shaken in its authority.

In the narrow little passage, however, she remembered the reporters, the detectives—all those people in the house. What were they doing, she thought—taking fingerprints? Measurements—hunting, with all the resources of modern crime detection at their disposal, for clues?

Clues; that meant material clues. Such as she and Dennis might have left in the springhouse without knowing it.

She could not just then face them all; could not cross the hall through the confusion and strange faces and observant eyes; could not run the gauntlet of those cameras. The door of the unused music room was at her elbow, and she opened it and went in. There was no one there.

It was an unpleasant room, not too well lighted, and seldom used. Someone sometime had filled it with cabinets of music and cabinets for trinkets; ugly massive mahogany and black leather, and Amelia had never changed it. The piano had been moved out and into the drawing room for the wedding, and its moving left a bare space over in the corner. The room was chilly; and seemed, because it was so seldom used, far from the rest of the house.

Daphne went to a chair. They had been wrong, terribly, dangerously wrong to undertake that deception. Law had its own innate force, its own crushing momentum. You couldn't do things like that and escape.

But she hadn't killed Ben. Dennis knew she hadn't; he'd found her there and Ben dead in the darkness of the springhouse. But she hadn't killed him, and Dennis knew it.

Dennis knew it. But if anyone else had come and found her there, would be have believed her? Would, say, Rowley have believed that she didn't kill him? That she knew nothing of his murder? Well, Rowley had believed Dennis. Or had he? Was it belief that induced him to accept Dennis' explanation, or was it for some dark purpose of his own?

Rowley was always indirect; Rowley had never really liked Dennis.

And Gertrude—she was thinking of Gertrude when the door opened and Gertrude came into the room.

"There you are," Gertrude said. And glanced over her shoulder into the hall and closed the door with a suggestion of stealth. "I thought you might be here."

She crossed to Daphne and pulled a small chair up near her. She was excited. Her tight, large bosom rose and fell jerkily, and there was a faint bluish tinge around her mouth and in her cheks. Her very light blue eyes were still shiny and the pupils in them bright and black. She said to Daphne in a rather husky voice, as if she were trying to lower her habitually loud and forceful tones:

"I was looking for you. See here, Daphne, I've something to say to you. And I think this is a good time. There's no sense in beating about the bush; I'm like Father, I come straight out with things. Never hesitate."

This wasn't true. But Gertrude had no notion at

all of the subtlety and wiliness that lay under and
dictated old Rowley Haviland's purposeful brusque-
ness, his pose of heartiness and bluff directness.

"What are they doing?" asked Daphne.

For an instant Gertrude wavered and looked
rather bleak.

"I don't know," she said. "Everything's upset—
men all over the house. That little detective poking
his nose into everything—upstairs, downstairs—not
saying anything." She stopped and mused and said
with a defeated air, "I don't like him. But Amelia
would have the wedding here. If we'd been in town
there'd have been the Chicago police force—much
better." There was in her manner a suggestion that,
wherever they were, the thing would have happened.
"But, of course," she said, "there's nobody can deny
it's a most fortunate thing."

"Fortunate——"

"For the company," said Gertrude. "For us all.
For the Haviland family. There's no need to pretend, Daphne."

The instant of bleakness and of defeat had passed.
Her eyes were shining again, and as always with
Gertrude there was something reverential about her
when she spoke of the company. Gertrude loved
exactly three things in life: the company and the
memory of her father, which were bound up in each
other; herself and the memory of her father, for
she felt she was very like him, and honor paid to certain qualities old Rowley Haviland had had was
next door to honoring Gertrude herself; and her
son, Rowley, who was named for his grandfather,

whom she expected to take his grandfather's place, but who was, regrettably, not at all like Rowley Haviland. Or, at least, so Gertrude felt, for she was able to perceive certain hidden traits in Rowley Shore no better than she had observed those same traits in her father.

She leaned back in her chair and kept her eyes fastened upon Daphne and said slowly, "There's no use pretending, Daphne."

At first and inconceivably Daphne saw no danger. She was used to Gertrude; accustomed to the air of hidden significance with which she invested quite unimportant and obvious things.

She did not see danger except that she did see that there was something triumphant about that bright, light gaze, fixed and shining, as if two marbles had been set in Gertrude's face.

Then Gertrude smiled slowly, as if she did not know she was smiling. She said, "Ben Brewer is dead. He's dead, and the company is saved. Nothing can bring him back now. The way is left open at last for Rowley."

"For—Rowley?"

"Certainly. Rowley ought to have been made president when Father died. Everybody knows that. He is the obvious choice——"

"My father," said Daphne. "He——"

"Johnny!" exclaimed Gertrude, her eyes snapping suddenly. "Not at all! Johnny is no business man. Johnny can manage the social end of things— he always has done that and most successfully. But Johnny has no business instinct at all. Anybody can sway him when it comes to business. Oh, of course, he doesn't realize that himself. I expect he thinks he's a model of business acumen. But he isn't, and it's a good thing my father left no real responsibility to Johnny. He has no business judgment at all. Why, all this year, Daphne, he has done exactly as Ben Brewer said to do—voted with him always. With Johnny's block of stock, he and Ben and the stockholders could always far outweigh my vote and Amelia's. Most unfair, of course, but there it is. Now, though——" Gertrude's bosom swelled a little, and a slow smile crept around her mouth again. "Now it will be different. Rowley will have the presidency and salary. Ben Brewer's stock, I happen to know, was willed to you. Johnny's stock——"

"To me!" Daphne sprang to her feet. "Ben's stock to me! Oh no, no!"

Gertrude eyed her coldly.

"Didn't you know that?"

"Oh no, no! I knew nothing of it. Aunt Gertrude, I—I can't take it. I won't take it. Nothing can make me."

"Oh, come, come, Daphne. There's nothing to get so upset about. After all, it was his will to his wife. Nothing more proper, I'm sure."

"But I don't want it. I knew nothing of it. I wasn't—I'm not his wife. Are you sure, Aunt Gertrude?"

"Of course I'm sure. I don't make mistakes. Sit down again, for heaven's sake, Daphne. You'll have the police in here."

Police. Daphne sat down and looked at Gertrude.

It wasn't possible that Ben had done that. He had said nothing to her of his intentions; no one had told her. No, it wasn't possible.

"Don't act like a baby, Daphne," said Gertrude. "He made the will about a week ago. Perfectly right and proper. Certainly, you'll take it. Think what people would say if you didn't. And it gives you— with Rowley—a controlling share of the company. That is, Rowley, of course, as president will have, sometime, my stock. The two of you——"

Gertrude was all at once trying to be subtle. She was floundering a little, watching Daphne with those shining light eyes.

But what was she trying to say? What on earth could she mean? Ben leaving her that stock because he had expected her to be his wife! And now she was not his wife, and there was that stock in the Haviland Bridge Company; a large block, a paying block. Well, there would be some way out of it; there must be. They couldn't force her to accept it. She could give it away. She could—— *What was Gertrude saying?* A word or two caught her confused thoughts and focused her attention sharply. An incredible word:

". . . the way clear for Rowley," Gertrude was saying. "So you and he can marry."

She stopped and looked at Daphne, and Daphne stared back at her. Certainly Gertrude had been talking of Rowley. And she'd said something of marrying—but what it sounded as if she said was altogether impossible. She couldn't have said that. Daphne pressed her hands to her temples confusedly.

"Aunt Gertrude—I—I don't think I heard you.
Who is Rowley to marry?"

"Who?" said Gertrude sharply. "Do pull yourself together, Daphne. You, of course."

Gertrude had gone out of her head. The excitement and the inquiry and Ben's death and—— She
was talking irrationally, as she did sometimes when
she was about to have one of her nervous headaches.
She——

"Don't look like that, Daphne. There isn't time
for a lot of talk about it. But I want you to understand exactly how things stand."

Daphne shook her head helplessly.

"But, Aunt Gertrude——"

"Hush. Look here, Daphne. I see you don't understand. Rowley has always had an—an affection for
you."

That wasn't true, either, thought Daphne. Besides, if he had had, Gertrude would have been
jealous; would not have talked of it, granted it as a
fact.

"Always," said Gertrude. "Of course, during your
engagement to Ben he was obliged to say nothing of
it. But now—it will be an ideal marriage. You and
Rowley. Ideal. Of course, we can wait awhile. It
wouldn't do to be too abrupt about it. But eventually . . ."

It was actually true. Her ears had not lied, and
Gertrude was really saying all those things. Really
meant her to marry Rowley.

Daphne stood up quickly.

"Look here, Aunt Gertrude," she said, "if you

mean that I'm to marry Rowley, you'd better know right now that I'm not going to."

"Daphne!"

"I won't marry Rowley. Never. It's impossible. Besides, Rowley doesn't want to marry me."

Gertrude stared glassily up at her a moment; then she rose slowly and rather ponderously.

"That," she said, "has nothing to do with it. Your marriage with Rowley will practically insure the future of the company."

You mean, thought Daphne, suddenly given a moment of insight, it would insure your control of it. Gertrude liked power; half of her hatred for Ben had been because he would have no interference. Because she could not influence him; because he belittled her business acumen.

She stood there facing Gertrude, so near that she could hear Gertrude's short, panting breaths. So near that she saw again a curious little snap and flash in Gertrude's eyes, as if something had opened and closed with the swiftness of the flash of a snake's tongue.

"But I'm not going to marry Rowley," Daphne said again steadily, and Gertrude's eyes snapped once and she said, "Oh, aren't you?" and laughed.

It was a queer, deep little laugh, as if she were really amused. Queer because Gertrude had no humor at all and laughed only when other people laughed.

But she laughed now. Laughed and said, "I think you are, Daphne. You'll make him a good wife once you are married to him. I'm sure of that. You see, my dear—I know something——" She stopped and leaned nearer Daphne and said in a kind of panting whisper, "I know something the police had better not know."

She came so close to Daphne that Daphne was pressed back against the chair. She said again, panting, "I know that you and Dennis planned to go away last night. To leave Ben. And I know that Ben knew it and tried to stop you. Who killed him, Daphne—you? Or Dennis?"

"I—I—we didn't——"

Gertrude laughed again with a deep, jubilant note.

"I don't care who killed him," she said. "It's good riddance. But it would be much better if the police did not know what I know. So I think you'll marry Rowley, my dear."

CHAPTER 9

LATER Daphne could not remember what she said. She knew she tried to deny it; she knew she had a confused but strong feeling that she must not say too much, must admit nothing, give Gertrude no satisfaction. She did attempt to question her, but it was difficult to question without admitting.

"I didn't kill Ben," she said once. "The police——"

"The police," said Gertrude, "are already doubtful as to there having been any burglar. I myself wasn't taken in for a moment. Not after I remembered that someone had been walking about in Ben's room—*after Ben was dead.* Was it Dennis? It doesn't matter. I know that Ben tried to stop you. So Dennis killed him. Or you. But I think it was Dennis."

"That is not true," said Daphne. (Had Ben come to the springhouse to stop that flight, not knowing that already she had realized it was impossible? And if so, how had he known? She had told him, in that last ugly interview, that she didn't love him. He had known it was Dennis. But he hadn't known what Dennis had persuaded her—momentarily—to do. Unless—unless it was Ben who had opened the library door.)

"Oh, isn't it?" said Gertrude unexpectedly. "Well, there's no use in talking of this. I know what I know. Never mind how."

"Does Rowley know of this?" asked Daphne suddenly.

"Rowley," said Gertrude, "will do as I tell him. That's all, Daphne. You are a sensible girl. And a bargain is a bargain. The police are out there now looking for evidence leading to the murderer of Ben Brewer. Murderer," repeated Gertrude lingeringly, holding Daphne with her eyes. "But, of course, I shall tell them nothing of what I know of the matter——"

It was just then that Amelia opened the door quietly, looked into the room, said: "Ah—Daphne!" and entered.

"I was looking for you," she said. "The house is full of policemen—really——" She crossed to Daphne, took her hands and kissed her cheek. It was rather a remote and cold kiss, very brief, but it was a kiss. "I'm extremely sorry for you, Daphne," she said, keeping to the letter of the truth. "This is most distressing. What do you know of the matter, Gertrude, and what matter were you discussing?"

She said it very quietly and turned and looked fully at Gertrude.

There was, actually, a kind of family likeness between the two sisters, although Amelia was dark where Gertrude and Johnny were fair like their mother. But there was a smallness and neatness of bones, a kind of delicacy of feature which was very like Gertrude's, except that Amelia was very slender and looked frail—though no one had ever known of a day's illness on her part. Her eyebrows were dark and heavy and came to a peak like Dennis' and like old Rowley Haviland's, thus shadowing her eyes a little so they seemed withdrawn and incalculable. Her hair was gray and curled; her nose unexpectedly strong, with thin, delicate nostrils; she dressed with the utmost care and elegance and liked fineness of material and cut and finish. Her voice was always very soft and very kind. It was particularly gentle and kind when she spoke to Gertrude then.

Gertrude flushed and blinked rapidly.

"About the murder," she said.

"Ben's death," said Amelia, veiling it so gently that the word "murder" immediately took on its full measure of ugliness and horror.

But Gertrude was still triumphant. "Ben's murder," she said, "and also of Rowley's marriage to Daphne," and looked at Amelia.

There was a sharp silence. Daphne said, "No—no, Aunt Amelia——" and stopped.

For a moment Amelia and Gertrude faced each other without sepaking: Amelia, delicate, frail, eyes withdrawn and thoughtful; Gertrude, flushed and oddly defiant. Then Amelia put out her small, lovely hand—soft and delicate in gesture as a butterfly's wing—and touched Gertrude's thick blue arm. And at the touch the strangest look came into Gertrude's face, and she shrank back a little and said in a breathless way, "Amelia——"

Amelia interrupted, so kindly it was not interruption.

"It might be better," she said, "to talk of Daphne's marriage later. Just at present—well, it's not in the best taste, is it, Gertrude?" Amelia smiled a little and took Daphne's hand again. "Just now we are in a rather difficult position. For I'm quite sure the police do not think there was a burglary. They are asking," said Amelia, "too many questions. Come, my dear, let's join the others upstairs."

Too many questions.

It was an observation that became increasingly apt as the day went on. As strange men came and went, as cars whirled up the long drive to the door, paused and whirled back down it to the highway again. As in a businesslike way that was remarkably thorough the police took over the house and grounds and all that was there.

The telephone was in constant use, but none of them knew what were the results of the low-voiced conversations that took place from the small telephone closet under the stairway in the lower hall. Gertrude complained of it. "I tried to hear what they said," she told them, unblushing, "but all I could hear was somebody talking about—well, it sounded like airplanes."

"Airplanes!" cried Johnny, jingling the keys in his pockets.

"The eleven-o'clock plane, somebody said."

"Is that all you heard?"

"Yes," admitted Gertrude. "A man in a brown suit with a hat over his eyes came and took the telephone extension right out of my hands. Isn't there anything we can do to stop them, Johnny? They are all over the house, looking at everything."

Johnny looked out the window.

"I'm afraid not, Gertrude."

About one-thirty Laing and Maggie served a rather scattered lunch in the old playroom on the second floor to which the family had drifted, seeking refuge from the strangeness and the seething activity on the first floor. It was also, as Rowley observed, coolly attacking the chicken salad which had been intended for the wedding—it was also a vantage point.

"An observation post," he said. "We can see everything that goes on from these front windows. Did anybody remember to stop the caterers or are these wedding-baked meats?"

"Laing telephoned them at once," said Gertrude. "I wonder why they are questioning Dennis for so long a time. He's been down there for an hour or so."

"They'll probably take us in turn," observed Rowley. "If you have any secrets, prepare to shed them now."

Amelia put down her teacup gently and said, "Rowley!" and waited till he looked at her. "It isn't exactly a joking matter, my dear," she said then kindly.

A slow little flush crept up over Rowley's sallow face. And Gertrude said suddenly, wheezing, "If you

don't stop jingling those things in your pockets,
Johnny, I'll scream."

She hadn't seen Dennis since she had left the
library, thought Daphne. Why were they keeping
him there so long?

She wondered, glancing at Rowley, if he knew of
his mother's incredible plan. Incredible, and yet
thought out and determined upon in the coolest possible way, as if Gertrude felt—as certainly she did
—that it was altogether right and just. Rowley to
take his rightful place at last. Gertrude to be the
power behind the throne—at last. And Ben Brewer,
at last, ousted.

Well, she had had every reason to think Daphne
could do nothing but agree to her plan. There wasn't,
thought Daphne, staring at the plate Johnny had put
in her lap, anything else to do. If Gertrude told the
police what she knew, it would be horribly convincing evidence against Dennis. Dennis . . . stealing
another man's bride at the very moment, almost, of
the wedding. Persuading her to go away with him.
And Ben knowing it—going to the springhouse to
stop them. And being found there murdered.

That was, almost certainly, why he had come to
the springhouse. But what had happened before she
and Dennis came, too? What had taken place, who
had followed Ben there and met him, in that black,
mysterious interval before she herself had gone
through the snow and darkness and had entered the
springhouse?

"Please, Miss Amelia," said Maggie from the
doorway.

"Yes, Maggie."

"Those—those men. Policemen," said Maggie, looking shaken. "They are looking in your desk, all through it. Drawers out and papers——"

"I can't help it, Maggie," said Amelia kindly. "It's their duty."

Maggie gave her a horrified look, said "Yes'm" dubiously and vanished.

"Had Ben no relatives at all?" said Johnny suddenly, helping himself to more salad. "He never spoke of anyone——"

"Only those Hartford cousins," said Amelia. "I wired them some time ago."

Quite suddenly Daphne looked up and met Gertrude's eyes. They were light and shining and secret. Altogether assured in their knowledge. Altogether certain of power.

Daphne rose. Someone spoke to her as she left the room—Amelia, she thought, but she did not stop. In the narrow hall she came upon a man who was blowing faintly ochre powder upon a doorknob and then bending to look intently at the old brass knob. He glanced at her questioningly but stood aside to let her pass.

In her own room again, she locked the door and sat there staring at nothing, thinking in weary, desperate circles.

Once she remembered the dress. She ought to do something with it. And she must tell Dennis what Gertrude knew and what she had threatened. He must know it at once, although she didn't know what he could do.

It was cold in the little room; cold and dreary, and the sky dark gray above a gray, cold world. She pulled the green wool cover that lay folded on the foot of the chaise longue around her and out of sheer physical fatigue went suddenly to sleep.

It was dark when she woke, and somebody was pounding at the door.

Maggie, her face ghostly in the shadow of the little passage, said that the detective—"that Mr Wait," said Maggie—wanted to see her.

She stumbled to the little bathroom adjoining her room and washed her face in cold water and ran a comb through her hair so the gold in it shone. She powdered, too, and put on crimson lipstick with hands that shook a little. On the way through the bedroom the wedding veil, a soft white wraith in the semitwilight, brushed against her hands and clung softly to them.

She pushed it away. And just then Dennis came to the door, glanced swiftly behind him and entered.

"Daphne, my dear," he said and pulled her away from the door so they could not be seen and took her in his arms.

"Where have you been? What have they——"

"Questions. Routine stuff. Getting—oh, identification. Nothing to worry about." But he looked worried, she thought swiftly. Worried and tired, with a queer, wary look in his eyes. "Are you all right, Daphne? Have they——"

"He sent for me just now. The detective."

His arms held her tighter, and there was a quick kind of tautness in his face.

"Well, then," he said, "it 'll be all right. But mind, Daphne, stick to the story. You know nothing of the murder. Nothing at all. Don't worry about anybody else. Don't let them trap you or frighten you into telling something. And look out for the unexpected—the thing you aren't prepared for. Promise me you'll do all this."

"I—I'll try, Dennis."

He looked down into her eyes searchingly, as if testing and plumbing her strength. "Oh, my dear," he said suddenly with something like a groan, "if I could have kept you altogether out of it! I love you so," said Dennis and held her tight against him, his face against her hair. "I love you so."

It was a long, inexpressibly sustaining moment.

She did not think of Gertrude until he put her away from him.

"You'd better go now, Daphne. And remember——"

"Oh, Dennis, Gertrude knows. She knows I promised to go away with you. She knows we were to meet at the springhouse. She says that Ben knew, too. She says he tried to stop us—and that we—that we murdered him," finished Daphne in a jerky, incoherent whisper.

"*Gertrude!*"

"She says," whispered Daphne stiffly—"she says she won't tell. And that I'm to inherit Ben's stock and marry Rowley and he'll be president of the company."

"To marry——" Dennis' eyes suddenly blazed in his white face. "God! So that's Gertrude's plan!

How——" He stopped, thinking furiously. "It's like Gertrude," he said. "She's just stupid enough and vicious enough to do it."

"What can we do, Dennis? How can we——"

"I don't know. I don't know. I'll try to think." He stared at her for a moment, not seeing her, his eyes withdrawn under those peaked black eyebrows. "I'll have to think, Daphne. We've got to shut her up somehow. We—— Look here, you'd better go down. They'll be sending for you again. Don't be afraid, my dear. And don't think of anybody but yourself. Remember!"

"Yes, Dennis."

He kissed her then. Swiftly, but so hard and deep a kiss that it seemed to remain, there on her lips, long after she had gone.

There was no longer the confusion of strange men and voices and cameras and smoke in the hall, although it had a disorderly look—and many and muddy feet had entered that wide door and trooped across the worn old rugs. Two men, plain-clothes men, were standing near the door, talking, and they stopped to turn and look at Daphne as she passed.

It was then about six o'clock. A cold, gray winter twilight with the feeling of impending snow. A twilight like the one twenty-four hours ago when Dennis walked up the road through the shadows of firs and falling snow and—before he came on to the house—climbed that steep little path to the spring-house.

And Jacob Wait, lounging against a table in the library, with his hat over his eyes, looked up when she hesitated in the doorway and pushed his hat farther back. "Come in," he said. "Sit down. Tony!"

The policeman with the shorthand tablet sighed and got up from the divan and came again to the little table and opened his tablet. It was fat now with notes—queer, irregular little lines. He wished Wait would call it a day. After all, they'd talked to everybody in the house from the cook on up, and they had enough material to keep an ordinary man busy for days. He thought rather grimly of some of the things that had come out during the course of those long, grilling interviews.

He sharpened a pencil meditatively. Queer old place. He didn't like it. If he had the money these people seemed to have, he'd live somewhere that was bright and cheerful. In town, where there were lights and people and traffic sounds. He didn't like the way night fell on those snowy, fir-dotted slopes.

He tried the pencil. Adjusted his long, bony frame to the stiff little chair. It looked as if Wait was going to try to push the thing through that night. It was like Wait, smart of him, to get all the dope he could and then go after the girl with it. The weakest link. The one most likely to break. She looked scared. Looked as if she was about to faint.

Schmidt, the man in plain clothes, was looking at Wait, too. Looking at him and waiting, as Daphne was waiting, for him to begin. He turned suddenly and fumbled for the curtain and pulled it across the window. The wind was rising and whispering around the house, and chill little drafts were creeping along the floor. You could never get these old houses shut up tight, he reflected and thought of his lumbago. He was due for an attack as sure as the wind shifted to the east. He shivered a little and wished Wait would get on with the job. He knew damn well one of them had killed this Brewer; well, then, why not just take the whole lot of them to jail?

Pretty girl, he thought. But she looked scared. Well, she'd probably spill the whole thing. They were about due for a break.

"Sit down," said Jacob Wait. "In that chair."

The chair was directly under the light, and it glared down into her eyes. She sat down, clasping the arms of the chair so her hands would not tremble. She had a curious feeling of being hedged in. Of being the center of a steadily encroaching and advancing circle.

It was so strong a feeling that she turned and looked behind her. Three other men had come from somewhere and were standing in the shadow by the closed door, watching.

Her fingers tightened on the arms of the chair. Her heart suddenly was pounding in her throat.

"All right, Miss Haviland," said Jacob Wait. "Who was the woman who left this house shortly after midnight last night?"

CHAPTER 10

I<small>T HAD</small> come.

All along, during those incredible, packed hours since midnight, she had been waiting, preparing, armoring herself against this hour. Answer him, then; evade; watch for traps.

She moistened her lips. Someone had seen her leaving the house and told of it. But if he had known it was she, would he have asked her in just that way? It had been dark, and there were no lights in the house. Whoever it was might have seen only her figure wrapped in the coat, veiled by flying snow, obscure in the darkness.

"My room is on the south," she said. "It only overlooks the back door."

"Don't evade," said Jacob Wait. "There's no sense in it. It just takes time. Shortly after midnight last night a woman left the house, walked down the drive to the gate and took a taxi which was waiting for her into town. The taxi driver left her at Diversey and Central. She paid him and went into the drugstore, and he got a cup of coffee and drove back out to St Germain. Now then, who was the woman?"

"I—— But I don't know! I know nothing

124

of——" It had given her a queer kind of shock; a surging relief that was, actually, dangerous itself because it threatened the tight guard she had placed on herself, because it was outside all the questions whose answers she had ready. "I don't know," she repeated.

"Come now, Miss Haviland. Think. Who was at dinner last night?"

"Just—just the family. My aunts. Myself. My cousins, Rowley Shore and Dennis Haviland. And— and Ben Brewer."

"All right. Then where did the woman come from?"

"I don't know. I haven't any idea. She was not here. I'm sure of that."

"Could she have been here without your knowledge?"

"No," said Daphne and stopped and thought, This old house. Rooms over the garage. A dozen places where one might hide if it were necessary. "I don't know," she said. "I suppose it's possible."

"The telephone call for the taxi came from this telephone," said the detective. "We traced it. The call was made about eleven o'clock. A man's voice told the taxi driver to be at the gate at twelve and wait until one or after. That he couldn't say what time exactly he would have to wait. Do you know who made that telephone call?"

"No," said Daphne immediately, sure that she did know. "No."

"Well, I know," said Jacob Wait in a bored way. "It was Dennis Haviland. Why did he want a taxi?"

"I didn't know he had called one," said Daphne. "If he did, I suppose he wanted to go somewhere."

"Where?"

"I—I don't know." (A taxi; waiting to take her away with Dennis—away to the station, into the Loop and trains; where? And she must not permit herself to think of it for fear her thought would become telepathic and would transfer itself to the ready consciousness of the man questioning her.)

"Dennis Haviland arrived yesterday, I believe."

(He meant that he knew; that he'd inquired.)

"Yes."

"About what time?"

(About this time of day, wasn't it? And she'd been sitting in the very chair where Jacob Wait sat now. She'd been looking into the fire and thinking of her marriage and of Dennis . . .)

"About what time?" said the detective again, his voice suddenly a little deeper and richer, as if in spite of his hatred of it there were moments of deep, instinctive excitement about this business of catching a murderer.

"About—about this time, I think," said Daphne. "I'm not sure."

"Did you see him when he arrived?"

"Yes. Yes, of course."

"What did he say?"

"Why—why, that he'd come back and—just the usual things."

"Did he say there was any particular reason for his coming?"

"No," said Daphne faintly, closing her mind to the thing Dennis had said.

"Did he know that you were to be married to-day?"

"Yes."

"Who told him of it?"

"I think—I think Aunt Amelia wrote to him about it some time ago." (He hadn't got the letter, she remembered suddenly. But Amelia had written.)

"Then he came from South America to attend the wedding?"

"I don't know. No, I don't think so. I think he was ready to come home. He'd been traveling for nearly a year."

"Why did he take a plane from New York?"

"I suppose he preferred it to taking the train."

"A train would have brought him here this morning. In plenty of time for the wedding."

(No need to reply to that; there wasn't any reply.)

"The plane brought him here last night. And at midnight Ben Brewer was murdered."

(No reply to that, either.)

"What is your feeling about Dennis Haviland? Are you in love with him?"

"My—— Why, I—— He's my cousin. We've grown up together."

"Were you ever engaged to him to be married?" said Jacob Wait coolly.

"*No.*"

"Did you love Ben Brewer?" There was a curious, brutal impatience about the question; murder was a brutal, ugly affair, said Jacob Wait's manner; there-

fore, why scruple about the tools of detection one
used?

"I was going to marry him," said Daphne.

"Look here, Miss Haviland," he said with a kind
of bored disgust. "Several times you have tried to
evade my questions. Why do you do that? It only
takes more time. There are things I know. I know
that Dennis Haviland had been making a leisurely
trip home from South America. I know that in New
York, quite suddenly, he decided to get home yesterday. I know that in one of his pockets there was
a picture of you, taken from the New York edition
of a Chicago paper. A picture of you and a notice
of the wedding. I know that he got hold of that
picture *in* New York. I know that immediately he
took a plane for Chicago and came straight out to
St Germain. I know he saw you last night. I know
that he telephoned for a taxi, telling the driver to be
at the gate at midnight and wait. This in itself
argues indecision—not so much indecision, perhaps,
as, for some reason, that he did not know exactly
what time he would be leaving. Well then, why didn't
he know? If he wanted to get a train, he would have
known the time. If he had some engagement, he
would have known the time. Why didn't he know
exactly what time he would leave?"

"I—I don't know."

He looked scornful.

"And when a passenger came to the taxi, why
wasn't it Dennis Haviland? What had happened to
change his plans? And who was the woman who
finally came?"

"I don't know," said Daphne again, feeling as if her voice were remote and distant from her body.

He looked at her and, suddenly, went back to her marriage.

"Did your family approve of your marriage to Ben Brewer?"

"Yes," said Daphne. "That is—yes."

"There were altogether friendly relations between your aunts and your father and Ben Brewer?"

"I—— No, not exactly."

"You mean they objected to the marriage?"

"No."

"What then?"

"My aunts and Ben—— Well, they have never been—friendly. But my aunts approved of the wedding. They—they made all the arrangements. They did everything."

"Everything," said Jacob Wait. "Except that the wedding didn't take place."

(No answer to that, either; suddenly she saw again—as she had seen so many times—the sprawled bulk of blackness on the floor of the springhouse. No, the wedding hadn't taken place. A little wave of sickness and faintness caught her. Perhaps she would faint, she thought, and did not know then that the merciless tension of inquiry had barely begun. She tried not to think of the moments in the springhouse.)

"Why were your aunts opposed to Ben Brewer?"

"There were—business reasons."

"Ben Brewer was president of the Haviland Bridge Company, wasn't he?"

"Yes." (He knows all this, thought Daphne. Probably everybody in Chicago knows.)

"He was made president and general manager by the will of your grandfather, is that right?"

"Yes."

"And your aunts did not approve of this provision of your grandfather's will?"

"No."

"They have been, in fact, trying in every possible way to get him out of his office?"

"I——"

"Don't tell me you don't know. You do know."

"Yes."

"Why?"

"They—they think his methods of management are all wrong. They think that he will—he would have done a great deal of harm. They thought the provisions of the will were unwise; that Grandfather was too much under Ben's influence."

"Do you know the provisions of the will, Miss Haviland?"

"Yes. Yes, of course. There is no secret about it. There was quite a lot of talk of it at the time he died, and when his will was probated. I'm not just sure about the exact figures of the blocks of stock held by my my father and my aunts. I think, roughly, the stockholders have nearly half of the stock and the family the other half, divided equally between Aunt Gertrude, my father and Aunt Amelia. Except, that is, for the stock that Ben owned."

"Stockholders, forty-five per cent. Benjamin

Brewer ten per cent, and a deciding vote in matters
of general management. The remaining forty-five
per cent divided equally between Mrs Shore, your
father and Miss Haviland. Cash bequests to servants; cash bequests of five thousand dollars apiece to
Rowley Shore and Dennis Haviland and to yourself.
Personal property and real estate divided between
your father and your aunts." He said it all rapidly,
with half-closed eyes. "Did you think this fair, Miss
Haviland?"

"Yes."

"Was everyone concerned satisfied with it?"

"It was my grandfather's wish. He felt he had
made the best possible arrangements. He only
wanted to protect us all."

"Yes. He seems to have wanted to do that and to
have felt he was successful." He quoted rapidly,
with his eyes half closed, as if the will itself were
written on his eyelids: ". . . 'with the knowledge
that in case of a future period of economic depression and financial need the said company and corporation is amply protected and duly provided for
under the now existing agreements and provisions.'
Sounds smug," remarked the detective, opening his
eyes again. "However, he, at least, was satisfied with
what he had done. Or do you think he referred more
specifically to Brewer?"

"I don't know. I never thought of it. I only remember the main provisions of the will."

"And your aunts did not think it fair?"

"They were afraid that—that Ben would wreck

the company. They didn't like his methods—the things he did. I'm not exactly sure about the details."

"You needn't be. The main thing is that your aunts were determined to get Ben Brewer out of the company. Why, then, did they permit you to marry him? If they wanted to get rid of him, it wasn't a good plan to tie him into the family by marriage. Or did they hope to influence him through you?"

"No. I couldn't have done that. I mean——"

"What do you mean?"

"I never tried to influence him. He told me——"

"What did he tell you?"

"That—that I couldn't," said Daphne. "That there was no use——"

"No use?"

"No use—trying."

"Had you tried to change him or influence him in any way?"

"No," she said faintly, perceiving the entangled threads around her feet too late.

"Then why did he say that? Why did he warn you?"

"I—don't——"

"When did he say that to you?"

"Yesterday," she said huskily.

"At what time?"

"After—dinner."

"Exactly what did he say?"

"I—— That is all."

He knew it wasn't all. She could see it in his eyes, his whole expression, the shrug he gave, as if her resistance mattered so little, was so slight that he could break through it any time he wished. He drew a small, shining object from an inner pocket and held it in his hands.

"Ben Brewer was not murdered by burglars," he said. "He was killed by somebody in this house. This whole setup was arranged afterwards—and not too skillfully arranged. He was not killed in the house: the bullet came from a thirty-two caliber revolver, and the sound of the shot would have been heard. His dress coat was hanging in the wardrobe off his bedroom, and there are dust marks and what look like cigarette ashes on the back of it; around the shoulders. The coat has been sent to the North-western Laboratory. I'll soon know the story it has to tell. There is no dress shirt and collar and no white waistcoat in his room which shows any signs of wear. Those he wore when he was killed have disappeared; but we'll find them. There would have been bloodstains on them. Powder burns. He was killed probably shortly after midnight. Yet at two o'clock Mrs Shore heard him walking about in his bedroom, which was next to her own. Dead men can't walk, you know. Who was it, then, in his bedroom; who was it who crept up and down stairs arranging all this? Putting a bathrobe on that heavy, dead body; arranging footmarks on the rugs near the window. Disposing of the telltale dress shirt and waistcoat, hanging that coat up in the wardrobe. Heaping up wedding gifts. Opening—too late—the windows of the drawing room. Who did all this?"

Her heart had quite literally stopped beating. She watched with a kind of still, fascinated horror while he tossed the small object upward so it flashed, and caught it again.

"To whom was Ben Brewer so great an obstacle that he had to be removed? There are many to whom his death conceivably would be a boon. But why should he have been killed the night before his marriage to you? Why was his marriage to you a crisis? Why did he become, only then, so great a menace that he had to be killed? What did he do—where did he go? I think you know the answers, Miss Haviland."

He was very near her now: so near she could see the small, ruby glow away back in his eyes. No one else moved: it was so still that, in spite of that hedge of listeners, it was as if she were alone with the detective.

"Is this your wedding ring?" he said.

She looked then at the delicate circle of gold in his palm. She recognized it immediately. Ben had shown it to her, holding it in his thick fingers for her admiration, calling attention to its exquisite simplicity.

"It—was to be."

"A thing of immemorial symbolism," said the detective, his voice suddenly rich and musical. "Hope and love; devotion, deception; death. The whole gamut of human emotions are bound up in a wedding ring. This one was in Dennis Haviland's possession. The bullet that killed Brewer came from Dennis Haviland's revolver. Will you tell me, now, what you know?"

It was the unexpected. The thing she wasn't prepared for. The thing Dennis had warned her against.

She tried to speak: she tried to tell him it wasn't true, it couldn't be true. But she could not take her eyes from the small gold circle. A symbol, the detective had said: and there was nothing in all that hidden story of the murder, as she knew it, to account for Dennis' possession of her wedding ring. For his revolver.

There was a sort of commotion at the door; there were voices, and someone spoke to Jacob Wait.

"We've got the woman," he said. "Only it isn't a woman."

CHAPTER 11

I𝚃 WAS, at least, a release for Daphne. For Jacob Wait put her wedding ring in his pocket and walked out the door and did not return.

They waited awhile, Daphne and the plain-clothes man and the policeman with the shorthand tablet, in the chill, quiet room. A room familiar to Daphne and yet poignantly unfamiliar just now, as if the thing that had happened were like a lens coming between her and old familiar things so they were sharply and strangely distorted and out of their known and natural order.

It was dark now, dark and very cold, with the windows shining and reflecting, where there were no curtains, the room and the waiting policemen and Daphne, a small huddled figure in brown, her face pale, her hands locked together. It would be an exceptionally cold night, with the windowpanes frosted later on and the snow blue and crisp under one's feet. Not soft and silent as it had been the night before.

So that was the line of inquiry. They knew, or had known somehow all along, that there were no burglars. They had to have the murderer, and they had to have the motive. And every question the detective had asked her led directly or indirectly to Dennis. Built link by link a chain which already, she realized, had dreadful strength. Quite small and trivial things such as the newspaper clipping in Dennis' pocket—a natural thing to do, after all, to tear out and keep that clipping—were suddenly high-lighted, made of significance and meaning. Dennis had foreseen all this; she had not.

The wedding ring had a dozen explanations; the most probable was that during that hideous moving and arranging of the body (suddenly she thought with horror of the physical strain it would have to be —sliding and fumbling and panting for breath down that slippery little path in the snow, getting that inert and heavy burden along the drive, through the window among all those vases and flowers and ferns)— sometime during all that the wedding ring had dropped out of Ben's pocket and Dennis had picked it up and thrust it into his pocket. It was not an explanation they could give the detective, for she began to see, coldly now and with certainty of reason, that Rowley and Dennis had been right. Rowley from his own point of view, perhaps, but Dennis decidedly from his and from her own.

For the police had to have a motive. And failing any other motive, that of love and jealousy and hatred remained. And with ugly aptness it fit. What had actually occurred—except that it had stopped short of murder. Dennis *had* returned as soon as he heard of the marriage. Ben *had* been murdered the very night of Dennis' return and the night before his wedding. And again with ugly aptness the thing the police wanted was exactly the thing that had occurred. That was the truth. Dennis *had* tried to stop that marriage, he had used desperate and extreme measures, and she, overwhelmed no less than Dennis by desperation, had agreed to run away. To leave Ben the night before a widely known and talked-of marriage. It had been, of course, a dreadful thing to agree upon; a cruel expediency which, if they had been cooler, if they had been less driven by the pressure of time and circumstance, they would never have considered even momentarily. But, besides the need for haste because the wedding was so near, they were, Daphne realized now, a little drunk with love.

Dennis had returned at just the time when she realized poignantly that her wedding to Ben was a tragic mistake but one that to all intents and purposes was already accomplished. There was, she had felt, no possible escape. She was set in a mold, and she could do nothing but remain in it. So she had said good-by to Dennis and good-by in a strange way to herself.

And then Dennis had returned. Had taken her in his arms. Had told her she could not marry Ben.

And in the sheer madness and drunkenness of those moments she'd agreed. They had planned the thing that seemed, then, their only way of escape.

She looked incredulously at the big brown chair before the fireplace. There was no fire there now; the room was cold and had undergone that singular translation so it was no longer familiar. But last night, at about this time, it had been warm and softly lighted; flames in that hearth and herself—alight, too—in Dennis' arms, promising anything, everything, overwhelmed as was Dennis.

But Dennis was stronger. And Dennis was not bound by all the fetters which bound her.

She had talked to Ben; she had realized she could not keep that mad promise to Dennis. That it was, again, too late.

She had gone to tell Dennis that; in her heart she had wanted another and a last moment with him. In her heart perhaps she had hoped against hope that he would find a way to save her.

She shivered a little, thinking of the way that had been made. But not by Dennis.

Not by Dennis. If the truth were known, it would be the motive the police needed. But it wasn't Dennis who had killed him.

She leaned her head wearily on her hand and thought of the revolver. He might have been lying —Jacob Wait—in order to get some reaction from her—in order, even, in some wily and hidden way, to trap her into giving evidence. But instinctively she believed he had told the truth. Not probably from any scruples or even habits about truth, but simply because he didn't bother with anything but direct methods. Short cuts.

If true, it was of course a horribly incriminating thing. Add to that a proved motive, and the police had all that they needed.

She thought of the revolver; going over in a kind of weary perplexity all possible contingencies whereby the revolver could be proved not to have been in Dennis' possession. It was a futile attempt; she knew

too little of the thing. The bare statement left no
loopholes, no ground for speculation. She would ask
Dennis; did he know—had they asked him—what
had he told them? It was again part of the dizzying
nightmare of questions—to which there were no discernible answers—which had overtaken them all.

But had overtaken more perilously herself and
Dennis. Had overtaken them so it was already like
a trap.

She had never in her life before consciously seen
or talked to a detective. She had known them as
newspaper figures, or less remotely as rather stolid
gentlemen, well dressed and standing about at unexpected points at weddings or fashion shows, keeping rather obviously unsocial and cold eyes upon
jewels. Now they represented in their persons in-
describable menace and power. It was their right to
question her about all those things; to delve insistently into her deepest thoughts and emotions and
motives. She thought, with a kind of sick shudder, of
what she'd read of murder trials and of suspects.
Suppose they took her to prison—questioned her for
hours and hours and hours until she was fainting
with exhaustion and the hypnosis of nagging, persistent, repetitious inquiry. Suppose—— Where was
the county jail? That would be the place. What kind
of room would they take her to? A cell—away from
her people—away from . . .

She caught herself up shortly; such thoughts were
dangerous.

Why didn't Jacob Wait return? Who was the

woman who had left the house? Why—— It was no good thinking.

The two plain-clothes men exchanged a word or two; a man came to the door and summoned the policeman with the shorthand tablet, who sighed and unfolded his thin length and went away.

"You can go now, miss," said one of the plain-clothes men. "There 'll be more later. All persons are instructed not to leave the house until further notice," he added mechanically and held the door open for her.

There were voices in the music room. As she left the library, the door of the music room opened and the policeman (stenographer, was he?) entered, and she heard Jacob Wait's voice and a few words: " . . . at exactly what time . . ." The door clicked, and Daphne went on. New evidence; she took a little courage in the thought of its being important enough new evidence to distract the detective, at least for the time being, from questioning her.

Dennis was waiting in the hall, pacing up and down, smoking. He threw down his cigarette and came to her quickly.

"Did they——" he began and stopped abruptly; it was with a quick feeling of incredulity, a stabbing sense of the unreality that had overtaken them, that she saw him glance quickly along the passage, as if to be sure no one could overhear before he continued. This, in the ordinarily peaceful house where up to now they could have shouted anything they wanted to say. Police all over the house, free to come and go and watch and listen. No reticence, no defense against them. Themselves under guard, under unrelaxing surveillance; knowing that a word, a whisper—a look even—might betray them. And in that surveillance was a chill, ever-present reminder that a man they had all known intimately, a man who'd been one of the small, tight circle and an important one, was dead and was murdered.

Death must always be a shock; sudden and unexpected death, and one that strongly affects the lives and destinies of others, a still greater shock.

But murder has its own being; its own aftermath; its own insidious and inexpressibly ugly shadow. It was as if the air were suddenly tainted; as if the house and the old familiar stone and wood had taken on a different and strange dimension. As if they themselves were touched and threatened by it in a way that went deeper than their obvious danger from the police—although that, thought Daphne wearily, was ugly enough.

It was, of course, the secret repudiation of man's inheritance of law and social pacts that was in itself terrifying. That secret loosing of bestiality. Of ruthlessness. Surely such an experience would leave its mark forever upon the murderer; stamped as if in letters upon his face. But no one of them was any different, no one of them—— She checked herself: that thought, too, was dangerous. And Dennis said in a matter-of-fact voice, "We're having some din·ner in the dining room, Daphne. You'd better come along. There's a fire there, too." He was looking at something over her shoulder. She looked, too, and a policeman had emerged quietly from the kitchen passage and was simply standing there looking at them. Dennis went on: "It's going to be frightfully cold tonight; Laing has stoked up the furnace, but there's not much chance getting this house warm. Thank God, there are fireplaces. Come on, Daph, and have something hot."

They were at the door of the dining room. She whispered, "The revolver—they say it belongs to you," and he nodded briefly and whispered, "I know. It 'll be all right. Don't worry."

He knew of it, then; and he must have given the detective some sort of plausible explanation, as otherwise he would have been under arrest. But the reassurance in his voice and face was too marked. And she had no time then for further questions, for they were at the door of the dining room.

There were tonight no candles reflected in silver, no red lake of roses. The lights from above were garish and bright: a bright, hot coal fire made the room stuffy but warm; the red curtains were drawn across the windows, and the entire family was at the table.

Amelia looked up quickly and sharply.

"Coffee, my dear," she said very gently, and Rowley jumped up and pulled out a chair at the vacant place beside his own, saying, "Here you are, Daph. You look all in. What had the detective to say?"

It was natural for every one of them to want to know any fresh developments; at the moment, however, it seemed to Daphne sinister and unnatural, as if among them might be one who hid guilty, gnawing anxiety as to the course of the inquiry. Well, that, too, didn't bear thinking too much about. She sat down in the chair Rowley held for her and said, "Just general questions. I answered—there wasn't anything that I knew of any real evidence." (Parenthetically she hoped it was true.) Gertrude, watching her fixedly, bit slowly into a grape she had held poised at her mouth for an instant or two, and Johnny sighed.

"I do wish they would let you alone, honey," he said worriedly. "I tried to tell them you knew nothing about it. But this Wait insisted——"

"Oh yes," said Daphne suddenly. "They stopped questioning me because they found out who the woman in the taxi was."

"The woman——" said Amelia and stopped, and Gertrude cried, "The woman in the taxi! Why, they asked me about that, too! They insisted that someone was here overnight—that is, was in the house last night and left about midnight or a little after. I told them there was no one, that there could be no one—— *Oh!*" She paused sharply, her blank blue eyes wide and glassy. "Why," she cried, "that means there really was someone! But it's impossible. It——"

"Who was it, Daphne?" asked Johnny.

Rowley, eating steadily, said nothing, and Amelia, pouring coffee in a steady amber stream, said, "They asked me that, too. I told them no one could have been in the house without my knowledge. Laing would have told me at once. Anyway, the thing is ridiculous. However, if they've found the wretched woman, I suppose she must have been somewhere about outside. Probably having come to see Ben." She filled the cup and gave it to Daphne. "I do hope it wasn't some woman who——"

"Who had claims upon Ben?" cried Gertrude excitedly. "Oh, my——"

"I was about to say," continued Amelia, "who was, or had ever been, his mistress."

"Really, Amelia——"

"It would be most unpleasant. Do have more grapes, Gertrude. But at any rate it would settle the thing without dragging us all into it."

Rowley put butter on a piece of roll. "You say they've found the woman, Daphne? When?"

"I don't know. But she's here now. In the music room, I think, being questioned."

"Oh," said Rowley. "Well, in that case you'd better know."

"Know?" said Amelia. "Know what, Rowley?"

"Rowley," said Johnny in a tone of sudden comprehension which had something despairing in it, "do you mean to say——"

"Oh yes," said Rowley. "He came last night. Wanted to see Ben."

Johnny put down his fork slowly, staring fixedly at Rowley with troubled blue eyes, and Gertrude stopped another grape on its way to her lips, shot one blank blue look at Johnny and another at Rowley, and a slow wave of crimson crept painfully over her face. Amelia said, "Oh—so that's it," quietly, and Gertrude thrust back her chair with a violent gesture and surged to her feet.

"I will not stay under the same roof with that man," she shouted with explosive, vehement passion. "Rowley, you've been writing to him! You told me you wouldn't! You promised me! You lied to me! You've been lying to me all along! How dared you do it! You let him into the house. You knew he was coming. You were going to let him talk to Ben. What about? What was it you had plotted? Why did he want to see Ben?"

"Gertrude!" Amelia put a beautiful small hand upon Gertrude's arm. "The police—they'll hear you. Stop shouting. You are childish."

"I am not childish," shouted Gertrude and began to wheeze so her voice was spasmodic and hoarse. "I am not shouting. He—my son—Rowley, tricking me——"

"Now, Mother, sit down. Nobody's tricking you. He wanted to see Ben——"

"Why?" demanded Gertrude hoarsely, leaning over the table and planting both her hands upon it. "Why did he want to see Ben? Because you were plotting, that's why. Because you——"

Rowley slid to his feet and said sharply, "You'll give yourself a headache, Mother. And you'll have the police in here. And it does no good to shout and rage and get asthma. He said he had business with Ben."

"What kind of business?" asked Johnny quickly. "He couldn't have had business with Ben. That's absurd. I don't know what he told you, Rowley, but——"

"He didn't," replied Rowley slowly, "tell me just

what business. He did say, though, that his allowance had been cut off."

Amelia glanced at Johnny, who drummed the table with his fingers, cleared his throat reluctantly and said, under the compulsion of Amelia's look, "Well —yes. That is, no. That is—well, dividends are low, Rowley. You know that. His allowance came from a small block of stock. There was nothing else to do. We had to cut it down."

"Serves him right," muttered Gertrude. Rowley said, "Of course he *is* my father."

"Your father——" began Gertrude, her voice thick with rage and hoarseness and scorn, her wide face hot and flushed, her eyes shining. "Your father——" she cried, and Johnny got stiffly to his feet.

"Oh," he said in a small voice and looked beyond the table to the doorway. "Oh—hello, Archie. Come in and have some dinner."

CHAPTER 12

Johnny's talents as a professional diner-outer, said
Rowley later, had never been of more use to the family. He said it unkindly and with a malicious gleam
in his dark eyes, but it was true and continued to be
true during those strange and horrible days and
nights following the murder of Ben Brewer. For
automatically, with innate tact and unimpaired social
manner (except for somewhat shaky hands and a
tendency to worry his neat blond mustache), Johnny
bridged many an awkward gap and soothed many a
stormy moment.

He did so then, when the others turned to follow
his eyes and saw Archie Shore standing in the doorway. It had been years since Daphne had seen him,
yet she recognized him at once.

Johnny pulled his waistcoat nervously, touched his
mustache worriedly and went around the table to
shake hands with Archie and find him a chair at the
table. Amelia helped, for she said rather grimly, "So
you're back, Archie," and rang for Laing. "Set a
place for Mr Archie," she said. "You've had no dinner, I suppose, Archie?"

"Thank you, Amelia," said Archie Shore. He was a

thin, dark man, like Rowley except that he was older and his narrow face deeply lined and his eyes shifty; he was a little shabby, too, although he looked almost too able to take care of himself, and there was a wolfish thinness about his smile which just lifted the corners of his mouth and showed two very long and yellowish teeth.

"That's kind of you," he said. "How do you do, Gertrude."

Gertrude, crimson and speechless, stared at him with stony blue eyes, and he lifted his eyebrows a little and turned to Daphne. "Daphne, I suppose it's not out of place to offer condolences. I'm really sorry, my dear, that it happened to you."

Daphne found her hand taken, pressed gently and somewhat damply, and released.

Rowley said coolly, "Do sit down, Father. How did they find you?"

Archie Shore shrugged, sat down and accepted soup. Daphne looked at him and remembered in a scattered way things she'd heard of him and tried to recall her childhood impressions of the man. It was too long ago, however; she could remember only dimly the turmoil in the house, long sessions of lawyers and of the adult members of the family, and Gertrude, a red-eyed, defiant and determined storm center. Then Uncle Archie had vanished, and the children had been instructed not to speak of him. What had he done? she wondered. Come into combat with Gertrude, certainly. And what had he done since then?

Gertrude, her flushed face set, was obviously torn

and perplexed. Should she leave the table in a rage, or should she remain?

She decided to remain, and Johnny, in a low and placative voice, made the decision easier (so it became an act of graciousness) by coaxing her.

"Do sit down, my dear. We've got to make the very best of this horrible situation Ben's—Ben's death has brought upon us," said Johnny, with his ringed hand on her arm. "Come, Gertrude." He hesitated, swallowed and said desperately, "Be brave, Gertrude."

Archie's upper lip drew back a little, wolfishly.

"That's noble of you, Gertrude," he said, with a mocking edge in his voice. "Very kind of you all, I'm sure, to welcome me. However, I assure you it's no easier for me than for you, Gertrude, except that I have better manners."

"Now, Archie," said Johnny despairingly, "don't! Why did the police bring you here?"

"Of course," said Amelia, "you are the woman in black."

"Always astute, Amelia. I am the woman in black who departed in a taxicab which was fortunately standing at the gate when I needed it. I don't understand the taxicab," said Archie, almost gayly, except his eyes kept shifting from one face to another. "But there it was in time of need."

There was a sudden, queer little silence. It was as if all at once and simultaneously everyone at the table had been recalled from the slight diversion of Archie Shore's unexpected return and were thinking of its possible and extremely unpleasant significance.

Amelia voiced it:

"But, Archie, just why did you leave by this mysterious taxi? At midnight?"

"Anyway, why was he here?" burst out Gertrude, pointedly not speaking to Archie but to the others. "Why was he here in the first place? What did he come for? And—why did he leave so suddenly? Rowley said he came to see Ben. Well, then——"

Johnny got up nervously and went to the door, glanced into the hall and closed the door again. The wolfish smile vanished from Archie's thin, rapacious face.

"How you would like to make me the scapegoat, Gertrude!" he said as softly as a snake swishing through grass. "But you can't. I had no quarrel with Ben."

Rowley reached nonchalantly for cake and said nothing. Johnny, obviously distressed, hovered near the door and said, "For heaven's sake, don't talk so loudly." Dennis, an enigmatic look in his eyes, watched and listened, and Amelia said, "Leave the room, Laing. Now then, Archie, suppose you tell us just what you were doing here. I did not know you were here, and you certainly know, so there's no reason to make any pretense to the contrary, that you are not welcome in my house."

"I know nothing better," said Archie. "I came, however, to see my son."

Rowley opened his mouth, shut it again and looked at the cake on his plate. Gertrude wheezed and struggled to talk, and Johnny went around and patted her heaving back perfunctorily.

"I came to see my son and also to see Ben. I wanted to find out why I'd not been receiving my"—he lifted his eyebrows and said, "my usual check. I thought it best to come directly to the head of the company," said Archie. "Is there anything wrong with that?"

"Who let you into the house?" asked Amelia succinctly.

"Rowley."

Again Rowley looked as if he were about to speak, changed his mind and ate more cake appreciatively.

"Is that true?" said Amelia, observing his detachment.

Rowley shrugged. "Really, Aunt Amelia, I can't do anything about it if my parents choose to quarrel. I have nothing to say."

A glint came into Amelia's deep-set eyes.

"You'll talk to the police," she said gently, and Gertrude gave her a startled look and turned to Rowley.

"Do tell us the truth, Rowley," she said with a sort of gasp. "After all we—we can't afford—we don't know—— It *is murder.*"

"Very well," said Rowley. "I don't know when he arrived. Sometime after or during dinner. I don't know how he got in."

"Walked in the back door," said Archie, his eyes going rapidly here and there, as if continually testing the qualities of their tempers. "Am I going to have any further food, Amelia?"

Amelia put her beautiful hand on the bell. "Certainly, Archie. What then, Rowley?"

"Well, when I went up to my room about eleven,

there he was. In my room, sitting in the armchair, smoking."

"How did you get there?" demanded Gertrude savagely and directly.

"Walked," said Archie. "Nobody saw me; everybody was busy, I suppose. I'm not in my dotage, you know, Gertrude. I remembered Rowley's room."

"Then what?" said Amelia, addressing Rowley.

"Well, he said he'd come to see Ben. That he was only waiting to see him alone. I didn't think it would do any good for him to see Ben and tried to talk him out of it."

"Did you see Ben?" Amelia asked Archie.

Rowley looked at his cake again, and Archie replied at once, "Certainly not. And a very good reason. I waited in Rowley's room until he came up about eleven; we talked for a while, and then I left. Rowley convinced me it wasn't a good time to approach Ben, and there was no point in my staying. I intended to walk into town, but this—taxi was there in the road, so I took it into town."

"How did the police get you?" asked Dennis suddenly.

Archie gave him a quick, sharp look which was still not direct.

"I don't know exactly," he said.

He was lying, thought Daphne. Fluently, as if he had had long practice. For no good reason the fantastic notion came to her that he'd given himself up. Why? Because he would be perhaps a material witness; because it was a chance to edge into the family circle again—or, which was more likely, because for some reason he could get something out of them. Fantastic, she told herself, and horridly suspicious. But something about the man bred such suspicions. Something a little flashy, a little shifty, a little furtive.

But a witness—a material witness. That meant he had seen something, knew something of the murder. And he had been in the house during that mysterious hour preceding Ben's death. He had left the house, by his own story, at shortly after midnight. She glanced at Dennis, to discover that he, too, had realized it and all its implications.

It was in his eyes; a look of wariness, of being on guard against another danger. Another and unexpected hurdle in that treacherous course. The more dangerous because Archie Shore was not a man even momentarily to be trusted. And because in all probability he knew something of the real story of Ben's death; the real story, at least, of its discovery. For Rowley had told him of it; that was it. Rowley had told him, and he had seen the immediate necessity for his escape and had disguised himself by getting into a woman's clothes—something taken from an attic or a store cupboard—and had gone.

But that didn't work out, either. For Rowley had had no chance to warn him. Rowley had come upon the murder as they (herself and Dennis) had come upon it; there had not been time, while Dennis took her to the house and returned to Rowley waiting in the springhouse, to permit Rowley himself to go to the house, reach the second floor, warn Archie and return to the springhouse.

But someone had been in the hall; someone on the

stairway. Had it been Archie, then? Had he been, perhaps, on the grounds—leaving—when Rowley had seen the light in the springhouse and had gone to investigate? Had Archie followed and remained outside—peering in through that narrow dark slit at the door—listening and watching and drawing his own conclusions? Had he followed Dennis and herself to the house through those muffling veils of snow? Followed her up the stairway and forgotten, because he'd been away so long, that the third step creaked? Had he gone into a closet and taken a woman's coat and hat, obsessed then only with a wish to escape now that murder had occurred and before the police came? At the gate the taxi Dennis had called was waiting. That was the taxi Archie had taken into town.

Well, then, why had he returned and given himself up to the police?

If he had returned of his own volition, there was only one motive. And that was because he knew something and intended to put it to his own use. And because he had had time, now, to think it over and to lay plans to do so.

She had had, always, a kind of feeling of sympathy for the underdog. The underdog, in this case, being Archie Shore. He had been literally pushed out of the Haviland family and from his job in the Haviland company. There had never been anything good said for Archie Shore, and instinctively and because of this she had felt that he might not be so bad after all. But she knew now that all they had said, those

Havilands, had likely been true. All that and more. You could not look at the man and trust him. You could not hear the false timbre of his voice and credit, for one instant, any motives of decency and honesty.

And, besides, he had probably hated the Haviland family, part and parcel, for all those years. Probably a perfectly comprehensible desire for revenge had smoldered all that time. And now, quite suddenly, he had them in his hands.

A man to be feared.

And everyone there knew it. The knowledge was like a live thing, running on swift and furtive feet around that table, laying a still finger on everyone's lips.

"How did the police discover you?" asked Dennis again. For if the police had found him, if he had not given himself up, there was still a hope.

But again the man was evasive.

"I don't know," he said, helping himself to potatoes. "I don't know."

That falseness in his voice. Well, then, what did he know?

Johnny said, leaning forward, "Archie, do you mean you didn't see Ben? Not at all?"

"Certainly not," said Archie, avoiding Johnny's eyes and busying himself suddenly with his knife and fork. "I tell you Rowley talked me out of the interview with him."

"When did you first know of the murder?" That was Amelia, eyes very deeply withdrawn.

"The afternoon papers," said Archie. "They certainly gave it a spread. Pictures all over the back page. It's the romance, I suppose——"

"Archie," burst out Gertrude furiously, "you keep evading. What have you told the police? Why did you leave here in a woman's clothes? What do you know? What have you——"

"One question at a time, Gertrude." He waited pointedly for Laing to leave the room. As the pantry door squeaked, he continued coolly enough but with a touch of arrogant defiance: "Here it is in a nutshell. First, I did not see Ben. So you need not be grateful to me for providing another suspect for the police and thus further distributing the guilt——"

"Archie!"

"Second, I left here in woman's clothes—they belonged to you, I believe, Amelia, and were hanging in the closet under the stairs. I'll return them to you in good condition—with thanks. I left here in Amelia's coat and hat, and a veil which was rolled up inside the hat, because I chose to do so. Because Rowley had impressed upon me the desirability of my absence and my not being seen and recognized. That is what I told the police. And I told them that I knew nothing of the murder. That my—disguise was merely in case anyone saw me as I was leaving. If you must have the truth, I did it because I didn't care to be recognized by, say, anyone at the railway station. For, of course, I expected to take a train into town. I did not know a taxi would be waiting."

"You knew of the murder," said Dennis grimly. "You were afraid——"

"You go too fast," said Archie. "I'm telling you

what I told the police. What I might have told them is another matter. As I told the police, I saw no one and no one saw me. And"—Archie's mocking, railing tone changed suddenly and became again edged and thin—"and I have told the police nothing further, so far."

"So far," said Johnny slowly and stopped.

For there it was. Out into the open—if it had ever been concealed.

"You've told them," said Dennis, "anything you thought would keep you in the clear."

"Do you mean," said Archie imperturbably, "to imply that I'm lying?"

"I know damn well you are," said Dennis. "You knew of the murder when you went away. And you have—or think you have—evidence involving the family in—in unpleasantness, or you wouldn't be here now. What is it?"

"That," said Archie, "is for the police. Unless——"

He stopped short, with an air of purpose and definite meaning.

"Archie, Archie!" cried Johnny suddenly with a kind of groan. "What have you done!" And then he, too, stopped short and with a queerly desperate gesture put his face in his hands.

Rowley looked at his plate, and Dennis, thoughtfully, looked at Archie. The pantry door squeaked a little. Laing, probably, listening.

Amelia took a long breath.

"Really, Archie," she said calmly, "that sounds like a threat. Or a confession. I might almost prefer it to be the latter, but you wouldn't have returned if you had feared arrest."

"Make him tell what he knows," muttered Gertrude. "Make him tell, Amelia. He can't sit there looking as if he knows something—as if he's already told the police—as if——"

"Hush, Gertrude," said Amelia gently. "Just what will you take, Archie?"

"Amelia, you wound me!"

"Wound——" burst out Gertrude, and Amelia silenced her again.

"I don't know whether you have happened upon something that you think would be injurious to one of us in our present trouble or not," she said. "I do know that you're quite evidently here to do us any possible harm you can do. Well, then, we are in no position to haggle. And we are ready to act, as always, as a family. You may," said Amelia simply, "name your price."

Johnny lifted his face and cleared his throat.

"I suppose you are right, Amelia," he said. "Still ——" He hesitated and turned to Archie. "You wouldn't tell the police anything that would—would harm any of us, would you, Archie? After all——"

Archie grinned. It was again a wolfish tightening of the corners of his thin mouth so it showed narrow, yellowed teeth.

"Oh, wouldn't I!" he said. "Wouldn't I! My dear brother, I have what it takes. You are in my hands," said Archie and put out his hands, which were in all truth ugly and grasping and predatory as claws.

CHAPTER 13

It was actually the unsatisfactory and wholly inde-terminate end of the thing for that night.

Archie kept on grinning and ate grapes vora-ciously. Amelia repeated in so many words her offer to pay him for silence. Gertrude stared and wheezed. Rowley said nothing at all, and Johnny was for once a handsome frozen image of despair.

Dennis felt and said that the sooner Archie Shore left the better for all concerned.

Archie kept on eating grapes.

"You are perfectly right, Dennis," he said, favor-ing Dennis with an extremely ugly look above that rapacious smile. "But, you see, you don't know the thing I could tell the police if I chose. You don't know the things I could do to the company if I chose. The rumors—the doubts—how circumstantial I could make stories of, say, embezzlement, of failure, of imminent bankruptcy. What reasons I could hint at for Ben's murder—if I chose. So far I have not chosen to do so. I'll tell you what, Amelia, I'll think it over. Give me two days."

"Two days!"

"One day, then. Say, till——" He paused to remove seeds with the utmost deliberation. "Say, till tomorrow night. Twenty-four hours."

"So you can frighten us—terrify us into giving you anything you want," cried Gertrude. "It's your one chance to get back at us. What is it you think you know? Nothing!" She turned to the others. "Don't you see he's only bleeding us for every cent he can get? And we are going to let him. I'm not afraid of anything he thinks he knows. I didn't kill Ben. Why, we are as good as admitting that we are afraid of something when we let him——"

"Gertrude," said Amelia, "stop that! Certainly you didn't kill Ben. I didn't kill him. None of us killed him. I'm not offering to pay Archie because he has any real evidence against any of us: I know that he has none," lied Amelia blandly. "I'm paying him because he is obviously here to make trouble. Most unfortunately,"—she looked coldly at Rowley—"he was here at the time of the murder. If he tells the police he saw this or that—any made-up story he wants to tell—they are likely to credit it at least until it is disproved. According to my notion, it is much simpler to pay him to keep his mouth shut. I am not at all afraid of him or of what he may say. Not, that is, concerning the murderer. He might damage the company. And I do wish to keep this dreadful affair as quiet as possible, to wind it up as quickly as possible."

"And quite right you are, Amelia," said Archie imperturbably. "Except that you somewhat underestimate my capacity for observation."

Dennis got up.

"Look here," he said, "can I kick him out, Aunt Amelia?"

Archie slid to his feet and got behind a chair, his grin changing to a kind of snarl, and Amelia said hurriedly:

"No, no! It's a bargain, then, Archie. Until tomorrow night. If in the meantime you say one word to the police which involves any of us, I pay you nothing." She rose. Johnny sat as if transfixed, staring at the tablecloth, and Dennis opened the door. "That's all," said Amelia and then added with a characteristic touch, "But remember, Archie—I—none of us—are as rich as we once were. That's why your allowance had to lapse. The Haviland Bridge Company, though you may not know it, has had a very lean year under Ben Brewer's management."

Archie, still standing, reached coolly down for cake but kept the chair between himself and Dennis.

"The Haviland Bridge Company," he said, "ought not to have suffered. It was well prepared for emergency."

Johnny pushed back his chair abruptly and went to Amelia.

"Good night, Amelia," he said. "You are perfectly right, of course. Archie, will you take one of the guest rooms? I'll loan you pajamas."

"Thank you, Johnny. I could do with a shirt or two."

"You can have mine," said Rowley.

"Good God," said Dennis violently, "are we going to let this man——"

Amelia put her hand on his arm. "Will you take me upstairs, Dennis?" she said gently.

He shot one look at Daphne and turned to Amelia.

"I think you are making a mistake, Aunt Amelia. You are simply playing into Shore's hands. Let him tell them anything he likes. He can't——"

"Come," said Amelia.

At the door he looked back at Daphne, and she followed them. Up the stairs, hearing the rustle of a taffeta petticoat under Amelia's handsome black crepe gown, pausing when Amelia paused to call to Laing to be sure that all the windows and doors were securely bolted.

"There's a policeman in the kitchen," said Laing, appearing at the bottom of the stairs. What did he think of it all? Daphne wondered, looking down at his long pale face and bald head. "A policeman in the kitchen," he repeated. "And two in the library. They wish to stay here all night, ma'am."

Amelia hesitated. Gertrude, coming into the hall, said, wheezing, "Of all the nerve!"

"I suppose they are obliged to," said Amelia. "Very well, Laing. Tell cook to put out sandwiches for them. And coffee."

They went on up the stairs, a queer, trailing little procession, its fortitude and its assurance shaken. Shaken by Archie Shore's return and the bargain he had driven with them—a sinister bargain, with the ugliest of implications. Shaken by the day's inquiry. Shaken by the unwonted things that had been happening to them.

And by night dropping down so coldly, and with such impenetrable blackness, upon the house. Isolating them in very fact as the thing that had happened the night before had in another sense isolated them. And in the same way binding them together.

Daphne had no chance to talk further to Dennis. Later, however, Amelia came to her door and knocked and came in. She wore a purple flannel bathrobe, had her hair in a net cap and carried an eiderdown.

"I thought you might need this," she said and put down the eiderdown. "Oh, and—by the way, you might lock the door tonight." She hesitated, looked at Daphne with eyes that had receded until they were mere shadowed sparks, said tensely, "With that man in the house——" and went away.

Daphne locked the door.

And after lying in bed staring at the black ceiling for what seemed an hour or two, she got up, shivering in the cold, and tried the latch to be sure.

Twenty-four hours, she thought once incredulously. All that had happened in twenty-four hours.

And she must talk to Dennis. She remembered and sought refuge in the memory of the long look he had given her there at the head of the stairs. Gertrude was beside her, and Rowley was coming up the stairs. Dennis said something casual, meant for their ears, but his look, guarded though it was, both reassured and warned her.

In the morning she would see him. Tell him—ask him—map some defense before the detective pounded at her again.

It was still in the house. Still and cold. She supposed she slept, but she was haunted by dreams and
a persistent feeling of consciousness. In the middle
of the night she remembered the yellow dress and got
up, shivering, and found it and tried to burn it, but
the last ember had burned out and there were no
matches. She returned, shivering with cold, to bed.
And once she was sure she heard footsteps in the dark
passage outside the door and sat upright to listen
over the sudden pounding of her heart. But if there
had been footsteps there was then nothing.

Probably there was not much sleep anywhere in
the place that night, yet there was no sound of motion. Except that after midnight, when things grew
quiet, the house itself came alive and creaked and
moaned a little with the cold and whispered along
the narrow corridors—so that the policemen were
restless and could not settle into sleep themselves
and sought each other's company as they'd been
ordered not to do and finally cleared off one end of
the table in the library and started a game of poker.
It was a desultory game, however, subject to interruptions. The third time one of them got up, swearing, and opened the door to look along the corridor,
it came to an end.

"It's cold in here," he said. "Let's go to the kitchen."

"Oke," said another, and the third stopped watching a window curtain, which certainly seemed to move
now and then, and agreed with some promptness.

In the kitchen they found the coffee and sandwiches
and ate them but were not greatly cheered, for the

house continued its secret rustling, and it was extremely cold.

It wasn't, they agreed, that anything was likely to happen; it never did right after a murder. But Wait had left them there to see that none of the suspects got away. So every hour or so two of them took flashlights and saw their revolvers were on their hips and made a somewhat sketchy round of the lower floor.

But if, during those cold, black hours, anything alive found its secret way in and out the twisting old corridors, no one knew it. And indeed, in view of later occurrences, it is probable there was only the wind and the creaking of old wood.

Morning was dark and cold. Breakfast trays duly arrived according to custom, with Maggie uncommunicative, owing to a cold in her head.

Except that she had a message for Daphne.

"Mr Dennis," she said, pulling the curtains apart and letting cold morning light into the little room, "Mr Dennis is in the old playroom and wants to see you. He wanted to bring you your breakfast, but I told him you were a young lady now and he couldn't. The idea!" She put the tray in Daphne's lap and handed her a wool bathrobe. "Better put this on, miss. It's cold as Blixen."

It was Maggie's swear word. She went away, growling about the cold and sneezing with a kind of martyred emphasis.

It was still early, and though there were sounds of showers running and coal fires crackling from behind closed doors, no one was in the corridor. Daphne,

clad hastily in her warmest sweater and tweed skirt,
found Dennis again pacing and smoking.

"There you are, honey," he said and took her in
his arms for a hungry moment and shut the door.
"Now then—wait till I put some coals on the fire."

He did so, swearing a little as the battered old
tongs pinched his hand as they had always done if
you gripped them too fervently.

"Nothing ever changes here," he said. "The stairway still creaks. The tongs still pinch." Flames shot
up and crackled, and he put down the tongs and
pushed aside the old brass coal scuttle with the loose,
coal-blackened cotton gloves hanging over the rim,
and stood with his elbow on the mantel. Daphne sat
on a cretonne-covered stool she had pulled close to
the fire. He looked around the room, remembering.
"Same old couch. Same old pictures—Stag at Bay
and Sir Galahad. I was terribly upset to discover a
woman posed for that. Same old rug—remember the
time we burnt that hole in it? Gertrude half killed us.
You were a little girl, Daph. Yellow pigtails—steady
blue eyes. I was always terribly proud of you." He
knelt down suddenly and took her again in his arms.
"I think I was in love with you always, Daphne," he
said shakily and kissed her face and mouth as if he
would never stop kissing her. "And I'm going to
marry you, and not all of them can stop it. I nearly
lost you once. But now——"

"Gertrude," said Daphne. "Rowley——"

His arms tightened.

"Gertrude can go to hell. And her precious son
with her. Just what did she say, Daph?"

She repeated it. In the warmth and security of Dennis' arms it had lost much of its threat. Yet as she spoke she could see suddenly Gertrude's flushed face, her blank, bright blue eyes. Gertrude, she realized, was dangerous because of her lack of common sense; because in her mad rages there was no balance, no caution.

"She said, then," said Dennis thoughtfully, "that she knew we had planned to leave that night. That she knew we were to meet at the springhouse, and that Ben knew it."

"And that he intended to stop us."

"That means, then, that whoever saw us in the library told Ben."

"Or that Ben himself opened the door and listened."

"If it was Ben, he wasn't likely to tell Gertrude. And he—— I was about to say he would have taken steps about it—I mean, when you talked to him, Daphne, did you think that he knew anything of our —our plan? Anything definite, that is?"

Daphne thought back to Ben's cool acquiescence when she told him she hadn't loved him—he'd known it all along, he'd said. But it didn't matter.

"No. No, I'm sure of it, Dennis. He didn't know it then."

"I think he knew it later," said Dennis, frowning into the fire. "It explains his presence there in the springhouse. But someone else knew it, too. Suppose the murderer knew we were to meet there, told Ben in order to get him out of the house where the shot would not be heard, and followed him there. If that's the way of it, the murderer is likely to be the person who opened the library door and saw us and heard our plan. And certainly Gertrude knew——"

"Gertrude!"

"Well," said Dennis thoughtfully, "you know what she's like when she gets in a nervous state. She always hated Ben. No matter how fully she seemed to approve your wedding to Ben, she still hated him. And with him out of the way, it leaves the coast clear for Rowley. The coast clear for Rowley and us actually playing into her hands. For if she once tells the police what she knows, it provides the——"

"The only thing they need. I know. A motive for you. It fits so—so horribly. Our meeting at the springhouse; Ben finding us there. Stopping us— and——" Her voice shook a little, and Dennis took her hands.

"And my revolver," he finished. "It *was* my revolver, Daphne. But I don't know how it happened. You see, I had the revolver all right when I came home Monday night. I'd taken it out of my bags when we went through customs and put it in my pocket. I'd never used the thing; don't know why I ever bought it. I've had it for—oh, three or four years. Got it here in Chicago, and it's registered——"

"Oh!"

"So there was no use in my not admitting ownership. But—but I didn't shoot Ben!"

"Where was it?"

He told her briefly. In the springhouse. He'd taken it absently from his pocket; had put it down to light a cigarette. Had quite simply forgotten it.

"Bright, wasn't it? But how was I to know what was going to happen in the place that night?"

And it had been used to kill Ben Brewer. He had seen it at once; recognized it.

"I picked it up when I bent over Ben to see if he was still alive. Put it in my coat pocket. Then—that moment when I turned off the flashlight——"

"I remember. And your voice seemed to come from the doorway instead of from where I thought you were standing."

"Did it? Funny Rowley didn't notice. I did go to the door. Went to the door and buried the thing in snow outside the door. I expected to have a chance to get hold of it again before the police did. But I— had no chance. They found it. Somehow—they—they do things so much more thoroughly than you think they will. With all that snow—none of it melting—— Oh well, the point is they found it."

"What did you tell the police?"

"Told them the truth," said Dennis, staring into the flames. "There was nothing else to do. Besides, I might have made up some more plausible explanation, but even if one has little if any regard for the truth there's always the matter of perjury."

"Perjury! But that's when there's a trial."

"Exactly," said Dennis. He turned and added quickly, "Don't look like that, Daphne! They haven't arrested me yet. And if they had a good tight case against me they'd make a murder charge pretty tout suite. There must be evidence we know nothing about which tends to clear me."

There was an alternative which he did not tell her;

conflicting evidence, or the detective wanted such conclusive evidence against him, Dennis Haviland, that the murder charge would hold before the grand jury; that it would be tantamount to a conviction later on. The newspapers had hinted at it. But there was no use talking of it to Daphne.

"So far," he went on, "they know only about the revolver. They've not proved any motive, and they won't if Gertrude keeps still."

"And," said Daphne. "If Archie Shore——"

He nodded swiftly. "Of course, there's Archie. I was talking to your father about him. He said Archie was gone from the company before Ben ever came. He said Archie and Ben didn't really know each other; oh, they may have met, we can't be sure. Archie has no feeling about the company as Gertrude and Amelia have. He wouldn't be actuated by what's almost an obsession on the part of the aunts to get rid of Ben. The only possible motive Archie could have would be Rowley."

"Rowley?"

"I mean, he might feel, as Gertrude makes no bones of feeling, that with Ben out of the way Rowley would have more chance. It occurred to your father and to me, but it doesn't seem very reasonable. Archie Shore doesn't impress me with having any particular affection for Rowley; at least, certainly not a crazy devotion that would lead him to commit—murder. Gertrude, of course——"

He stopped, and Daphne said, without being quite aware of what she said, "Gertrude—does such queer things."

Dennis glanced at her quickly.

"Yes. Yes, she's always been like that. Doesn't seem to weigh things properly. Her bargaining with you—trying to force you to marry Rowley—is exactly like Gertrude. Get her in a rage, and God knows what she might do. And certainly she knew of our meeting in the springhouse; and she knew that Ben knew. I always come back to Gertrude, somehow. It's so—so like her." He rose and stirred up the fire again and absently went to the door and made sure it was closed before he came back to stand there at the mantel, tall and brown, with his peaked eyebrows thoughtful. "It's impulsive—as if somehow she—well, suppose she met Ben there—sent him there really by telling him we were planning to go away together—suppose she saw the revolver, picked it up, shot him. I mean, it's an impulsive sort of murder; as if it hadn't been planned at all. We know it hadn't been planned, because no one could have known my revolver would be there—so readily at hand. And that's like Gertrude, somehow; oh, everything about it—she's horribly impulsive, scarcely knows what she's doing when she's in a rage, and she has no sense at all. Never has had. Of course——" He paused thoughtfully. "Of course; if somebody sent Ben to the springhouse with the intention of following him and murdering him, the murderer must have known my revolver was there. That would argue he had gone to the springhouse earlier for some reason—had seen my revolver—had planned. Or that he saw my revolver before Ben saw it, snatched it up and fired."

"Or," said Daphne, "whoever murdered Ben might have planned to shoot him and arranged to get him to the springhouse and followed him out there with his own gun——"

"Whereupon he saw my gun and thought, What a lucky break! I'll use that gun and they can't trace me," finished Dennis. "Lucky for him. Everything handed to him on a platter. We provide an excuse to get Ben to go to the springhouse, and then, just to do it up right, I leave a gun for him. Yes, it might have happened that way, too."

"Gertrude knew about us," said Daphne again.

They always came back to that.

"She's hated him from the beginning," said Dennis. "She's been certain he was mismanaging the company. Perhaps he was. Dividends have been almost nonexistent. But it isn't entirely Ben's fault. It's the times. At least, so Johnny thinks. And even Rowley admits his mother's feeling about Ben was mostly sheer jealousy. Her sun rises and sets in the company and in Rowley."

It was a long talk, and they were conscious of the house, of the sounds of movement now and then in the corridors, and kept their voices low instinctively, as if someone passing through that narrow corridor might pause at the door and listen. It was not nice, that feeling of surreptitiousness.

It was not nice, either, to realize that at the end they had arrived at no conclusion—no conclusion, that is, other than to continue the course they had been obliged to undertake.

"However," said Dennis, "if worst comes to

worst, I do have an out." And showed her the thumb-print and told her all he knew of it. The gruesome little lines in reddish brown, fine and small, affected Daphne, as they had Dennis, with a frightening sense of their sinister potentiality. So small, so fine and faint to mean, perhaps, so much.

And she did not like the memory of the moment on the stairway when she had turned and whispered into the cavernous darkness below and then fled from whatever stood there on the third step.

"I've tried twice," said Dennis, "to take it into a crime-detection laboratory in town. A private one where I can get a print of it without the knowledge of the police. Once I got as far as the gate before they stopped me."

"Is it the murderer's thumbprint? How can you be sure?"

He couldn't be sure, of course. But neither he nor Rowley could remember getting blood on their hands during that grisly transaction. They'd been very careful about that. He hadn't told Rowley about the thumbprint. But he had asked him about blood on his hands. He took the sliver of wood bearing its horri-ble little burden from her fingers.

"I'm pretty damn sure," he said confidently, "the police and the crime-detection laboratories can do things—have secured convictions on less evidence than this. So you see, Daph, if they do arrest us—I mean me—here's this."

"Why don't you give it to the police now?" she said, watching him put it carefully into an inside coat pocket.

He gave her a very queer look. "It's better," he said shortly, "to wait. After all, Daphne, it was on the stairway—someone going upstairs——"

"Oh. Oh, you mean someone in the house," she said and swallowed with a tight throat.

He nodded. But they'd known that. Known it from the beginning. He meant, then, to give it to the police only if he had to. To save himself—to save her. Besides, to give it to the police would be to tell them the whole story of the murder as only she and Dennis knew it. And suddenly she understood: saw through all his excuses. He had found her alone in the springhouse, alone except for Ben—murdered at her feet. And his whole object was to keep that knowledge from the police.

Her eyes blurred suddenly so she couldn't see him distinctly, and he turned, saw it, and told her briskly to cheer up.

"At worst there's the thumbprint," he reminded her. "And at the very least it will give its owner something to explain. So don't worry too much, Daphne—I mean if we—I—you—finally are charged with murder, there's always this." He patted his pocket and gave her a kind of smile, meant to reassure. "It may save both of us yet," he said. "And look here, my girl, don't get any notion that I'm intent on sacrificing my young life for—for anything," he said. "Suppose the police do find out we were in the springhouse——"

"I was there first. You found me with him. I could have murdered him before you came."

"But you didn't. And as to that, I could have mur-

dered him, left the springhouse and returned later to
meet you," said Dennis cheerfully. "I didn't, but I
could have. So there's no question of sacrifice, and
don't be a little idiot." He went on quickly to other
things: Could they, he asked her, depend upon Rowley? Rowley had never been exactly trustworthy. But
here his own interests—safety, even—were involved.

"He may turn state's evidence if——" Dennis
checked himself and said, "Eventually."

They talked, too—fruitlessly—of Archie. Of
Amelia's offer to pay him off. Of the progress the
police had made or had not made.

"They found the revolver near the springhouse,"
said Dennis. "Seems odd that they happened to look
just there. But if they know the murder occurred in
the springhouse they've not yet said so. To me, at
any rate."

But he hadn't known about the wedding ring. And
he stopped poking up the fire again and turned
abruptly to face Daphne when she told him of it.

"Wedding ring!"

"Yes—oh, of course, I knew you had only taken it
—without thinking what you were doing while you
and Rowley were—were——"

"I didn't take it. It didn't roll out of Ben's pocket,
if that's what you were going to say." He frowned.
"I know nothing about this, Daphne. In my pocket,
you say?"

"Yes. I—I was so sure that was how it happened. I didn't attach much importance——"

"Do the police? I mean do they seem to—to em-
phasize it?"

"Yes," said Daphne miserably and told him.

He stared somberly into the fire for a moment and then poked it vigorously and took the heavy, bronze-handled fire tongs in order to adjust the lumps of coal so they would burn.

"And you are sure it was the wedding ring?"

"Yes. Ben showed it to me before dinner that night. He put it back in his pocket. I'm sure it is the ring."

"That means, then, that whoever took the ring from his pocket knows we were in the springhouse— knows at least something of what we did that night —and is trying to—well, to frame me." He gave a short, dry laugh. "Pleasant, isn't it? And God knows there are enough clues involving me if the murderer knows of them and can bring them to Wait. Well, it's to be war, then. And with an unseen enemy. Working in the dark. How about this will of Ben's, Daphne? Your father told me of it, and you say Gertrude knew it. What are you going to do about it?"

"I can't take the stock. I won't——"

"You'll have to," he said. "You see, your father says Ben told him of it, and said he had given your name as Daphne Haviland when the will was drawn up and it was to be changed to Daphne Haviland Brewer immediately after the wedding. It was his lawyer's doing; merely a matter of accuracy at the moment of making the will. But the result is, his whole property comes to you."

"I won't take it."

"It doesn't matter," said Dennis, "whether you do or not so far as——"

"Motive?"

"Well, yes." He said it reluctantly, hating to add to the dark care already in her eyes. She was pale that morning, with small, dark shadows under her eyes, and she looked very young in her red sweater and tweed skirt. He thought of how he loved her and wondered why he had ever gone away. First Ben stood between them, and now Gertrude and Rowley and the ugliness of the thing they threatened to do. Well, he wouldn't let them. He wouldn't let her marry Rowley. It was a monstrous suggestion on Gertrude's part; a queer, half-hysterical undertaking. But it was, he thought, in the future. They couldn't press the thing until all this had died down. Until the murderer was found—or until the quest for him was given up. Until people had stopped talking.

He went to her and took her quietly in his arms. "I love you so," he said. "Sometime, Daphne, soon —you'll be my wife."

"I'm afraid."

"Of what?" he said, holding her more tightly against him.

"Of everything—of Wait—of the house—of all these things——"

"Nonsense!" He tried to laugh. But he thought of Wait, too.

"And the wedding ring," she said suddenly. "It— it terrifies me, Dennis."

He didn't like it, either. But he smoothed her brown hair and told her he loved her and things would be all right and hoped it was the truth.

"Why should anyone take the wedding ring?"

He didn't know. He looked over her head into the fire. In the drive below, cars were arriving—police cars, he supposed. Every now and then someone passed the door of the playroom; once he had thought someone paused in the hall outside, and he had listened for the creak that would tell of retreating footsteps. But Daphne hadn't noticed it, and he hadn't wanted her to; they couldn't hear, he told himself. And forgot the thinness of the old walls; the remarkable ease and swiftness with which sounds in that echoing old house traveled.

For he was thinking of the wedding ring.

Why would the murderer of Ben Brewer take the wedding ring?

"Daphne," he said suddenly, "don't think I've gone out of my head, but did your father really want you to marry Ben?"

CHAPTER 14

Mʏ ғᴀᴛʜᴇʀ!"

"Yes. Oh, I know Johnny. But that wedding ring——"

"If it hadn't been for my father I wouldn't have promised to marry Ben," said Daphne wearily. "He didn't urge me to; he wouldn't have tried to make me marry Ben against my will. But he liked Ben; he thought he would be a good husband as he was a good business man." She shook her head slowly. "My father wouldn't have murdered Ben to keep me from marrying him. Even if—if he thought I'd be unhappy; if he'd made some—some dreadful discovery about Ben. Oh, he loves me—he loves me dearly. But he——"

"I know," said Dennis. Johnny was innately selfish, hated trouble as a cat hates water and avoided it with the most affable determination. Of course, the most affable and social of persons might pluck up the desperate and momentary courage to do a murder. But there had to be a motive: Daphne herself profited by Ben's death. Rowley would profit by it, if Gertrude could (but he wouldn't let her) carry out her plans. But no one else. So far as money went, that is. "You're sure both the aunts wanted you to marry him?"

"Perfectly. Oh, I don't mean that they or my father brought—pressure to bear upon me. It was just that—somehow they made me see it was the thing to do. Made me do it——"

"And Rowley. Was he, too, in favor of it?"

"Why, I—I suppose so. I can't think——"

"You see," said Dennis, "Rowley may be in love with you, too." He smiled a little as he said it, but his eyes searched her own deeply just the same.

"If Rowley's in love with me," said Daphne somewhat crisply, "he's certainly done a good job of concealing it. Of course he's not in love with me."

"Oh, come, come, Daph. Don't be so disgustingly modest. You're kind of a nice girl. I'm in love with you. Why shouldn't Rowley be?"

"Well, he isn't," said Daphne definitely. "Gertrude's plan for us to marry is probably altogether news to him."

"Oh yes," said Dennis, looking thoughtful. "Gertrude."

It was just then that, with somewhat grim appositeness, Rowley came to the door, rattled it and called out, "Dennis!" impatiently.

"It's the police again," he said when Dennis opened the door. "They want to fingerprint us. Oh, of course they have no right to do so. But Jacob Wait—the detective, you know—asked us if anyone wanted to make a formal objection. Naturally no one did. What have you two been talking about so long?"

"Suspects," said Dennis. "And you."

Rowley's eyes narrowed a little, and he looked quickly at Daphne.

"See here," he said. "Have either of you told the police? I mean—told them about the—the spring-house?"

"No," said Dennis. "Have you?"

"Certainly not." Rowley looked at Dennis and at Daphne and back again. "But why, then, do they keep asking me about what I did that night—whether I was out of the house—if I saw anybody—all sorts of questions?"

"Probably to find out whether you killed Ben or not," observed Dennis.

For just an instant Rowley looked remarkably like his father. Then he smiled. "You *will* have your joke, Dennis," he said. "But this isn't really a joking matter."

"You are perfectly right," said Dennis. "Did you burn the shirt and waistcoat? I didn't ask you yesterday, but was checking things we might have forgotten."

"Why, I—— Yes. That is, I tried to. They wouldn't burn—too wet." He glanced quickly at Daphne and said hurriedly, "That is, they wouldn't burn."

"Good God!" said Dennis and took a quick step nearer him, so that Rowley stepped backward involuntarily. "Well, what did you do with them?" said Dennis between his teeth.

"I took them out on the river; made a hole in the

ice and stuffed them in. Nobody saw me. Best I could
do, and it's just as good as burning. Just as———"

"Oh, you fool!" said Dennis, his eyes blazing.
"Oh, you fool!"

"Dennis!"

"What else have you done—or failed to do?"

"Nothing, Dennis. Nothing, I swear it."

One never knew when Rowley was telling the
truth. Dennis said, "Look here, Rowley, I was trying
to remember exactly what was in his pockets."

"I don't know," said Rowley sullenly. "I remember when we took his shirt and waistcoat there was a
lot of blood. I don't think we looked in his pockets.
At least, I didn't. Why?"

"There might have been some clue," said Dennis
slowly.

"You might inquire of the police," suggested
Rowley with a lifting of his upper lip which was very
like his father, and Johnny stopped in the doorway
and said, "Hello there, children. Morning, honey,
how are you? They're waiting for you downstairs."

Dennis shot one warning look at Rowley and said,
"Okay. Come on, Daph." And Rowley stepped suddenly toward Daphne and put his arm around her
waist.

"I don't like your airs, Dennis," he said coolly, his
anger hidden suddenly and showing only in the extreme paleness of his face. "I think you'd better
know that Daphne is to be my wife."

All her life afterward Daphne was to remember
that moment, although at the time it was only a kind

of blur from which certain things floated. The sense
of Rowley's nearness, her body pressed against him
and his arm tight around her. The crackle of the coal
and the faint smell of coal smoke and breakfast. Another car driving up outside and the closing of its
doors—one, two, three. More police, she thought
vaguely. Her father's face, gray, with wide blue eyes,
and the nervous way he patted his tie and pulled
down his waistcoat and tugged at his mustache and
still did not speak. No, he was never violent; always
wanted things to be smooth and polite and civilized.
    And Dennis.
    Dennis, white with something besides rage; some-
thing more than momentary and purely physical jealousy. Dennis, with his eyes blazing again from under
those peaked eyebrows. Dennis, starting forward
furiously and checking himself within a foot of Rowley. Checking himself obviously at the thought of
Gertrude.
    She'd told Rowley, then. And they'd joined in that
ugly, devilishly ingenious compact.
    Johnny was talking: "Daphne, is this true? Are
you and Rowley—— Dear me, wouldn't it be best to
wait a little? What will people say? What——"
    Rowley's voice cut through it, cool and malicious:
"Congratulate me, Dennis—that is, if you have any
—affection—for Daphne."
    "You damn cur!"
    "Dennis—Rowley—good God, what's the matter
with you!" cried Johnny, pulling his mustache wildly,
but cautiously refraining from getting between them.
"See here, you two. Keep your quarrel till this thing

is safely over. Good heavens, does it matter? Now? When there's been a murder here and any of us are likely to hang for it? Good God! Dear me!" He twisted his mustache, ran his hands through his blond hair and turned in anguish to Daphne. "My dear, do tell them to stop. Tell them anything—tell them——"

"Daphne doesn't need to speak," said Dennis. He took her hand. "I'll speak for her. She'll do as she pleases and——"

It was then that Daphne saw him standing in the doorway. His hat over his face. His dark eyes somber.

"Dennis!" she cried in a choked way. Both Dennis and Rowley saw him then, too, and stiffened.

"Don't mind me," said Jacob Wait, his dark eyes shining deeply. "Go right ahead. You were about to say?"

"We were just going down to be fingerprinted," said Rowley coolly. "Coming, Daph?"

Somehow she moved. For an instant or two it looked as if the detective did not intend to permit them to go, but he moved aside then and followed them downstairs.

And they were fingerprinted.

Which was out of all order. But none of them refused.

It was the beginning of a queer and unpleasant day. A day that seemed long because such strange and unaccustomed things took place. And that yet passed swiftly.

In the first place no one knew what Archie Shore

would or would not do, and it was an ever-present
and immediate source of anxiety.

"But he'll keep his mouth shut till tonight," said
Amelia once. "We can count on that." But she would
not discuss the thing at length; nor would she say
more of her willingness to pay him.

Gertrude's asthma was worse, and she was in and
out of her room, wandering about with washcloths
wrung out of steaming water and pressed over her
face, which grew blotchy and red. After lunch the
family doctor came and, meeting Daphne in the hall,
stopped her and pulled her to a window and looked
searchingly into her face.

"It's a bad business," he said. "Stick out your
tongue."

She did so, and he looked at it and at her throat
quite as he had always done.

"It's the damnedest cold house," he said grumpily.
"You'll all likely get pneumonia. See here, Daphne,
who did kill him?"

She shook her head hopelessly.

"Well, what about the Haviland Bridge Company? All my savings are in it, as you know. It's all
right, of course—don't look so scared. But——"
He paused and glanced down the hall. "You know
this stockholders' meeting scheduled for January
first?"

She nodded. They had intended to be back for it;
back from that strange honeymoon in Bermuda.

"Well," said the doctor, "they do say there was a
pretty strong movement on foot to oust Ben. Of
course, they've always wanted him out—your aunts,

I mean. Everybody knows that. But it looks as if
they were doing things this time that—— Yes, yes,
Maggie. Tell Mrs Shore I'm coming." Maggie vanished, and he said to Daphne, "Keep yourself
wrapped up and take some soda. No sense getting
down sick. Why Amelia insists on living in this drafty
old barn——" He went away grumbling.

Other people came, too. The corporation lawyer
with a clerk carrying a fat brief case. The family
lawyer, flurried and carrying another brief case. Two
or three stockholders to see Johnny and Amelia. A
steady succession of Western Union boys with tele-
grams.

And always the police.

Always that knowledge of them working secretly,
constantly, with all the powers of crime detection at
their service—hunting, seeking, questioning, discov-
ering things of which one knew nothing. Drawing
conclusions.

And there was no way to know what.

Jacob Wait did not question Daphne again that
day; did not, indeed, as far as she knew, question any
of the family at length. She had, however, a strong
feeling that it was only because he was gathering evidence against them.

He was away from the house that day, too, for a
long time—visiting Ben's apartment in town, his
office in the Loop and at the plant. Searching, always searching for evidence.

"It's elimination," he said shortly to Johnny and
Rowley, who met him by appointment at the Loop
office. "Do you have keys to his desk?"

They had not, but the senior member of a corps of secretaries had. And if Wait found anything that was evidence, he did not say so. He lingered with the secretary after Johnny and Rowley, accompanied by a plain-clothes man, started on the cold, long drive back to St Germain. Lingered and had the company safe opened and looked at the shelves and boxes, asked many and sundry questions.

"There are no secrets," said the secretary. "Here are all the records. The auditors are working on the books. Everything is open to inspection. There are no secrets."

No secrets. On the way back to St Germain, Wait stopped at police headquarters and looked again at the articles of clothing—the billfold, the penknife, the handkerchief, the small change which had been in the trouser pockets. Looked and did not find something that ought to have been there and went on, driving himself and skidding a little when he turned into the well-rutted drive leading up to Amelia Haviland's house.

Later he interviewed the servants; a long interview from which Maggie emerged red-eyed and with her customary defiant air somewhat subdued. Laing spoke to Daphne of it.

"They want to know such—such strange things," he told her worriedly. "Such as locks on the doors— how they open, who locks them. And———" He paused abruptly, dusted a table which ought to have been dusted that morning and said, "And other things."

"What other things, Laing?"

"Well,"—he was reluctant, but below the reluctance was a suggestion that she ought to know—"well, about members of the family, Miss Daphne. Their private affairs. It did no good for me to tell them I didn't know. They—especially the person called Wait—were very insistent. Kept at me, you know. Kept at me. They wanted to know, for instance—if you'll excuse me, Miss Daphne"—he shot one worried look at her and went back absorbedly to dusting a chair which he had already dusted—"they wanted to know if there was ever anything between you and Mr Dennis. Anything of a romantic nature. They were very insistent."

"What did you say?"

"I said I knew nothing of such matters. At least, I said that at first. When they insisted, asking what I'd seen or heard, I was obliged to answer directly. But I said"—he bent over so his face was hidden—"I said, no, Miss Daphne. Was that right?"

"That was right, Laing."

"And they asked a great many things about what occurred the night Mr Ben was murdered. About the—dinner. A great many what I should call trivial questions, except that they impressed me with a sense of strong purpose behind them. I was—a little upset about it all. They wanted to know if you had had anything like a—a private interview with Mr Ben. Immediately before or after dinner. I said I didn't know, but Maggie had happened to see you and Mr Ben coming from the library while the florists were arranging the flowers, and the others were standing together in the drawing room watching, and I—I'm

afraid she told them. Without wishing to do you any
harm, Miss Daphne." He looked at her anxiously.

She thanked him and reassured him, telling him
the truth couldn't hurt any of them. But she wondered how many meaningless, trivial things extracted
from the servants were to be given a meaning and
taken as evidence.

She remembered later that, as Laing went away,
looking relieved, he hesitated in the doorway, and
she had a fleeting impression that he was about to
say something else. But Rowley came in just then,
and the old man vanished.

Rowley looked very cool and untroubled, his sallow face sleek.

"Well," he said to Daphne, "whatever Ben did,
the affairs of the company are all straight. They've
been going over the books with a fine-tooth comb,
and they found only a thirty-two cent mistake in a
total. It embarrassed Jenkins much but was scarcely
a motive for murder."

"Jenkins," said Daphne. "That's the auditor, isn't
it? Rowley, what about this meeting on January
first? Was there anything in particular to come up?"

He hesitated. They were again in the old playroom, Daphne sitting on a cretonne-covered couch
below the window. It was by that time close to five
o'clock and rapidly growing dark. Below, in the
drive, a car started up with a roar, headlights swept
in a curve and turned into the fir-bordered drive.

"Well, yes, there was," said Rowley. He crossed
and sat down beside her. "Look here, Daphne, I
want to talk to you. I think we should have a definite

understanding. Of course, I understand from Mother that the thing is settled. Fini. But I didn't like your attitude this morning."

"Oh, Rowley, please——"

"I think you'd better understand here and now, Daphne, that—well, if I must put it brutally, Dennis is out."

"Rowley, you have no right——"

"Oh, don't I!" said Rowley, taking her hands and leaning close to her face, so that she shrunk backward against the arm of the couch. "Am I going to be obliged to remind you of things that——" He stopped abruptly, his narrow face close. "You're awfully pretty, Daph," he said suddenly in a different tone. "I might do worse. Don't draw away like that, Daph. You needn't be so touchy. After all——"

"No, no, Rowley!"

It angered him.

"Look here, Daph. Don't forget that I know what really happened that night. I will say you and Dennis put up a convincing demonstration of innocence and surprise when I found you there in the springhouse leaning over Ben and saying you knew nothing of it. But since Mother's told me what really happened— that you and Dennis had met there, actually intending to elope—to leave Ben in the lurch—— And Ben knew it and came to the springhouse to stop you. And was murdered. Any jury in the world can bridge that gap. I never liked Ben much; I don't care who killed him. But would you like to see Dennis hanged?"

"*No. No, Rowley! Don't!*"

"Well, then——"

"Dear me," said Amelia from the doorway. "Who's here? Oh, it's you, Daphne. And Rowley. Why don't you turn on the lights?"

Rowley gave her an unpleasant look, released Daphne slowly, and Amelia walked to a table lamp and jerked the cord.

"Go and find Johnny," she said to Rowley. "And your mother."

"Really, Aunt Amelia——"

"Do as I say," said Amelia with horridly marked gentleness. "Your father has issued something in the nature of an ultimatum. It is most unpleasant, I assure you. I'll pay him the money he asks. But I'll tell you now, Rowley, that you were a great fool to let him remain in this house for a single moment. It's my house——"

"I'll go, Aunt," said Rowley and went away.

"What is it, Aunt?" cried Daphne.

Amelia gave her a long, appraising look and told her.

"He says he knows something of a motive for the murder. He won't tell what. He says he knows the motive for Ben's murder and"——she cast one look at the doorway and finished in a whisper, soft and gentle as a summer wind——"he says he'll keep what he knows a secret for"——the gentle voice choked a little——"for a lifelong position in the Haviland Bridge Company. And a sum of money. If he has any responsibility at all in the company, he'll ruin us. It would be worse than——than Ben," finished Amelia in a whisper.

There was a silence. Daphne looked at her, a

small, handsomely clad figure, with beautifully
curled gray hair and a delicate face and eyes that
were sparks of light in deep shadow. Outside, more
cars started, and the sounds of engines were clear
through the frosty air.

The motive for Ben's murder: did that mean,
then, that it was Archie Shore who knew what she
and Dennis had planned to do? Gertrude knew—but
was willing to trade for silence. Well, Archie wanted
to make a bargain, too.

Motive. Did he mean that motive which would be
fatal to Dennis? Or did he know the real motive?
"What are you going to do?" said Daphne finally.
And Amelia looked at her with deep-set, unfathomable eyes and said gently, "What *can* we do?"

It proved to be a consensus of opinion to which
even Gertrude concurred. She was calculative about
it, though; scheming, playing for time to mature her
own designs for Rowley. It was in the secretive look
of her broad, blotchy face.

Oddly, no one insisted on Archie's telling exactly
what is was he claimed to know. Instead there was a
tacit agreement that it were best not to inquire; to
give him, at this emergency, anything in the world
that he wanted to insure his silence.

"Whether he really knows anything or not," said
Amelia, "he is here to make trouble. It's best to
agree—just now."

Nobody said, "Just what can he do?" Nobody
said, "He can't prove something that is not true."

Johnny said, sighing, "It won't be pleasant—having him in the company again." And Gertrude,

wheezing and looking at Rowley, said, "Well, it can't last forever. But, just now, I'm for giving him what he wants." Dennis was not present at the curiously brief family conference. He was in the library, somebody said, with the detective again.

He turned up, however, at dinner and managed a brief and reassuring word with Daphne. He wasn't yet arrested, he told her. And apparently they knew no more. Except that they had questioned him about the possession of the ring—that small circle of gold —and didn't seem to believe him when he denied knowledge of the thing.

He looked taut, though, and pale. But then so did everyone.

Archie Shore had the grace to take dinner on a tray in his room. But for those in the dining room it was exactly as if he were there with them, reminding them at every turn of the loathsome hold he had— or claimed to have—over them. It was an unpleasant meal; no one talked and no one ate, and it was cold again, so that the red curtains over the windows moved now and then softly, so you expected someone to emerge from their folds.

Which was nonsense, said Daphne to herself.

They separated very shortly after dinner.

The police, Laing said, had gone—except for the two who were to remain there that night and who were having dinner in the little breakfast room adjoining the kitchen—so for the first time since the murder Amelia led the way to the library, where Laing served them coffee.

It had been cleared and straightened, and there

was again a fire blazing on the hearth. The wedding presents had been put away pending their return, and the long table moved. There was nothing at all to remind them of the turmoil and nightmare of the past two days and nights.

But there was a reminder there. Stalking about on silent feet, sighing with the wind, creeping in the shadows of the room; hesitating like a black shadow at the closed door into the drawing room.

Daphne looked at that door and wondered what they'd done with the flowers. Wondered what Jacob Wait was doing just then. Where he was. He had not talked to her that day. Why? His silence was almost as threatening as his questioning.

"Liqueurs?" said Amelia questioningly, but Johnny shook his head and ran his ringed hand over his blond hair.

But the Haviland Bridge Company was safe. There were no defalcations of funds on the books, no faintest shadow of anything involving the company. They had proved that. They had talked of it exultantly, Amelia and Johnny, Gertrude and Rowley.

"I can't help thinking," said Gertrude suddenly, staring into the fire, "that, after all, the company has been saved. Even if Ben——"

She stopped. But everybody knew what she'd been about to say. She said, "I think I'll have some brandy, Amelia, and go to bed."

It was a welcome suggestion. Except that Dennis brought in whisky and soda and nobody noticed the difference.

On their desultory way upstairs, with Amelia pausing in the hall below to see to the locks of the front door and Gertrude complaining loudly to Johnny of her asthma and leaning heavily on his arm, Dennis came up beside Daphne.

"The old playroom," he whispered. "When the house is quiet."

She nodded. Rowley, waiting in the hall for Amelia, looked up at them, but she was certain he could not have heard.

There was a fire in her room. The little corridor approaching it turned so she could not see along it to the door of Amelia's large, long room, which was nearest her own. She could, however, hear their voices; could hear doors closing and the gradual cessation of motion in the house. She sat down to wait.

It was then that Archie Shore came to the door. She did not hear his approach, and the furtive knock on the door frightened her.

But she opened it, and it was Archie Shore. And he'd come to tell her something, he said. Something she ought to know.

"Only to reassure you," he said. "I thought it might worry you, and since you have all agreed to give me what I want—— You see, I know you came upstairs shortly after midnight the night Ben was killed. I know, too, that Dennis was there—that you were expecting him."

"*You*——" said Daphne and choked.

His thin lip lifted and showed those sharp, rapacious teeth.

"I was on the stairway," he said and added, "It

creaked," thereby convincing her. "But since you have all been so—so agreeable to my offer——"

"Why are you telling me this? I have nothing to give you—to pay you."

"Hush. There's no need to shout." He smiled again; his thin, long face loomed yellow, like a candle from the shadow of the corridor. "I only want you to know I'm your friend. As I'm sure you and Dennis," he said, marking each word, "are my friends."

Daphne's knees were shaking. She tried to speak, and her throat was dry, and Archie laughed silently.

"Talk it over with Dennis," he said. "He'll understand."

"Wait," whispered Daphne painfully. "Is this the thing—the motive—you claim to know?"

"This!" There was real surprise in his sharp whisper. "Oh no."

He chuckled evilly. "Oh no," he said again and turned and vanished, silently as a cat. As a panther stalking.

She closed the door and bolted it. She went back to the chaise longue, and presently, without knowing it, she was cold and pulled the eiderdown around her.

It had been Archie, then.

Archie Shore had murdered Ben. Murdered him and returned to the house to get Amelia's hat and coat. Archie.

Why had he told her? To secure her favor, her agreement to any demand he might make then or in later years. She would inherit from Johnny, she knew. And there was Ben's stock.

And he felt himself safe in admitting his presence because he had covered it in that circumstantial account he and Rowley had given the police; the account which provided them—falsely, she believed— with an alibi.

All at once she realized that the fire had died and the house grown silent, and the little clock reached twelve and was striking the hour huskily. Dennis would be waiting. Dennis must know.

She rose, cold and too conscious all at once of the house surrounding her. She went to the door. There was, as was customary, no light in the corridor, but it was only a few steps to the playroom.

She was at the turn of the passage, groping with her hand along the wall, when she heard the sound. A short, hard sound, as if a door had thumped once, hard, against a rubber doorstop. It was padded, yet curiously hard and loud, too.

And it was a queerly and horribly arresting sound.

Quite suddenly she heard footsteps running along the corridor. Pattering softly toward her.

CHAPTER 15

D<small>APHNE</small> could not move. For one thing there was no time, and for another thing she was gripped by a kind of nightmare of paralysis. Her throat ached to scream, her muscles strove to move and she could not.

It was for only a few seconds that the thing lasted. But they were rather dreadful seconds, for she could hear that quick little patter through the darkness toward her, and she could hear quick panting breaths, and she knew that in the narrowness of that black lane that was the corridor the thing running there must come upon her.

Then somehow she broke through the fetters of that queer paralysis and instinctively, as a frightened animal might do, she flattened herself against the wall.

The thing passed her.

She knew it because of the motion felt through the darkness, the nearness of it, the faintest brush of contact against her—nothing to which she could put a name, but it was there.

And immediately a door flung open somewhere along the corridor, beyond the turn by the stairs.

Light streamed thinly, and someone cried out, "Who's there? What——"

Gertrude's voice, was it? Hoarse and strained. Rowley's? Whose?

The thing was behind her now. She could think only of lights, the proetction of lights. Without knowing quite what she did, she ran along the corridor and stopped at Amelia's door and pounded upon it with her fists and called out.

She thought she was answered. Quite suddenly she saw that the door to Archie Shore's room opposite was open and was a black cavern of shadow.

And from somewhere near her came Dennis' voice.

"Daphne—where are you? Is this——" His hands were on her, touching her shoulders. "Daphne, what are you doing here?"

"Something is there," she cried. "Down the corridor. Toward my room."

Other doors were opening. There were indistinguishable sounds and voices. Then someone turned on the lights above the stairs.

It was bewildering, unutterably confusing—the voices, the lights streaming out in lanes, leaving the rest of the hall in deeper shadows.

Someone—Rowley?—was asking what had happened. Everybody was asking. Johnny was there beside Daphne and pounding at Amelia's door. Nobody ever knew exactly what was done or said during that moment or two and could never tell with degree of certainty or clearness.

Except that it was Dennis who turned on the lights

of the playroom and found him and shouted. They all crowded to the doorway. Amelia was there then, too, wrapped in her purple bathrobe.

After one look, Daphne turned blindly to her father, and he took her in his arms, hiding her face on his shoulder and staring above her at the thing on the floor.

"He was killed instantly," said Amelia out of the shocked silence. "He couldn't have lived one instant with a wound——" She stopped there.

It was true. No man could have lived. Archie Shore must have died instantly. He lay sprawled heavily on his face.

He had been killed with the heavy, bronze-handled fire tongs. They were there on the floor beside him.

Dennis bent over the sprawled body and gently turned him so he could see his face, but there was no need to do so.

"He's dead," he said. "He—— There's nothing we can do. Give me something to put over him."

Gertrude whispered hoarsely, "Rowley—come— help me." She put her hands on his arm and appeared about to faint, but Rowley, staring downward, eyes like black slits, did not move. Johnny put Daphne gently away, went next door and came back with a blanket, which he and Dennis put carefully over the thing on the floor.

"Don't touch the tongs," said Johnny. His hands were shaking, his thin, blond hair tousled, his face bleak and sick-looking. "Don't touch anything."

There were running feet suddenly in the hall; voices. Police.

"Hey there, what's going on here? What's all this commotion? What——"

Amelia moved aside to permit them to enter— three of them, inexpressibly comforting in their solid-blue bulk.

And inexpressibly threatening.

For they looked; pulled off the blanket and squatted down there on the floor briefly.

"He's dead, all right," said one, looking rather green around the mouth. A revolver was in his hand. He looked up and said, "Consider yourselves under arrest. You can stay right here, all of you, in this room. Braley, go to the telephone and call Wait."

He rose. One of the policemen went hurriedly away, running heavily down the corridor. The other covered Archie Shore again and went to the door, standing there as if on guard, his revolver in one hand, the other busy buttoning his tunic. They'd been playing poker again in the kitchen. Wait would in all probability raise hell. But how'd they know there'd be a murder?

"You can sit down if you want," said the policeman who had taken charge. "It'll be some time before Wait gets here. You can all sit down, and one of you"—his revolver singled out Dennis and pointed at him—"can fix the fire. There's coal there. You don't need to go out of the room. Now then, look here, folks. We've got to wait awhile for Wait"— he was not making a pale attempt at humor; he was in deadly and rather sick earnest—"you can make yourselves comfortable. But one move out of any of you and it's just too bad. Understand?"

The policeman at the door had got his tunic buttoned up and was feeling more efficient. He said briskly, "The servants—what about them?"

"They're out of this," said the other. "They are all out there in the place over the garage. Nobody got in the house the back way. Nobody——"

"Search the house?" suggested the other, bent on redeeming himself.

"When Braley gets back. Yes."

Dennis was fixing the fire; putting on coals with his hands, taking time and care to arrange them over the small bed of embers. Gertrude had collapsed on the couch and was sobbing hoarsely but rather quietly in the ruffled sleeves of her pink chiffon dressing gown. Amelia, wrapped in purple wool, a tight black net cap over her head and tied under her chin, looked straight and severe and a little witchlike, for her nose and eyebrows jutted out, and her eyes had retreated to two points of light. There were no sobs from Amelia.

No tears from Rowley, either, though his face was like a yellow wax mask with only his dark eyes alive. He, too, had seized a dressing gown, and so had Johnny. Daphne was still fully dressed, and she caught the eyes of one of the policemen traveling over her slowly, from her smooth hair to the tips of her brown oxfords, and then going with suggestive directness to Dennis who, too, had obviously been still dressed and about instead of sleeping in his bed as he ought to have been.

It was a hideous wait. The fire began slowly to crackle and smoke and then at last burst into flames. No one spoke; there was nothing they could say. The heap on the floor was terribly accusing. Archie Shore dead. Well, then, he no longer threatened them.

Or didn't he?

If only, thought Daphne once, if only the little playroom were not so full of memories. The spot on the rug they had burned, she and Dennis and Rowley, years ago, was there just at the murdered man's feet. On the wall hung an old thumbmarked and yellowed map of the world, traced once with an indelible pencil; Dennis' pencil it was, marking the trip around the world he had said he was going to make.

Johnny at her side coughed. The policeman returned from telephoning, and he and the other one talked of searching the house and did so, the third remaining, watchful, his revolver poised in his hand. In the silence they could hear the two going the rounds of the house—opening doors—searching, talking—always, it seemed, together. The sounds grew more distant as they went downstairs. Johnny coughed again, and the policeman guarding them had his whistle halfway to his lips before he perceived it was only a cough and dropped his hand.

They could not communicate; they could not say all the things they would have said. Gertrude had stopped sobbing and was simply staring at the floor and twisting the pink ruffles of her dressing gown in her strong white hands.

They all heard the car—distantly at first, so they only listened—now nearer, so Amelia and Gertrude and Rowley, Daphne and her father and Dennis all stirred a little, exchanging glances. Curiously furtive glances that engaged and instantly shifted.

It turned in the drive. It came, loud in the silence and cold of the night, up to the door. They could hear it stop, just below the windows, and the thumps of the doors. And then another car came, hurriedly, and another.

The front door was flung open—there were voices and footsteps on the stairs and at last along the corridor.

Jacob Wait entered. The big policeman stood aside respectfully and started to explain, but Wait stopped him with a single motion of his small, supple hand. He stood there looking at them, his black fedora shadowing his face, his tweed overcoat dusted with snow. After a moment he went to Archie Shore and knelt and pulled back the blanket. There were others in the hall, peering, crowding; the detective, too, turned the body over a little. Gertrude took a long, sucking breath and covered her eyes.

Then Wait got to his feet.

"He's yours, doctor," he said. The medical examiner came in, his cheeks pink with cold, his bald head shining.

"Skull fracture," he said. "H'm. The prodigal, isn't it—this Shore fellow? Nothing to do here, Wait. All right, boys."

They carried Archie Shore, a heavy, moveless burden, into the hall. Out there was some kind of stretcher; they could hear the men speaking: "This way—look out for the turn."

The doctor said to Wait, "There's your weapon," and pointed to the heavy tongs.

Wait nodded and bent to look more closely at the tongs, putting his hands experimentally over the handles but without touching them. They were all obliged to watch. Presently he stood up and went to the fire, taking off his overcoat and his hat.

"All right, Kellogg," he said, addressing the policeman who had taken charge. "What about it?"

The policeman knew nothing about it save the bare fact. He stammered a little telling of what they had done.

"They was all here," he said, "when we got upstairs. All here in this room. I made 'em stay here——"

"Okay," said the detective. He looked tired and a little ill and was. The sight and nearness of violent death always gave him a kind of qualm of nausea and hatred for it. It was his curse to see the thing fully, deeply, to feel its implications, to taste with horrid poignancy the full flavor of the thing. God, how he hated it! And hated them—people, staring at him, holding secrets back of every still face.

He lighted a cigarette; it was rank and bitter in his mouth, as if he had had recently a more acrid taste.

One of them in all likelihood had killed the man. He made the provision because he was truthful; in all likelihood. Well, there were motives. And he'd have to begin. The sooner he began and plunged into the noisome mess the sooner he'd be out of it.

Those two old women; scared to death, both of

them—determined to fight him. They didn't care, probably, who killed Ben Brewer or who killed this Shore fellow. All they wanted was to cover the thing up. Hush it, keep any family skeletons decently covered; if one of them had killed him and the other knew it, still she wouldn't talk.

Of course, it would have taken strength this time. Shooting was easy, anybody could do that; but breaking a man's skull with a bronze-handled pair of fire tongs—that took a certain amount of physical strength. But not enough to exclude the two—no, three—women; the girl might be stronger than she looked. She was slender but not thin; there was considerable nervous strength and toughness in her. He looked at his cigarette and decided to tell them what he knew. They wouldn't be prepared for that. But mainly it would be a short cut. Would hurry the thing along. He'd have to close the case; make an arrest or two; let the inquest take place; have his evidence ready.

Because one murder wasn't enough.

Because whoever murdered Benjamin Brewer was ready to do murder again and had.

Yes, he'd have to stop it. Stop it if he put them all in jail.

But it put the murderer in a new light. The murder of Ben Brewer might have been impulsive; might even—though it was doubtful—have been done in self-defense. But another murder changed the thing. It was as if some incredibly malignant disease were spreading, creeping, putting out its loathsome tendrils.

Whoever did it, the girl was mixed up in the thing. The woman Brewer had been about to marry and who had certainly some elements of beauty. He looked at Daphne, considering her deeply, as he had already many times considered her. Well, one thing was certain: she had not been in love with the man she was to marry. That or he was entirely mistaken in her character—her strength and her ability to love and grieve. She was frightened and horrified; she was in the grip of some extremely strong and devouring emotion. But she was not, now, in grief.

As to that there was very little grief displayed anywhere. They were, of course, relieved to see the last of Benjamin Brewer, and he knew, now and pretty definitely, why. And probably they were relieved in their hearts because this Shore fellow was out of the way. Even the son, Rowley, didn't look exactly grieved. He was shocked and frightened and not at all inclined to respond to his mother's glances, but still he did not seem to be in grief. Not that he was of a particularly affectionate temperament; still there might be some regard for his father.

He took a long puff and looked at his watch. One o'clock. Time for decent people, leading decent, orderly lives, to be in bed and sleeping. Untroubled by monstrous things like murder. Unaware of it. He wondered if he would ever be able to lead a sane, decent kind of life—he envied deeply the inhabitants of the darkened, peaceful houses they had passed in their headlong swoop through the snow-laden roads.

They'd waited—the coroner and county officials —about the inquest. They would wait, he knew (unless it was too prolonged a wait) till he gave the word.

But as things were it wouldn't be safe to prolong his gathering of evidence. It was not at all complete. Not nearly as complete as he would like it to be before proceeding with the coroner's inquest.

But he didn't dare wait much longer.

And it proved, he thought wryly, that the murderer had nerves. Was in a state of frenzy and desperation.

For self-protection was almost certainly the reason for the murder of Shore. There couldn't, really, be another motive. Yes, he'd tell them what he knew —or some of it.

One o'clock. Night hours and day hours were the same to him. A part of his abnormal, out-of-plumb kind of existence. He closed his eyes for a moment and thought fleetingly and in the top of his mobile mind that he would like to marry again, a woman this time who knew about and would give him a rich, warm, tenacious way of living which was complete in itself, far apart and away from all this. . . . He opened his eyes, and the other part of his mind began to function, almost against his will.

"Wake the servants," he said to Braley. "Tell 'em to make some hot coffee. Put some more coal on the fire. Now then."

His voice had taken on richness and depth which almost insensibly affected them all. Johnny sighed and rubbed his eyes wearily and sat up straighter in his chair and looked anxiously at Daphne. Amelia blew her nose and folded her bathrobe tighter about her knees. Gertrude straightened up, too, and looked warily at the detective, and Rowley's dark gaze shifted toward him, and Dennis went to show the policeman that if you put chunks of coal on their sides they would slit and blaze up sooner.

"We'll have some coffee in a few moments," said Jacob Wait. "And it 'll soon be warmer in here. Who killed Shore?"

Nobody, of course, replied, although Gertrude uttered a kind of stifled scream. Wait looked at her disapprovingly, and she stopped with her hand over her mouth.

"Well, somebody killed him," he said, "and there was no one but you in the house. He was killed because he knew something about the murder of Benjamin Brewer. Isn't that right?"

Again, and naturally, no one replied. The detective's eyes were smoldering. He said abruptly:

"I'm going to tell you a few things. There's only two motives for murder. Three, if you include self-defense. One is for profit. One is because the murderer simply likes to kill. I think we can rule that out here—at least—at least we'll do so for the moment. Also self-defense———"

He paused very slightly there, but no one claimed that vantage ground. So he went on, hurriedly, as if the things he was saying were things they ought, all of them, to know that he knew. As if none of it would be news to any of them.

He hated talk; but when he had to talk he did so rapidly, fully, volubly.

"Archie Shore was here the night Brewer was

murdered. He came to see Brewer—in the hope, he
said, of getting a job. He had no money. His son"—
he looked at Rowley—"managed to persuade him to
leave without seeing Brewer at all. He did promise
him to intervene, to say a word to Brewer and to the
others and to try to get him—Shore—another job
with the Haviland Bridge Company."

"Rowley!" cried Gertrude sharply. "You did
that!"

"Don't interrupt me," said Jacob Wait. "I've got
things to do. So Shore promised to leave. According
to Shore himself and his son——" Daphne glanced
at Rowley, and he was looking subtly guilty; exactly
as he had always looked when he told tales as a
child. *What, then, had he told?* Her heart gave a
painful leap, and she looked at Dennis, and he, too,
had observed that subtle evasion in Rowley's long,
sallow face. He was watching Rowley with hidden
tension, waiting for it to come out. "—According to
both stories," said the detective, "Shore was in the
act of leaving, was in fact at the door, saying good-
by to his son, who stood beside him, when they heard
a shot. Owing to the snow and the muffled quality of
the shot they couldn't be sure where the sound came
from—whether from the house or from somewhere
on the grounds. Or so they say. But they did hear
the shot, and both identified it definitely as from a
small-caliber revolver—not, for instance, from a
forty-five, which would have made considerably more
noise. Then, according to their story, they decided it
was nothing. Shore went his way, first taking a
woman's coat and hat and veil from the closet off the

hall and wearing it. This point was, at his telling, obscure and threw some doubt on the whole story. However, he found a taxi waiting, as you all know, and went away." There was here a strong feeling of a reservation; of something withheld. The fire cracked as a large lump of coal fell apart, and the detective went on quickly, always with that queer impatience and haste: "At any rate he did leave; was taken into town and disappeared. Rowley——" (He looks so guilty, thought Daphne. He heard the shot and told the police. Is that it?) "——Rowley went back to bed. He did not tell his story of the shot until his father turned up again. His father, as you know, came forward of his own volition the next day; said he was the woman in the taxi and told what I've just told you. A story which, when he discovered that his father had returned, Rowley Shore corroborated in every detail. Giving both men, if their stories are to be credited, an alibi for the time of that particular shot. And it is not proved, but it is a strong supposition, that that was the shot that killed Ben Brewer."

Rowley was looking at the rug. Gertrude, panting and flushed, was twisting her hands and staring from Rowley to the detective and back again.

"According to the taxi driver, he left at exactly one o'clock. He did not hear the shot: his engine was running in order to keep the heater going, and the windows were closed. Thus, if we admit the shot heard to be that which killed Brewer, and the truth of the story Shore told—which his son corroborated with, so far as we know, no collusion—that shot must have been fired about ten minutes to one."

He paused.

But that was wrong, thought Daphne. Ben had been killed almost an hour before that. It could have been only a little after twelve when she arrived at the springhouse. She had a strong involuntary impulse to speak and remembered that she must not. The detective would say, "How do you know?"

"That would give," said Wait thoughtfully, "about ten minutes for the two Shores to talk of the thing, for Archie to get the coat, hat and veil and walk through the snow along the drive to the gate. He intended, he told us, to walk into town and did not want to be recognized by the fellow at the station. He did not admit that he was afraid that that shot meant murder or even any kind of trouble; he would not admit that he had any suspicions at all about it. He would not admit, either, that he or his son tried in any way to discover just what had happened. Which seems wrong," said Jacob Wait dryly, looking once at Rowley. "However, he did leave at that time. And he did return the next day, altogether uninvited. We did not discover the identity of the woman in the taxi; we probably would have, given a little more time. But Archie Shore did not wait to be discovered. He returned of his own volition, told us this not entirely to be credited story and took up his residence here in the house, apparently on the most peaceful terms with you all—this in spite of the fact that, by all accounts, he was not welcome and had not been welcome for a period of years. So—what did he know?"

He paused, and no one spoke.

"What did he know?" repeated the detective impatiently. "There was something. Something that made him, when he knew of the murder from the papers—or if he knew of it by other means—certain that he himself would not be accused of murder. Something that safeguarded him, something that, if he were arrested by any chance and charged with murder, he could produce as evidence to free him. He would not have run the risk of returning otherwise. Thus it must be evidence leading to the murderer. And it must be evidence for which you—all of you—one of you—were willing to pay. Otherwise you would not have permitted him to remain. Otherwise you would not have offered him money." He did look then directly at Amelia. And Johnny made a helpless motion and cried, "There, Amelia. I told you all not to talk so loudly. They heard—there were policemen everywhere——"

The detective glanced at him, too, impatiently. "Certainly," he said. "Why do you suppose they were here? To play games? Now then, what did he know? You may as well tell me, you know. Did he see the murder? Did he investigate after he'd heard the shot? Did he go up the little path to the springhouse and——"

"Springhouse?" cried Amelia violently.

"Certainly, springhouse," said the detective, looking at her as if he hated her. "Brewer was actually murdered in the springhouse. We've known that for some time. That," said the detective, "and some other things.—Oh, there you are. Put the coffee on the table. And bring enough cups for all of us."

CHAPTER 16

I HAVE them, sir," said Laing. Looking pale and frightened, and clad hastily in trousers and sweater, evidently pulled on over pajamas, with a woolen scarf tied around his throat, he came into the room, hesitated while Johnny cleared a space on the table, and then set the tray down. His hands shook as he began pouring coffee, and he darted quick, worried glances about the room—at Amelia, at the detective, at the fire. At the fire tongs on the floor, which he avoided carefully as he began to pass the coffee.

Jacob Wait looked at one of the policemen.

"Did you question him?" he asked, nodding toward the old man.

"Yes, sir. No go. But the housemaid—Maggie—the one with the cold——"

Wait nodded impatiently.

"Well, we got something sort of queer out of her."

"What?"

The policeman—the one they called Braley—was overconscientious.

"Do you—shall I——" He indicated with a dubious gesture the circle of listeners.

"Go on."

"Well, this housemaid, this Maggie, didn't want to talk, but we—we got it out of her, sir, we got it out of her."

"*What?*"

"About the hammer, sir."

"The——" Jacob Wait stopped short, gave the policeman a long look and said, "What hammer?"

But he was killed, thought Daphne, with the fire tongs.

"The hammer in the linen closet, sir," said Braley with ingratiating eagerness. "She found it. She found it yesterday morning. It belonged in the tool chest in the basement. She found it in the linen closet yesterday morning, and she took it to the basement and put it away."

"Oh," said the detective. "Well. If she put it away——"

"Oh, that isn't all," said Braley. "She put it away, and during the afternoon she went to the linen closet again for something, and there was the hammer again. Right where she had found it before."

"Did she knew who put it there?"

"She said she didn't know anything about it, sir. Not anything at all." He looked a little rueful, as if the force of Maggie's disclaimer had made a deep and not very pleasant impression. "I'm bound to say I believed her, sir."

"Did she leave it there in the linen closet?"

"No. Oh no, she put it away again."

"Are you sure she's telling the truth?"

"Yes, sir. At least she was very reluctant. If I do say it myself, we had to handle her adroitly."

"Huh," said Jacob Wait shortly. "That 'll do, Braley. I'll see her myself."

Jacob Wait jerked his head toward the door. Braley choked and vanished.

The cup which Laing was passing to Amelia rattled thinly on the saucer and stopped as Amelia's beautiful hand took it. The fragrance of the hot, black coffee filled the little room. The detective said, addressing a plain-clothes man, "See that the tongs are taken care of. Get me an analysis as soon as possible."

The plain-clothes man, wrapping the tongs as carefully as if they were thin glass, instead of bronze so hard that it had killed a man, went away. Jacob Wait said, "I'll take some coffee. Thank you. Know anything about this hammer, Laing?"

"No, sir," said Laing, his voice trembling a little. He went on, passing coffee, without adding to his denial.

But Archie Shore had been killed with fire tongs, thought Daphne again. And the hammer . . .

"Premeditation," said Jacob Wait and drank some coffee, leaving the word hanging in the air with all its grisly connotations.

They were all inexpressibly grateful for the coffee.

Johnny stirred sugar and said suddenly to the detective, his blue eyes harassed, "Mr Wait, what about the springhouse—did you really mean that Ben was murdered there and not in the house?"

"Yes," said Jacob Wait and finished the steaming coffee he held and took more.

"But how—are you certain, Mr Wait? He—it seems so strange——"

Amelia thought so, too, apparently, for she looked more witchlike than ever and said abruptly, "If Rowley and Archie heard the shot and were standing in the door at the time, they must have known the sound came from the springhouse."

"We asked that," observed Jacob Wait. "How about it, Mr Shore? Do you want to change your testimony?"

Rowley looked into his coffee cup and said "No" sullenly.

"You did hear the shot, though?"

"Yes. I told you that."

"But you didn't think of it coming from the springhouse?"

"No."

"You didn't go up to the springhouse and look?"

Rowley looked up suddenly and angrily. He said, "What are you trying to make me do? Confess? Well, I won't. I didn't kill him. I have an alibi. I mean, I—I had an alibi. For the time when the shot was fired."

"But," said the detective in a businesslike way, "it took two people to move the body of Ben Brewer—dead, then, or dying—from the springhouse to the house. I'm not sure of the motive for that, but I think I know. One person could not have done it; thus the murderer had an accomplice. An accessory after, and in all likelihood before, the fact. Now get this: I know how and why you—all of you, as a family—hated Brewer. I know that you had fought him for a year. I know the things you were doing to oust him from the company."

"We didn't murder him," cried Gertrude shrilly. "We didn't murder him. And our hatred was justified, for he was ruining us. Another year of his management and the Haviland Bridge Company would have been bankrupt. Ask anyone. He was taking the very bread out of our mouths. The thing my father worked his whole life to build up was being steadily torn down by this—this interloper. He was not responsible—he——"

"Can you prove all this, Mrs Shore?"

She stopped in full flight; her eyes glittered and she said, "Certainly. It is not my opinion alone. We have often thought that he——"

"Gertrude!" said Amelia softly and tenderly. Gertrude gulped and gave her a startled look, and Amelia said gently, "My sister was extravagantly fond of our father, Mr Wait. She felt, as you seem to know, that Mr Brewer was a danger to the welfare and progress, the continued existence indeed, of the Haviland Bridge Company. Her feelings, however, were not so violent as to—— Well, dear me, I assure you we wouldn't have been obliged to resort to murder. There would have been—if need arose—other means of removing Mr Brewer."

"Such as," said Jacob Wait, "having him committed to an asylum for the insane?"

Two points of light gleamed suddenly in Amelia's deep-set eyes. She put a slim, beautiful hand to the net cap she wore and pulled it a little looser about her throat. Gertrude's eyes were bulging like blue marbles.

Amelia did not, however, betray herself in words. He waited for her to do so, and as she didn't, and as Gertrude was mesmerized into silence, he said, "You have been trying to do that for months, Miss Haviland. Don't trouble to deny it, for we know it. Even after he became engaged to your niece you kept on— we found a list of things which you thought ought to be called eccentricities and which you had prepared to present to the stockholders in the hope of their making a petition to the medical commission."

"How did you know?" said Amelia, not troubling to deny.

Jacob Wait looked annoyed.

"It seems," he said, "that you don't know much of what we've been doing. What we always do. We know all this from the family doctor, from the doctor you went to for advice, from Mr Brewer's own lawyer—Mr Brewer was perfectly aware of what you were doing. From the stockholders who have been getting letters signed with your name and your sister's—violently abusive letters, casting doubts upon Mr Brewer's sanity. We know that you did everything possible to have him removed and were told that the only possible way you could accomplish his removal was to prove his mental inability to carry on business. We know that——"

"Letters?" said Amelia wonderingly and turned

to Gertrude. "I wrote no letters. I suppose you did that."

Gertrude's face was purple; she looked at Amelia and looked quickly away and shrank back against the couch so she seemed to cower before that ever-gentle little voice.

"I——" said Gertrude and mustered up defense. "I had to do something. Certainly I had to do something. You were talking to every stockholder—insinuating—seeing doctors. I told you all along that Ben knew. I told you he was only waiting till you had everything done you could do and he was going to turn around and—and make you sorry," finished Gertrude childishly. "He——"

Amelia's eyes flashed away back in the shadow of her deep eye sockets.

"Listen, Gertrude," she said. "If you are trying to make it look as if I feared Ben Brewer, you are not succeeding. I was afraid of what he would do as manager of the company. Everybody knows that. But I was not afraid of him physically."

"I didn't mean—— I never thought—— I didn't mean that, Amelia—I never thought you murdered him. Really I——"

"Be still," said Amelia and put her hand on Gertrude's knee. "Don't babble." Gertrude's silence assured so long as that small, beautiful hand touched her knee, Amelia turned to the detective. "Certainly I tried in every way I knew to get Ben Brewer out of the company. It made no difference to me whether or not he married my niece."

"Did you or did you not press this marriage?"

"I did neither," said Amelia. "You asked me that before. It was going to take place. Daphne was of age and my niece. I know my duty. But I brought no pressure to bear upon her. Did I, Daphne?"

If it was an attempt to shift the burden of questioning, it failed. Daphne caught her breath and started to speak, and the detective said, "Did you think that you could influence him through your niece?"

"Certainly not," said Amelia.

"If everything else failed, still you had him in the family. You had a tighter hold than you would have had otherwise. And he would be the husband of a niece whom you had cared for—who was under heavy obligation to you. It looks very much as if that was your plan, Miss Haviland. Otherwise why would this girl have been about to marry a man whom she was not in love with? Why, unless she had been urged to do so?"

"She was not urged to marry Ben Brewer," said Amelia flatly. "Ask her. Ask her father. Ask anyone."

"But on the night before the wedding something happened," said the detective. He paused. He hated talking so much. But they had to be beaten down— they had to be frightened—they had to realize that murder was nothing you could pass over, seal up, pretend hadn't happened, escape from. "I told you," he said rapidly, "that you didn't know what the usual routine of our work consisted of; it's this—masses of information from everybody. Look here—we know, for instance, the color of the gown you wore

at dinner the night Ben Brewer was murdered. We
know what time he left his apartment and how long
he was in his office and who came to see him. We
know when he arrived here. We know when Dennis
Haviland returned home. We know how long you
all talked before you went to dress for dinner. We
know—good God, we know what you ate. We know
what time the florists came. We know what flowers
they used for decorations and what you paid for
them. We know who suggested the decoration. We
know—well, we know that Ben Brewer quarreled
with the woman he was to marry and told her she
could never influence him and there was no use trying to do that."

"I told you that," said Daphne. "You made me."

He did not look at her.

"So you see, Miss Haviland, there's no use in
lying. We——"

"I see," said Amelia gently. "Do you know who
murdered Ben?"

For just an instant Jacob Wait did not reply. Not
because Amelia's petty sarcasm had touched him. But
because he saw, suddenly, that he was using a completely futile method. Futile, at least, with the two
elder women. The men understood the inexorability
of evidence, of law, of police methods. The girl, too,
was sensible. But the two women had been for too
long padded against the rebuffs and struggles of the
world; for too many years they had been secure. For
too long they had immersed themselves in the tight
little world of the Haviland Bridge Company and
the Haviland family.

"No," he said simply. "I still lack proof."

He let them wait for a completely still, shocked moment to understand—rather, to repeat to themselves—what he had said.

Daphne thought, He thinks it's Dennis. This tilt with Amelia means nothing: he only wants her— wants us all—to talk. He knows about the springhouse; he knows there were two. He knows they were people who had access to the house; he knows —and has known from the beginning—that there were no burglars. He knows what we did—but he can't yet prove it is Dennis. He can never prove it, really, because Dennis didn't kill him. He didn't kill Archie—Dennis couldn't kill anyone.

But there was Dennis' revolver—linked to the springhouse by that dark juxtaposition. There was that burden of evidence against Dennis, that inexorable heaping of one thing upon another. And there was the wedding ring.

A crime of passion—that was what they would call it. She was, too, appalled at the vistas of exploration—of inquiry and information—which the detective's swift words had opened before her. It was as if curtains around them had parted here and there and revealed unknown dangers pressing upon them.

Masses of information, he had said. All the day before and the day before that the police had worked, gathering information—any and all information—and out of it, quite evidently, they were going to construct motives, evidence.

And Amelia. Daphne had known, of course, that

Amelia never gave up; that her seeming acquiescence
and acceptance of Ben Brewer as president of the
Haviland Bridge Company was merely her way of
biding her time. Of carrying on that unremitting
program to oust him secretly. Under cover.

She glanced at her father, wondering if he had
known to what vicious lengths Amelia's desires had
carried her. He caught her look and tried to smile
reassuringly and put his hand over her own for a
moment. But he looked shocked; he hadn't known,
she decided swiftly, and hadn't been a party to it. He
had gone on trying to keep peace, hoping for the
best.

The detective was going to say something. More
questioning or more direct accusation. She braced
herself for it.

But it was neither. The detective turned and said
to one of the policemen, as if it were a forgotten
chore, "Get the hammer the woman talked about
and have it examined for fingerprints. Question her
more. Don't bring her up here yet." The policeman
vanished. Wait turned abruptly to Amelia again.
"Why were you paying Shore? What did he know?"

Amelia looked at Johnny. "He'll not believe us,"
she said to him, and Johnny looked up at the detective. "She doesn't know," he said. "We didn't know."

"Why did you pay him, then?"

"We hadn't paid him yet," said Johnny truthfully.
"But we were going to. The thing was, he was out
to make trouble for us. He threatened us. But he
refused to tell us what he knew, except that it was a
motive for the murder of Ben. Amelia and I decided

it was best to give him what he asked; we are not in a position at the moment to bargain. But we—well, we don't know what information he held. I mean," said Johnny, "said he held. It was all one so far as our feelings and situation are concerned."

"But you don't know exactly what. Well," said the detective shortly, "we'll have to see if we can find out. Who found his body tonight? One at a time, please. We'll begin with you, Miss Haviland. When did you first know of Shore's death?"

It was then about two, and the detective did not release them until five, but kept them there, questioning them.

And in the end it summed up to exactly nothing.

They had all heard the sound of the blow. Nobody, it developed, had been asleep. There was confusion about voices and about lights and about who saw what in the hall.

"But Dennis found the body," said Gertrude. "I remember that. And we were all there in the doorway when he turned him over and said 'He's dead.' "

Everyone agreed.

Daphne had told her own story wearily. She could not tell of Archie Shore's visit to her room, and that because of it she had been curiously, directly certain that Archie Shore had murdered Ben. But she had been wrong: she had to be wrong, for Archie himself was murdered.

So she told only what she had to tell. When she got to the instant or two in the darkened corridor, however, the sheer terror of it came over her again, and she was all at once horribly conscious of the

ring of eyes, all watching her. ". . . And whatever
it was passed me," she said and faltered, struck with
the thought that—incredibly—one of those pairs of
eyes might be hiding the truth of it. Because one of
those people had certainly passed her—running away
from the thing that had been done. Running down
the corridor toward her.

But it wasn't possible; she knew them all too well;
she had known them all too long, too intimately.

Yet people changed. And she'd been away at
school. She'd been engrossed herself in the business
of growing up, becoming an adult, changing. Then
why couldn't some of them have changed? Rowley
and Dennis had had to grow up, too; had been away
themselves. And the older generation—her father
and her two aunts—well, people did change. There
was some artist—she groped vaguely for his name—
who'd changed so much that even his paintings of
the earlier period showed no relation whatever to the
later period. There was the story of the famous
physician, known for his mercy and philanthropy
and charity, turning, in the last year of his life, murderer. People did change.

"Who passed you?"

"I don't know."

"Why were you up and dressed and in the corridor?"

It was like cold water dashed in her face, dispelling the mists of weariness and dazed horror, opening her eyes to the thing she had walked into.

"I was going to the playroom. This room."

"Why?"

Why?

Dennis stirred suddenly and spoke for her.

"I asked her to meet me here. I wanted to talk to her."

"Oh," said the detective, turning to Dennis. "Oh. You again."

CHAPTER 17

BUT Dennis' story was brief, clear and undeviating. The detective's questions could not shake or change it.

"I was in my room. I was about to go to the playroom. I heard the sound of the blow—except I didn't know, then, what it was. I hurried into the corridor and ran along it——"

"You were expecting something to happen?"

"No," said Dennis. "At least, no more tonight than any other time."

"Then what did you do?"

"Well, I ran along the corridor and heard someone knocking at a door. Then in the darkness I came upon Daphne pounding on the door to Aunt Amelia's room. I said, 'Is it you, Daphne?' or something like that. I was expecting her, you see. Then she said something, I don't know what—it's all very confused, because other doors were opening and people were coming out and wanting to know what had happened. Anyway, I went to the door of the playroom——"

"Why?"

"I don't know. I just did. It was near. Anyway, I

turned on the light and there he was. And that's all."

"You saw no one coming from the southern end of the corridor?"

"No."

Nor had anyone. Or, at least, no one remembered and admitted it. But then none of them had a very clear notion of the thing.

He kept on, making them repeat, asking a steady stream of questions about the smallest things. Who turned on the light in the playroom? Oh, Dennis Haviland. Who turned on the hall light? Oh, no one remembered. Rowley thought he did. Where was the switch? He turned to Daphne again and plied her with a hundred questions about that ugly moment in the corridor. Had anything touched her? Had the person who passed her spoken? Was it a man or a woman? She didn't know. Well, was there a kind of rustle of skirts? She didn't know that either. Well, how did she know the person passed her at all? Oh, just a feeling.

It went on and on.

The little room grew warmer as the cannel coal began to crack and blaze fiercely. Warmer, that is, near the fireplace. It was a bitterly cold night, with the windows frosted and little icy drafts along the old floor. There was a knitted scarf folded across one end of the couch, and once Gertrude got up with a rather desperate look on her face, took the scarf and wrapped herself in it. Johnny went to the fire and put on more coal, bending over, too, to take the chunks of coal in his hands. His neat black satin coat swung out as he bent over; the homeliness of it em-

phasized, as did the shabby, familiar room, the un-
questionable reality of the thing. He turned, dropping the loose cotton gloves on the coal scuttle, and
sat down again beside Daphne.

And Jacob Wait asked who had last talked to
Archie Shore. After some discussion it was found to
be Laing, who had brought him cigarettes.

"He was in the best of spirits," said Laing. "Very
cheerful, indeed. That was about ten o'clock."

"Your room is opposite the room Shore used, Miss
Haviland. Did you hear or see anything out of the
ordinary? Anything at all?"

Amelia decisively had not.

And the questions went on.

The detective did not make any further comments
concerning the activities of the police. Once or twice
his questions showed a startlingly complete knowledge of the household—its usual routine; occasionally he would revert to the night of Ben Brewer's
death, as when he turned suddenly to Rowley again
and made him go over, step by step, the events of
that night. Again there was that guilty look in Rowley's sallow, long face, but again he avoided the thing
that actually occurred in the springhouse.

"I went to my room after I heard the shot," he
said. "And the next morning I was told of the murder when I came downstairs. Maggie had found the
body in the doorway of the library."

It was, though Daphne did not know it, something of a feat for the detective to keep them
there, questioning them tirelessly, swiftly, constantly
through those dreary, cold hours—hours when re-

sistance is low, when human ingenuity is weakest.
When truth comes out and wears a mask and gar-
ments of foreboding.

Occasionally, too, one of the men with him would
take up that role of inquirer—once when Jacob Wait
asked Daphne something of the light in the southern
corridor and the distance from her door to the turn
of the corridor and disappeared, presumably to see
for himself, for they could hear him walking in that
direction. And again, when he went into Archie
Shore's room and remained there a long time and a
detective they called Tillie—fat and shining with
little, piggish eyes and a suave manner—asked them
a number of questions about Archie Shore. Gertrude,
reluctantly and with a kind of harried indignation,
answered most of them—pressing her hands to her
temples and saying a number of times that she knew
nothing of him in recent years.

"But I never," said Gertrude spitefully, "knew
anything good of him."

Rowley gave her a cold look and murmured, "De
mortuis——"

"Nonsense. This is no time for French. Or eva-
sions. The truth," declaimed Gertrude falsely, "must
come out," and put her hands on her head with a
little moan.

"It wasn't French," said Amelia. "You are talking erratically, Gertrude. Pull yourself together."

Rowley shot an uneasy glance at Gertrude and
said, "Now, Mother," warningly. Johnny said
quietly, "It's one of her headaches. Look here, Mr—
er—Tillie——"

"Tillinghouse," said the detective with a snap.

"Tillinghouse," said Johnny and rubbed his hand through his tousled blond hair. "Look here, can't you let my sister go now and rest? She's ill."

"You'll have to ask Wait," said Mr Tillinghouse.

"Let 'em go," said Wait from the doorway. "But don't let any of 'em leave the house. That's an order."

Tillinghouse looked at them and said, "Hear that? It's an order. You can go now."

It was then five.

They filed in a weary little line out of the room. Daphne, cold and exhausted, felt Dennis' hand for an instant on her arm.

"Keep your chin up," he said and tried to smile. It didn't reach his eyes, however.

In the hall Daphne heard Tillinghouse talking to another plain-clothes man.

"He's got to make the arrest," he said, and the other nodded.

They were both looking over her shoulder, and Daphne turned to follow their gaze. Dennis was talking to Amelia—answering some questions and nodding.

Dennis? Or was it Amelia they meant?

At another time the questions—answered either way—would have been sheer absurdity.

But she thought again, People do change. And she knew in her heart that, when all was said and done, Amelia was the man of the family.

She reached her own room. The light was still burning as she had left it—how long ago?

She closed the door. The fire in the little hearth was completely burned out. The radiator was hot, however; Laing or someone had seen to that. She crossed the room and sat beside it for a while, staring into space. Finally she got up and went to the closet and found the yellow velvet gown, still hanging where she'd hidden it. It was not possible that she'd left such horribly betraying evidence for so long. She took the dress and rummaged in sweater and coat pockets until she found a package of matches and went with them to the fireplace. It took a few moments to rip the bands of mink from the shoulders. It took longer to get a wavering blue flame to crawl up the sleek folds of velvet.

It was a stubborn little flame; it would burn a few inches and go out. She held the dress up with the small brass poker, turning it this way and that, so that the flame would follow the draft upward. It took a long time to burn the thing. And she felt curiously guilty and as if the dress had a living quality as she watched the flames creep upon those artfully stitched folds of yellow velvet.

That long-ago night when she'd worn it—it seemed months, and incredibly it was only a few days. Two nights.

Well, and there was another day to be faced.

He was going to make an arrest, the detective had said. "He" meant Wait, of course. And they had looked meaningly at Dennis and at Amelia, standing together, when they spoke.

She was too tired to think coherently. Her hands

were trembling. She felt actually ill and drugged with fatigue.

Desperately tired of that inexorable round of speculation. Who *had* killed Ben? And now—who had killed Archie Shore? She had been so sure, all at once, that Archie Shore was the murderer.

Rowley couldn't have killed his own father.

Rowley was thoroughly selfish; he was and had always been secretive; you never knew what he was thinking, what he was planning to do.

But he couldn't have killed Archie Shore.

She turned the dress so the flames spread a little and thought suddenly that she didn't really understand Amelia—or Gertrude. Knowing them so well, she still failed in that instinctive understanding she ought to have had. Well, that was because—one of them though she was—she was not actually of their blood. She could not really understand them because she was not like them. Because underneath she had not the same impulses, the same weaknesses, the same strength. She was one of them, certainly; never more closely a part of that family than now. But she lacked the inherent accord, the deep knowledge of each other which those of the same blood share.

Dennis had said, the crime—the murder of Ben Brewer, that is—was "like" Gertrude.

But Amelia was the one who had strength and will.

And Amelia had brains.

Were there really any clues to the murders? Any, that is, besides those that with such dreadful fatality heaped themselves up to involve Dennis?

She turned the dress again. Even after it was burnt it had a dreadful tendency to remain in stiff folds, showing clearly the soft nap of velvet. She was obliged to beat the crumbled brown heap with the poker, scatter it—for didn't they find all sorts of clues from things that had been burnt?

She was sitting there when her father came to the door and proved once and for all time that those who called Amelia the man of the family were wrong.

When she heard the knock she thought first it was Dennis and sprang up to answer. And then a second thought came to her, and she was afraid to answer —afraid to open the door. There were policemen everywhere, of course—yet Archie—and Maggie had talked of a hammer . . .

Then Johnny said, "Daphne!" and she ran to the door and opened it.

"Good God, it's cold in here," said Johnny. "You ought to have a fire. Look here, Daphne—I thought I'd better tell you before—you see—— Well, I'm going to confess. To the murder. Murders, that is."

He looked at her, blinked, and said hurriedly, "There, there, now, Daph. Here—sit down." He pushed her into the little slipper chair. "Don't look like that. Dear me, I've got to."

And as she still did not speak, he said simply, "There's nothing else to do. You see, Daph—— Well, now, my dear, if you're going to take it like that I won't. That is, well——"

He sat down on the end of the chaise longue and put his hands in his pockets. His blue eyes were puffy from lack of sleep; his face was not pink and healthy-looking as usual, but wore instead a kind of gray mask of fine wrinkles. He said abruptly:

"It's so simple, Daph. There's Amelia and Gertrude. There's Rowley. There's Dennis. There's nobody else. Daphne, answer me something truly. Do you love Dennis?"

"Yes," said Daphne.

"H'm," said Johnny. He looked at her lingeringly and then turned away and put his chin in his hand. "What have you been burning?" he said after a moment. "Smells like——" He sniffed. Daphne said, "A ——dress. Father, what are you saying! I don't—I can't think. I don't know——"

"I was saying," said Johnny, "that I'm going to confess." He was looking at the bands of mink lying on the cushion beside him in a puzzled way. "We can't go on like this. There's nothing else to do."

"But you——" Gradually she was beginning to understand that he really meant it. "Why, you can't do that. They'll—they'll arrest you—charge you with murder."

"No," he said, smiling a little. "I'll charge myself with it. What dress was it, Daphne? It seems to me I remember those little bands of fur——" Recognition dawned in his face. "Why, my dear—that was the dress you wore——"

"The night Ben was murdered. Yes."

He looked once at her, turned abruptly away and rose and went to stand before the fireplace.

"I see," he said finally, still not looking at her. He sighed lightly. "Well," he said, "that settles it."

"Do you think," cried Daphne past a suddenly throbbing, aching throat, "that I'll let you sacrifice yourself for me! That I'll———"

"No, my dear, don't. I'm not sacrificing myself for you. For anyone. Listen to me. It's all quite simple. Amelia and Gertrude are my sisters. They have been too sheltered; they do things in a headstrong, unthinking way. They cannot understand that there are certain penalties; that the world can reach out and grasp them. That—you know, my dear, how they are; they both have a kind of empress complex. It's partly my fault. I've always agreed rather than struggle with them. Amelia, of course, is smart—too smart for her own good. Neither of them is showing to very much advantage in this affair. Both of them were crazily determined to get rid of Ben Brewer. I didn't know they had gone to such lengths." He sighed again. All the debonair, social manner which was a part of Johnny Haviland was for the moment fled, and he was only an oldish, weary, helpless man with the look of blond handsomeness blurred and indescribably aged. "Don't mistake me, Daphne," he said. "I'm going to confess to it. Not to save Amelia or Gertrude. Not to save Dennis for you. Not to"—he turned, and his blue glance strayed to the mink bands which Daphne clutched in her hand—"not to do anything highfalutin. But it's obvious Rowley didn't do it— Rowley wouldn't have killed his own father. At least———" He paused and thought and then shook his head. "No; Rowley's mean, and he's always been cold-bloodedly cruel. Remember the bird———"

"Don't," said Daphne, remembering after all those years too well.

"Yes. Well, of course, he was well trounced for that. And he was just a boy; lots of boys have sort of instinctively savage moments."

"I won't let you."

"Hush, my dear. You can't stop me. I'll phone my lawyers at once. I'll arrange the most perfect defense that a man ever had. I'll fix it. I'll be through with it, and the thing will be ended——"

"You can't do this. You are trying to make me think it will be all right. But I know. A confession— just the mere confession—is enough to convict you. I know that. No matter what kind of defense you could arrange, there would still be the confession. And you——" Without warning she began to cry, great sobs tearing through her throat.

"Now, now, Daph. Don't." He waited and finally came over to her. "Now listen, my dear. Stop crying and listen. I promise not to do anything right away. But in the meantime, Daphne, think this over: I'll confess to the murders; just say I did it and offer no details or what would be incriminating evidence. I'll have my lawyers get me the best defense lawyer in town. Or—see here—construct the thing so there are loopholes—so it couldn't possibly happen that way—so it doesn't square with the evidence."

"It wouldn't," said Daphne, still sobbing, "work."

He gave her his handkerchief, and she wiped her face.

"Well, then, I'll talk to the lawyer first. The whole thing is this, Daphne: the first thing you know

Amelia or Gertrude or—or you—is going to be taken off to jail. We can't have that."

Havilands. The family—the company.

"What about the company?"

"I don't know," said Johnny rather bleakly. "But we'll fix it somehow. Who's that?"

It was Dennis. He looked relieved when he saw Johnny.

"I got to thinking about Daphne being off here in this long L alone. You ought to change your room for a while, Daphne. Move in to that couch in Amelia's dressing room—— What's the matter?"

She told him, expecting his immediate agreement. But he looked thoughtful and to her dismay considered Johnny's proposal thoughtfully.

"But," said Dennis calmly, "it isn't fair. Suppose we draw lots, Johnny. You and Rowley and I. The one that gets the short end confesses. We'll get the lawyer to word the confession; we'll fix it so——"

"Oh, you can't, you can't——"

"Be still, Daphne. It's really not a bad idea."

"But why?" wailed Daphne. "Why?"

"Because," said Dennis suddenly stern—"because we think Amelia did it. And we know damn well you are in danger. That's why. We don't propose to have you dragged through a trial. And we don't want to see Amelia spend the last years of her life in jail. At best," added Dennis. He paused, took a fold of Daphne's sweater between his fingers and looked at it thoughtfully. "Besides," he said unexpectedly, "they'll probably arrest me sooner or later. I don't know why they're waiting so long. If anybody confesses, it had better be me, because I do have, in a pinch, an out."

"That little piece of wood!" cried Daphne stormily. "That's what you mean. Oh, you are both stark, raving mad! How can you—— Go away! Go away, both of you!" She was sobbing, furious, helpless. So terribly tired.

She flung herself in a very luxury of fury face downward in the cushions and let them plead and soothe and comfort her. Let them bring her water and handkerchiefs and cologne. It was the cologne that made her feel very silly. She stopped sobbing and sat up and pushed back her hair.

"I think," said Dennis rather sheepishly, "you'd better rest awhile."

"Yes, yes," said Johnny. "Yes. We won't do anything, Daphne, until we talk to you again. I promise you."

"All right," said Daphne huskily and wiped her eyes. "But I'm right. It's too dangerous."

"You may be right," said Dennis. "It was only a thought. God knows I don't really want to get in any deeper than I am now. Look here, now, my dear." He bent over her. "You're cold and tired. You've no idea how much better you'll feel when you're rested. Now I'm going to fix you up."

He kissed her briskly. Then sat down beside her and took off her oxfords and took both her feet in his hands.

"Two small chunks of ice," he said and went to the bathroom and rummaged and returned presently with a little rubber hot-water bottle. "Its coat seems

to sort of slip," he said, fumbling with the quilted
satin cover. "But it's warm." He put it to her feet
and pulled the eiderdown around her, tucking it in.
He adjusted the pillow, pulled the eiderdown around
her chin and kissed her again. Tenderly this time;
loving her dearly.

And went away. Johnny, yawning, had waited.

When they had gone she remembered that she
hadn't told Dennis that it was Archie on the stairway. But it seemed, then, unimportant.

She couldn't sleep, she thought dully. And
promptly did.

And so passed most of that strange, cold day.

A crowded, busy day on the part of the police. On
the part of the crowds of newspaper men.

The sprawling, cold old house was a very beehive
of strange activity—alien feet tramping over rugs
and up and down creaking stairways. New, curt
voices; cigarette smoke from a dozen brands of
cigarettes mingling with the floating odor of flashlight powder.

Cars coming and going continually. A few hardy
souls parked along the highway for hours; people
who had no business there, who were simply curious,
watching, looking through the bare trees at the roofs
and gables below which two murders had taken place.

"It must be up there where that little hill is. See?"

"Two murders. I bet old man Haviland's turning
handsprings in his grave."

There were even a few skaters on the river. Cold.
Building a little fire. Finding remains of another fire.
Finding some things which were not quite ashes, not

quite charred. Finding them—consulting over them
—hurrying to the bank at last and taking off their
skates and bringing the things (in a body, five high-
school boys the later reports said) to the house.

For the reporters at the door saw it; scurried into
their cars and to St Germain to telephone, because
the police would not let them use the telephones in
the house. Shouting to rewrite men over telephones.
Lingering to get some hot coffee at Dutch John's on
the corner of Main and Charity streets. And to talk
of the Havilands. People in the village had never
done so much talking or had it so gratefully and
flatteringly received.

And then scurrying back to the house to get a new
story for the night editions.

It was late afternoon when Daphne awoke.

Maggie was pounding at the door.

She let her in and sat down and blinked sleepily.

"It's Miss Gertrude," said Maggie. She was
stupid and red-eyed with her cold and with fatigue.
She still wore her morning uniform of striped blue
broadcloth, and her first excitement had given place
to something still and deep and frightened. It was a
good place; she had been there so long that she
wouldn't know how to go about getting another
place. But she would have done it at once if the
police had let her. Laing could stay if he wanted to;
and his wife. But she was going. Although it would
be hard to leave. She looked at Daphne; it didn't
seem, just then, possible that she was now a young
lady. The years had gone so fast. "I'm sorry about
the hammer," said Maggie.

"It's all right. You couldn't help it, I suppose."

"No, Miss Daphne. I'll bring some tea and a sandwich. There's no need to hurry to see Miss Gertrude—she's in," said Maggie, "one of her tantrums."

But it was not exactly a tantrum.

Daphne took the tea and a hot shower, feeling as if she hadn't undressed for a month. She dressed slowly, grateful for the reviving cheer of the tea. It was quiet back there in the L; distant from the commotion and tremor in the rest of the house; far from the continually arriving and departing cars.

She even took care to put a little scarlet scarf at the throat of her blue wool gown, a small scarlet handkerchief in its pocket. And then, to match it, lipstick on her mouth.

She went to Gertrude's room, knocked, and Rowley said, "Come in."

Gertrude was lying in bed, but her fine, dry hair was done carefully, her face made up, and she wore a pink satin jacket. The curtains were drawn, and a low light was shaded from Gertrude's eyes, and a fire was going in the grate. Rowley was lounging, smoking.

Gertrude said, "There you are; close the door, Rowley. Now then, Daphne, it's all arranged."

There was a triumphant little snap and flash in Gertrude's eyes. She said, "He'll be here as soon as he can come. No one need know about it yet; it will be kept a secret. But it has been done and it can be done. I'm sure he'll consent. If not, of course, you can get one—but I'm sure he'll do it. After all, it's as binding, if there are witnesses——"

Daphne took hold of the polished mahogany railing at the foot of the bed.

"Who? What?"

"Reverend Dr Lonergan," said Gertrude. "Legally it will hold. Then you can get a license later and have it done over again. You and Rowley, I mean. Married."

CHAPTER 18

I suppose, thought Daphne, holding the footrail, that I ought to humor her. That's what they do, isn't it? Aloud she said, with the calmness of complete disbelief, "Aunt Gertrude, you cannot possibly mean that you expect us to marry. Rowley and I. Now."

"Certainly, I mean it. Dear me, Daphne, you aren't in a position to draw back. Not now. I've read and heard that it's quite legal. You needn't live together till this thing has blown over, and you can get a license and be married all over again publicly. But just now that isn't exactly practicable. No," said Gertrude, looking very shrewd and wise and nodding her head as if, though everyone else had gone out of their wits, she, Gertrude, could be trusted to keep a cool and wise grip on things. "No, it isn't exactly practicable now. But my idea is this: Reverend Lonergan is coming to see me. In fact, he's on the way now. I telephoned for him, and he said he'd come at once; that he was only waiting for us to call and wanted to be of any possible service to us. Well," said Gertrude smugly and closed her eyes, "he can be. And will."

"He won't," said Daphne. "He——"

"Oh, come, Daphne." Gertrude's eyes flew open, and she said, with inexpressible complacency, "We haven't supported his church for forty years for nothing."

"You needn't be vulgar," said Rowley suddenly.

"Vulgar," said Daphne. "Is that all you can say!"

Rowley rose and came toward her, his black head shining, his long, sallow face again masklike; his eyes shining.

"It's not a bad plan, Daph," he said slowly. "You'd do well to think of it."

"It's a good plan," said Gertrude. "You see, all he—Dr Lonergan—needs to do is to read the marriage service. I know exactly how it should be—I'll be witness, and we'll have—oh, Maggie, or somebody, witness it, too. That makes two witnesses. It will be binding to you and to Rowley—then later——"

"Oh," said Daphne. "I begin to understand. You want——"

"My mother thinks," said Rowley, "that it would be better to have no misunderstanding about our— our agreement. You see, once this affair is over with, she feels that you might change your mind about what you promised her——"

"I didn't promise anything."

"Oh, come, my dear, a bargain is a bargain," began Gertrude, and Rowley went on as if he had not heard her: "It's just as well to do as she wishes. She knows that once you and I make these sacred vows before a minister and before witnesses——"

Sacred vows, said Rowley!

"I won't!"

"—it will be perfectly binding. She feels—I'm sure, rightly—that neither of us would—ah—break such vows. She feels——"

"It 'll make your marriage certain," broke in Gertrude forcefully. "That's all I want. I don't like the way you're acting about Dennis, Daphne. I know all about his tender little love scene with you the night Ben was murdered. I know you would have run away with him then if Ben hadn't tried to stop you."

"Hush, Mother. Let me talk. There's no use getting upset—having any words about it. I think it would work out all right, Daphne. We'll keep it secret, of course; but, as Mother says, it would be binding. And perhaps you'd better know, my dear, that the police are getting closer and closer to the real truth of the matter. They found Ben's shirt and waistcoat today."

"You didn't burn them!"

His narrow shoulders shrugged lightly.

"It doesn't matter. It's only one more scrap of evidence. They know it actually happened in the springhouse. They found ashes on the back of Ben's coat which were the same as the ashes Dennis dropped at some time—earlier in the day, Dennis says—in the springhouse. On the floor. A nice little bit of laboratory work, that was. Nothing unusual, they say, but nice. It's only a matter of a few hours until they get at the real truth of it. Well, just consider what I can do for you. I can tell the truth—

that I walked into the springhouse shortly after the shot was fired and found you and Dennis bending over the body. Or I can tell them I was with you; that I met you both in the hall downstairs—or anywhere you like—and went to the springhouse with you. I can tell them—describe as vividly as you like —your surprise when you found Ben dead. Can corroborate Dennis' story of how and why we moved the body. That's going to be the rub, you know."

"I'm not going to marry you."

"Oh, very well," said Rowley. "But what will you do when you both—you and Dennis—appeal to me to uphold your story?"

"Our word is as good as yours."

"Oh, is it?" said Rowley. "When my mother has told what she knows?"

"Rowley,"—Daphne tried to speak quietly and reasonably—"please think what you are doing. You know what Aunt Gertrude's like when she——"

"What's that?" said Gertrude, sitting up. "What do you mean? I was never clearer in my mind. Thank God, it's like my father's. Always clearest and finest in time of need. Dr Lonergan ought to be here in an hour. Keep her here, Rowley, until he comes."

"Why, you are both mad! Do you really think I'll stay here—let myself actually be married? I'll tell Dr Lonergan. I'll scream—I'll——"

"Scream if you like," said Rowley. "It 'll cost Dennis something. Now get this, Daphne: This wasn't my idea. I'll admit it sounds plain nuts. And, of course, we aren't going to use physical force or

anything so absurd as that. —Hush, Mother!— But
the more I think of my mother's plan the better I
like it. There's good sense in it. After all," said
Rowley, "I'd rather have cash than a promise to
pay any day."

"I didn't promise anything. I won't. There is no
possible way you can carry out this—this—— Oh,"
—she flung out her hands toward them—"don't you
see how—how silly it is? How childish—how——"

"Oh, is it really!" said Rowley. "Well, we'll see."

That had been a mistake; opposition had always
fixed Rowley in his course. And ridicule had always
enraged him.

"I think," said Rowley, "we could even borrow
the wedding ring. From Dennis."

"From Dennis!" cried Daphne. "*Dennis*——"
And understood. She ought to have known at once.
How could she have been so blind! She must let the
detective know; it was as if she had suddenly found a
weapon and had seized upon it, but without investi-
gating its strength. For she cried, "You put the
wedding ring in Dennis' pocket. It was not taken
from Ben at all. He gave it to you. Gave it to you
because you were going to be best man. That was it.
I'll tell the police—I'm going to tell them now—it's
you, Rowley. You murdered Ben. That's why you
came into the springhouse just then. That's why you
wanted to cover everything—that's why—— But
how could you murder your own father——"

Gertrude cried savagely, "Stop that!"

Rowley had her suddenly in his arms and had his
hand over her mouth. She struggled against him,

writhing, gasping, crying out. Dimly she heard Gertrude's sharp whisper, "Her throat—get her——"

He was stronger than she. He did not, however, take her by the throat. Instead he flung her, hard, down into the chair from which he'd risen. And then —quite coldly—slapped her.

Gertrude watched.

"And that, my girl, is what you need. Now we'll have no more of this raving—— Never mind, my dear. Years from now you'll be grateful for this. We really are saving your life—aren't we, my son?"

The cold fury in Rowley's narrow eyes covered itself. He stood looking down at Daphne for a moment and said, "Sorry, Daph. But, after all, you can't go shouting around like that. Preposterous accusations——"

"Now, now, Daphne," said Gertrude suddenly, looking uneasy. "Don't look like that. Perhaps Rowley went too far. Sit there for a moment, Daphne. You——"

Daphne stood. She looked once at Rowley and then at Gertrude.

"Understand me," she said in a queer, unnatural voice. "I am not going to marry Rowley. Now or ever."

"Do you mean——" gasped Gertrude incredulously.

"You can do anything you please, say anything. I'm going now. You don't dare stop me."

"Now listen, Daphne," said Rowley hurriedly. "You know my temper. It was your fault altogether. You can't say things like that—I didn't murder Ben.

And you know I didn't. Suppose I did slip that ring into Dennis' pocket. I'm not admitting it, but suppose I did—what of it? Of course, I'll admit I rather lost my head just now. But I've apologized. Now let's be friends again."

"Get between her and the door," said Gertrude. "Quick, Rowley. Now look here, my fine young lady. Just stop for a moment and think——"

Someone knocked heavily at the door. She stopped, and Rowley stiffened a little, looking at the door. Daphne made a quick move forward, and Gertrude said suddenly, "It's Dr Lonergan. Good!"

But it wasn't. Dennis called, "Daphne—are you there?" and Daphne said, "Dennis! Dennis——"

"I told you to hold her," whispered Gertrude sharply. "Keep him out." But Rowley did not move, and Dennis flung open the door.

"Oh," he said and entered, looking from one to another. "What's the matter? What's going on?"

"Nothing," said Gertrude, "that's anything for you to interfere with. Please leave us, Dennis. At once."

"What's the trouble?" He ignored Gertrude and came to Daphne. "Look at me. What have they been doing——" He stopped abruptly, said, "What's that mark on your cheek? It looks like——" and stopped again and whirled around suddenly toward Rowley. "I've been wanting to do this for some time," he said. Quite neatly and expertly his fist shot out to engage Rowley's chin. Rowley made a flailing, futile motion and slipped sidewise over a chair and subsided. Gertrude uttered a stifled scream, and

Dennis said to Daphne, "Get out of here," and Amelia opened the door. Amelia and—behind her—Jacob Wait.

There was a moment of rather abruptly arrested activity. Jacob Wait looked at them.

And Gertrude pulled the pink satin jacket modestly about her throat and reached a peak in a long career of inanities.

"Boys," said Gertrude, "will be boys. Do close the door, Amelia, there's a draft."

Amelia glanced at Rowley and said gently, "Hadn't you better do something about him?"

Wait came into the room and crossed to the chair. He gave Rowley one brief look and said, "He'll be all right. Anybody got anything to say?"

"What do you mean?" began Gertrude with false indignation. He cut her short.

"Oh, all right," he said. "I'll draw my own conclusions. Haviland, you can go downstairs. This young lady, too. You're both wanted."

He turned around and walked out of the room.

Amelia said, "See here, Gertrude, why have you called Dr Lonergan? It's possible you need spiritual admonition, but not at all like you, dear, to realize it."

"Rowley's hurt. Why don't you do something? He may be dying—he——"

Dennis said to Daphne, "I suppose we'd better go down. What were they doing to you?"

They left Amelia very scornfully bathing Rowley's face with cold water, and Gertrude scrambling out of bed to see to him herself.

Daphne told him briefly.

"Gertrude," said Dennis, "has the mind of a two-year-old. If you can call it mind." He frowned, though, and added, "Next time I'll kill Rowley. Well, come on, my sweet, and face the music. I think the band approaches."

"But all the same," said Daphne, "they can do just what they said they'd do. Gertrude and Rowley, I mean. Perhaps——"

He stopped and put his hands on her shoulders so hard it hurt and turned her around to face him. "Don't say it. Listen: granted Gertrude is screwy. At the same time it would have worked; I mean it really would have been a legal marriage. Well, we can't have that, my lamb. And what I say is, Rowley can go to hell. And I think he will," he concluded cheerfully. "Come along to the slaughter." He pulled her arm through his and stopped to salute the newel post. "We who are about to die——" he said flippantly.

"Dennis, don't——"

"Now, look here, Daph, you'll have to pull yourself together. Do you think I want to take a wife out into the wilds who's going to have hysterics every time she gets a little scared?" He wouldn't, however, meet her eyes directly. And he kept on chattering until they saw people—men, smoking, watching their descent from the hall below. He stopped talking then but walked her briskly along to the library. The door was closed, and he stopped and whispered, "Remember, if it comes to arrest I still have the thumbprint. The murderer's thumb-

print——— Oh, my God!" said Dennis. "All we lack
is a couple of false beards. Smile, my girl!"

"I—can't, Dennis."

"Well, then, don't smile," he said. "But for God's
sake don't walk into this room looking as if you'd the
guilt of the world on your shoulders. Honest, Daph,
anybody looking at you right now would say, 'There's
the murderer,' and call the case done. Now then,"
said Dennis. "Here we go!" and opened the door.

Jacob Wait was standing, leaning on a tall chair.
Two plain-clothes men were with him, the man called
Tillie and the one called Schmidt. A little in the background the policeman, Braley, waited with a thick
look of expectancy on his face.

"There you are," said Wait. "You can make the
arrest, Braley. The young lady."

Dennis' hand on Daphne's arm tightened as if an
open electric current had touched him.

"Oh, look here," cried Dennis. "You're wrong. It
isn't Miss Haviland you want."

"It's Miss Haviland we are arresting," said Wait
wearily. "Daphne Haviland. On a murder charge."

Dennis was as white as the paper in Jacob Wait's
hand.

"You're wrong," he said again. "What are your
grounds? What——"

Wait put up one mobile hand and pointed to the
table. "Turn on that light, Schmidt," he said. It was
a dark day, growing darker. The little pool of light
from the lamp fell directly on the table, and in the
center of it were two slippers. Two small gold kid

slippers, with high heels and little jeweled buckles. Two gold slippers that were stained and brown and had been very wet and a little muddy.

"Don't bother to deny them," said Wait. "You wore them the night Brewer was murdered. You were at the springhouse. We found the heelprints on the cement floor. Matched. We know when you wore the slippers. We know——"

"Stop! I'll tell you the truth. I was there, too. I——" That was Dennis.

Wait looked at his watch.

"All right," he said. "But hurry up. The inquest is set for tomorrow. The boys out there are waiting for news of the arrest. Want it for the night edition. However, you can say all you want to if you don't take too long."

"Dennis, don't talk. They can't arrest me for murder just because my slippers——"

"Oh," said Wait. "Go ahead, Braley."

Braley advanced toward Daphne.

Dennis cried, "I was with her, I tell you. We went to the springhouse together."

"You were not together then," said Wait. "She left the house alone."

Was it a guess? Or did he know? Had someone seen her? There was no way to know.

"Didn't you, Miss Haviland?" said Wait.

"I—— Yes," whispered Daphne. "I was alone."

"Why did you go to the springhouse?"

"Look here, Wait, do I understand that you are making a formal charge of murder?"

"You do."

"Then she has a right to a lawyer. And a right to refuse to talk."

"Certainly," said Wait. "Send her lawyer to the Wrexe County jail. We'll hold her there for the night. Call that maid, Schmidt, and tell her to get a coat and hat for the girl."

"All right," said Dennis. "You win. I was there at the springhouse. I was with Daphne. Ben Brewer was lying there dead. We didn't kill him."

"But you were going to leave together?"

"No, no," cried Daphne. "I came to tell him we couldn't. I——"

"So you killed Ben Brewer. And then dragged his body——"

"We didn't. Rowley Shore came, too. As we were standing there—he said, 'Let's move the body. People mustn't know it was murder—or suicide——' "

"Why?"

"On account of the company. Dennis didn't kill Ben—I was there first—I——"

"Daphne! Stop!" Dennis gave her a blazing look. "I'll tell you anything I know," he said, again turning to the detective.

"So Rowley Shore was in the thing, too?"

The detective looked somberly at Daphne. "Will he corroborate your story? . . . I thought not."

Dennis was fumbling in his pocket.

"Look here," he said. "It's true just as we've told you. I'll give all the details you want. But I do have some evidence leading to the real murderer. I do have——"

"We've all the evidence we need," said Jacob Wait.

"And at every turn it leads to you. Has led to you, Mr Haviland, from the beginning. Don't misunderstand me. Daphne Haviland is under arrest. She had plenty of motives: Brewer's fortune willed to her as Daphne Haviland—not as his wife; her quarrel with him; her affair with you. Her slippers—— Oh, yes, she's under arrest. And so are you. They'll call it conspiracy. Collusion. You'll both appear before the coroner's inquest and later, for I know what the verdict will be, before the grand jury. I know what that verdict will be, too," said Jacob Wait softly.

"All right," said Dennis. "I'll confess, and you know it, before I'll let Daphne be—be taken away. But I do have a piece of real evidence."

"What is it?"

He was going to give him the little piece of wood, of course. The brownish red lines of that thumbprint which he had counted on as a last resort. A life line.

She saw him, searching again through the same pockets. She saw the queer white look of doubt come over his face. She heard him say in a tight, flat voice, "It—it must be here. It——"

"Is it this thing you're looking for, Haviland?" said Wait. He put his hand out toward him. It held a small, ivory-colored piece of wood. "Because if it is, it's your own thumbprint. Either one of you, of course, can turn state's evidence. Later."

It was just about then that the thaw began. That unexpected, sudden thaw which set the eaves and window sills dripping. The eaves around the dark little springhouse dripped, too, stealthily, steadily in the darkness.

CHAPTER 19

I<small>T WAS</small> true, and Wait convinced him of it.

"It is your thumbprint. We already had a finger-print record. This was immediately identified."

"It can't be."

"It is," said Wait simply and put the sliver of wood in his pocket.

"How did you get it?" Dennis was still trying not to believe—fighting a conviction of its truth—thinking of that gray dawn when he might have destroyed it. Realizing it was possible—that he could have left that bloody thumbprint without knowing it. Remembering how—later—he had scrubbed his hands. Cursing his own blunder. "How did you get it?"

"I got it," said the plain-clothes man they called Tillie, with something like a smirk on his large face, "this morning. You were in the shower, I could hear it running. Your coat was over a chair in your room."

"The door was locked."

Tillinghouse looked faintly but honestly surprised, and Wait said:

"Never mind that. What about the bloodstain? If you've anything to say, say it."

"And you ought to be thankful for the chance he's

259

giving you," said the plain-clothes man. "This is certainly blood. Why and how——"

"You don't suppose I'd have kept it if I had had reason to think it was mine!"

Wait made a small, impatient gesture. "I'm giving you a chance to talk, Haviland. The case is pretty strong against you and Miss Haviland. You called a taxi, telling it to wait. You and she met at the springhouse. The taxi alone is enough to suggest that you had planned to go away. Together, perhaps, which gives a motive for murdering Brewer. There's the revolver—the wedding ring—the thumbprint. I can see you don't want to talk," said Jacob Wait simply. "But you can't make it much worse for yourselves, short of confessing. And you might make it better." His look said he didn't expect the latter. "As it is, I've got practically a jury-proof case against you— circumstantial, but sound. If, between you, you murdered Ben Brewer, there's no occasion for you to speak. You can save it for your defense. If you actually didn't murder him, you'll better your chances by telling anything you know about it. Everything."

Dennis strove to remember what points of law he knew.

"I'll tell you anything I know if I can talk to you alone," he said. "Will you send these men out of the room?"

"You mean you might make statements which would be difficult later to reconcile with whatever defense your lawyer undertakes."

"Will you send them away?"

"No." Wait leaned back in his chair and glanced

at his watch. "After all, Haviland, the girl's already arrested. There's already an airtight case against her; you can't make it much more incriminating, and you might make it less so. That is, if she actually didn't murder him," finished Wait in a voice that did not conceal innate skepticism. A pretty woman—trouble—murder.

"She did not murder Brewer," said Dennis and told him their story. Everything. As it happened.

It didn't take long. The room grew duskier with heavier shadows in the corners. Once the man called Tillie went to the window and pulled the curtain across it, for in spite of the sudden thaw the air was damp and chill. Good pneumonia weather, thought Tillie, and returned to sit with his elbows spread upon the table and to listen and watch.

Dennis talked swiftly. So long as he was telling it, he must make it convincing by telling the whole truth. Telling it all. There is nothing, after all, so powerful as the truth, and it was their only hope.

But unfortunately the truth was damning. As she listened, Daphne was overcome by a horrible sense of futility, for it sounded so hopelessly false and weak.

Dennis, she thought, felt it, too, as he neared the end.

The two plain-clothes men and the policeman watched and listened, with blank, altogether expressionless faces and eyes that revealed nothing. Wait did not even look at Dennis or at her, but, instead, broodingly at the slippers on the table.

He listened, however.

And he checked Dennis now and then to ask a few questions.

"What time did you go to the springhouse?"

"About twelve. I don't know exactly."

"And Miss Haviland reached the springhouse before you and waited there for you?"

"Yes," said Daphne.

"She didn't know he—Ben—was there at all," said Dennis hurriedly and went on.

Wait asked, too, about the taxi.

"You ordered it before you went upstairs?"

"Yes. At the little telephone closet under the stairs. No one could have heard me. I told the taxi driver to come to the gate about twelve and wait."

"You didn't hear the taxi leave about one o'clock when Shore left?"

"No. We were trying to arrange the body—getting it down the slope, I suppose, at about that time. It was a—job."

"And you and Miss Haviland were not going away together?"

"I had gone to tell him I couldn't," said Daphne. "When I talked to—to Ben—after dinner, while the others were in the drawing room seeing to the flowers, I—I realized I couldn't do it. I had come to tell Dennis. And to say good-by to him."

"Did you tell Brewer you planned to meet Haviland that night?"

"No."

"Did he know it?"

Dennis replied, "Gertrude—Mrs Shore—says he knew. Certainly someone knew."

He had not omitted telling Wait of the door which had closed silently while he and Daphne made that mad plan.

"Yes, yes," said Wait. "Someone. And someone who saw fit to keep that knowledge from me. Go on."

There was not much more to tell. The locked door when they returned to the house, the open window, the step which creaked on the stairway. He shot one liquid, dark glance at Daphne when Dennis told it.

And Daphne cried, "Oh, Dennis, it was Archie."

"Archie! How do you know?"

"Shore!" said Wait. "Did you see him?"

"No—no, he told me. Last night. He came to my room."

"When? For God's sake, Daphne, what do you mean? What happened?"

She told them. "And I thought he was the murderer," she finished. "I was sure of it; I was so—so *afraid* of him. But I was wrong, for it was only a little later that he was murdered." Queer, she thought in a kind of dull acquiescence, that she could talk of killing, of murder, could speculate upon things that had been only a few days ago completely removed from her little, governed orbit. Unspeakable things then—unreal, too, because one didn't look closely at them, because one never peered below newspaper headlines into the murky, ugly entanglements that, she knew now, had to be there.

There was a kind of small ruby glow in Wait's eyes.

Dennis started to speak, and the detective said, "Tell all that over again, Miss Haviland."

She did so.

"And almost immediately after he told you that, he was murdered?"

"I don't know how long afterward—not an hour." Daphne didn't see the implication, but Dennis did.

"She couldn't have done it," he cried hotly. "No woman could bring those tongs down with sufficient force——"

"Oh yes, she could have done it. And she could have gone to you at once and told you about it and you could have murdered him. Reason: he knew too much. And proposed to use what he knew."

"But his own presence on the stairway ought to be explained." Dennis was snatching at straws. "If he murdered Ben——"

"Shore was murdered, too," said Wait. "And by his own story was in the house at about that time." He stopped; added: "The time's wrong. If you reached the springhouse at twelve or near it, and the taxi left at one—well, go on, Haviland, what next? You went back to the springhouse."

And Dennis took up the false-sounding tale again, going on to the grisly business of moving and shifting that terrifically heavy and inert body. Of taking the dress shirt and waistcoat. "Rowley was to burn them," said Dennis. Of arranging that stage setting —clumsily, amateurishly, thinking of possible clues and of the seriousness of the thing they had done.

"You did it to protect the bridge company?"

"No," said Dennis.

"The girl, then. What about your revolver?"

"That's as I told you. I left it accidentally—I

mean without knowing it—in the springhouse. When I put on the flashlight and saw Ben there on the floor, I saw my revolver, too. Daphne didn't see it. I took it and managed to put it, finally, outside in the snow. I didn't think it would be found, the snow was so deep."

The snow so deep. Well, it wouldn't be deep much longer. If there were anything else it had masked, it would soon be unmasked. Exposed. Discovered.

Wait turned to Tillinghouse. "Have you got the other revolver here?"

"Huh?" said Tillinghouse, startled. "Oh, the other one. The one Shore had, you mean? No, it's at headquarters."

"It's the only other revolver you found?"

"Yes. Nobody else in the house had a revolver. This one was in Shore's room in town."

"I know." Wait's somber gaze shifted to Dennis again. "He had a room of sorts in town. No evidence of any kind in it, but there was this revolver. A thirty-two."

"Then my revolver——" cried Dennis, but Wait put up his hand.

"The bullet that killed Brewer and that we took from his body came from your revolver. And Shore's revolver was loaded but hadn't been fired for some time." He stopped and gave his attention to the rug at his feet. There was a short silence. They could hear the heavy drip and murmur of the thaw. Presently Wait turned to Daphne.

"You say you unlocked the door when you left the house that night?"

"Yes."

"I've looked at the night latch—it's a sort of double button arrangement—which one unlocks the door, upper or lower push button?"

Daphne thought back.

"I don't know. I just assumed it was locked and— and changed it."

"Why did you unlock it? Why, rather, did you mean to unlock it?"

"So I could return to the house, of course."

"Then you may really have locked it. That is, if someone had preceded you out that door and un- locked it. Or, if you actually unlocked it, someone may have come out after you and locked it again—as you found it later when you returned to the house. You, Haviland, did you change the night lock?"

"No. I didn't expect us to come back to the house. The taxi was waiting."

"Did you have your bag?"

"Yes. I got it back to my room—I think without Rowley seeing it."

"You two and Rowley Shore," said Wait. "Brewer —Archie Shore. All out the door near midnight. Good God, it looks as if you'd have needed traffic signals to keep from running over each other. You still say you saw nobody? Heard nothing?"

"Nobody," said Dennis. And Daphne said, "Ex- cept on the path to the springhouse. I thought there was somebody moving."

"Where?"

"I don't know. Not on the path ahead. Somewhere

among the firs. I couldn't tell exactly—the snow muffled sounds."

"But you did think you heard someone moving?"

"Yes."

They couldn't tell whether he believed the things they had said or not.

"What about the wedding ring?" he said.

Dennis said, feeling again, as they had both felt, that the whole story sounded false and rehearsed, "I don't know anything about the wedding ring."

"Rowley was to be best man," said Daphne. Her voice was small and tired. She twisted her hands together and strove to speak calmly, with clearness, so it would convince. "Ben had the ring before dinner. He showed it to me then. I think he gave it to Rowley to keep until the wedding. Because Rowley was to be best man. Ben was—oh, efficient. Orderly. It would have been like him to do it."

"He had the ring, then, after he'd dressed for dinner?"

"Yes."

"And he didn't have it when you found him in the springhouse?"

Dennis saw it was a trap and said quickly, "We didn't look in his pockets at all. We didn't think of it. There was nothing in his waistcoat pocket unless —well, Rowley was to dispose of it—he might have got it then."

"In fact," said Wait, letting a tinge of melancholy enter his voice—"in fact, you are both determined to put the possession of the ring upon Rowley. Why would he go out of his way to involve you, Haviland? Any particular source of enmity between you?"

"No."

"Oh," said Wait. "You just knock him down from sheer cousinly affection."

Dennis reddened. "That," he said, "Rowley deserved. Gertrude——" He swallowed and decided to tell that, too. "You see Gertrude—Mrs Shore—is not too—too——"

"Bright," said Wait. "I gathered that. Well, what's she trying to do? Make a match for sonny?"

"Yes," said Dennis.

"And proposes to do it by—well, how?"

"She knew we had planned to—to go away. Daphne and I. She said——"

"Said she'd tell if you didn't agree to her demands. Nice family," murmured Wait. "Murderers—extortionists——"

Dennis said, "It's the money——"

"Not entirely," observed Jacob Wait with truth. "After all, money can be anything you make it. Natural depravity is something else."

Dennis, who didn't expect the detective to moralize, especially with such simple sincerity, was surprised. It was a fleeting surprise, however. There was too much to think of that was more important.

"So you think Rowley Shore had the wedding ring and put it in Haviland's dress coat to frame him?" said the detective to Daphne.

"I thought so. Yes," said Daphne. "I don't know, of course, I didn't see him do it."

"You would accuse him of it, though, in order to shift the thing from Haviland?"

She didn't, curiously, feel anger. She replied honestly, "Yes, if I thought it was right. It's like Rowley somehow—and he didn't deny it when I told him what I thought. And he did come to the springhouse that night."

For a moment the detective did not speak. Tillinghouse shifted his position and sneezed, and the lamp made a bright circle on the table and around the stained gold slippers. Dennis looked at them and thought, in an underlayer of his mind, Why didn't I tell her to do something about her slippers? I cleaned my own shoes—I brushed the snow off my clothes—I looked over everything for fear there was blood—I ought to have told her.

Then Wait said obliquely, "Rowley's alibi is also his father's alibi." And while Dennis looked at him, struck by the possibilities of interpreting it, Wait turned to Schmidt.

"Get Mrs Shore down here. And young Shore."

Gertrude. Daphne's hopes, which had risen a little as the detective questioned and seemed to listen, sank again. Gertrude in a rage, Gertrude getting over one of her nervous headaches, Gertrude baffled and furious with opposition. Any evidence she could give would not be friendly. And suppose Rowley stuck to his story. Maintained that he had not gone to the springhouse. But he couldn't do that; surely her word and Dennis' would more than balance Rowley's; it would be at least two against one. But there was a thing called collusion. There was prejudice. And even if Rowley told the truth, as she knew it, it would still constitute the strongest evidence against her and against Dennis, for he had found them leaning over Ben—Ben so shortly dead.

She understood then; Dennis had been right to tell the whole story. For, since she had openly defied Gertrude and Rowley, it was only a question of time before Wait was told how deeply she and Dennis were involved in the thing. Dennis had been right to tell the story first; before Rowley could tell it. Before Gertrude could tell it.

She looked at Dennis, and he rose and came to her and put his hand upon her own.

"Look here, Haviland," said Wait. "You say you didn't look in Brewer's pockets at all?"

"I didn't."

"During that business of getting him down the path from the springhouse, do you think anything could have slipped from his pocket and become lost in the snow without your knowing it?"

"I suppose so. Yes. But it doesn't seem likely. After all, you don't carry much in the pockets of a dress coat. And things don't fall easily from trouser pockets. And it wasn't so—so rough-and-tumble as it sounds. We made a sort of hammock of my coat."

"And you stayed entirely on the path?"

"Yes."

"You were not at any time beyond the firs—out in the shrubbery beyond the path?"

"No. I'm certain of that."

"You went to Brewer's room once—twice?"

"Yes. Twice."

"You took nothing from the room?"

"A bathrobe. Nothing else."

"And you would be willing to swear that you took nothing from Brewer's room or from his pockets?"

"Certainly. I am ready to swear to everything I've said just now."

"Well," said Wait rather grimly, "you'll have a chance to."

"Is Miss—— Are we still under arrest?"

"Why not?"

"Because she didn't murder Ben. And I didn't," said Dennis. And held Daphne's hand tightly, but would not look at her. In the silence the drip of the thaw beat an inexpressibly dismal tattoo on the window sill.

Jacob Wait got up and went to the table and leaned against it, facing them with his hands in his pockets.

"Did Brewer know you were leaving together?"

"I don't know. Mrs Shore says he did."

"You don't know. See here, Haviland, suppose he did know. Suppose he went to the springhouse. Suppose he found you there and tried to stop you— what would you have done?"

"I don't know," said Dennis, white to the lips, and his eyes two sparks of light under those peaked black eyebrows.

"Your revolver was there. Suppose he had tried to use force. He was by all counts something of a bully. He was a big man—accustomed to having his own way—had an ugly temper. What would you have done, say, if he had laid hands on the girl? What," said Wait slowly, *did* you do?"

"Nothing like that happened." Dennis was white and taut. "Nothing like that happened. But if it had, it would have concerned only me. Not Daphne."

Wait made again that curiously impatient gesture with one of his small, mobile hands and shoved it back into his pocket.

"There was nothing to prevent your arriving at the springhouse before Miss Haviland—meeting Brewer—killing him——"

"Would I have left my revolver there to be found? Would I have kept the thumbprint? Would I——"

"I'm asking you," said Wait, and there was a flurry and commotion at the door, and Gertrude swept in, green silk and the pungent smell of cologne swirling around her, and Schmidt a cautious three feet behind. Braley, forgotten in the corner, stepped forward as if he felt he might be needed. For Gertrude was plainly in a rage. Her face was red, her light fine hair violently askew, and her eyes snapping dangerously.

"*You!*" she cried and waved the cologne-scented handkerchief and put it with exaggerated flourish to her brow. "*You*—dragging me from a bed of pain——"

Rowley entered. He, too, was angry, but you had to know him as Daphne and as Dennis knew him to perceive that anger, for he looked merely pale and sullen. There was a smudged reddish spot on his jaw. He said crossly, "Oh, do hush, Mother."

"Even my son," cried Gertrude, "turns against me," and kicked the train of her house gown aside and sat down in a swirl of green silk and glared at the detective and then at Dennis and Daphne. She looked as if she might unsheathe claws and spring at any instant, and Wait got down off the table and approached her rather wryly. Braley, somewhat reluctantly, followed his superior and stood behind him.

Wait said directly, "Did Brewer know that Miss Haviland and Dennis Haviland were to meet at the springhouse the night of his murder?"

It startled Gertrude. She floundered, darted one look at Rowley and another at Daphne. "Well, he— that is—yes. Yes," she said with a kind of defiance. "Yes, he knew it." She waved her handkerchief, and Wait stepped back a little away from the aura of cologne, and she cried, her eyes flashing and snapping as if venomous little tongues were leaping out, "He knew it. He went to stop them. And they killed him. Dennis and Daphne. Killed him."

"How do you know Brewer knew it?"

"How do I know?" cried Gertrude. "Why, because I told him."

CHAPTER 20

You told him?" said Wait, and Gertrude touched her brow with her handkerchief and said, "Certainly. I agreed that he ought to know. Somebody ought to know, anyway, and stop the elopement, and Ben was better able to do so than any of the rest of us." She shot a look at Daphne. "After all, Daphne, you ought to have decided sooner that you didn't want to marry Ben. Why, even the wedding presents had come. Or most of them," said Gertrude. "We hadn't heard anything from the Wileys yet. Or the Andersons. Funny, how lax people are growing."

Wait moved a step nearer, and Gertrude stopped abruptly. He said, "So you wanted your niece to marry Brewer?"

"Oh," said Gertrude. "Yes and no."

"You didn't want anything to happen to stop the wedding?"

"Well, I couldn't stand Ben Brewer. Never could. But, after all, we'd invited people to the wedding. You can't do things like that—I mean not have a wedding after——"

Rowley said savagely, "For God's sake, Mother——"

Wait said, "So you told Brewer—just what did you tell him?"

"Why, I told him that Daphne was in love with Dennis and was going to elope with him. He didn't seem to like it. In fact he went absolutely scarlet, and I thought he was going to—have a stroke or something. I told him not to worry, that girls often felt like that just before a wedding—reluctant, you know. But that I thought he ought to do something about it. He seemed to think so, too," said Gertrude. "At least, he swore quite a lot and went to the spring-house."

"Where were you at the time?"

"When I told him, you mean? Why, I went to his room. After we'd all gone upstairs that night. He—well, really he all but pushed me out of the way and went right downstairs. Didn't even stop for a coat, and it was snowing. However, I still think I was right."

"But you admitted you were glad he died."

"Certainly I was glad. Thankful he was out of the way. And as to the wedding, well, you can't have a wedding if anybody dies, everybody understands that. But an elopement is different. Besides," said Gertrude with an effect of candor, "if Daphne was going to marry one of the two men, I thought it was better to marry Ben, much as I hated him. At least, we would keep him in the family—him and the company."

"I see. Now, Mrs Shore, how did you know about this—elopement?"

"She saw us," said Dennis. "She listened at the library door. She——"

"I did no such thing," said Gertrude. "Johnny told me."

"Johnny!"

"Certainly. My brother."

Wait turned to Dennis slowly. "So that's why whoever it was that opened the library door didn't tell me. It had to be someone who wouldn't put that evidence against you in my hands. It——" He stopped short as if he'd been thinking aloud. "Get Haviland—John Haviland—down here," he said shortly to Schmidt, who went to the door, spoke to a policeman and came back into the room. Wait had turned again to Gertrude. "Johnny told you. Why?"

"Why!" cried Gertrude. "Because he was terribly upset, and who wouldn't be! Do you realize what Ben Brewer could have done to us if Daphne had done that to him?"

"But I—I wasn't going away. I knew when I'd had time to think that I couldn't—I couldn't——" Daphne's small voice stopped, and no one seemed to have heard it. Gertrude was talking on: ". . . what retaliation—what revenge he could have taken upon us. Not that Johnny talked much of that. Johnny isn't farsighted as I am. Johnny isn't at all like his father—he simply doesn't see a crisis when it's under his nose. He——"

"Suppose you tell me just what happened. From the beginning. When did your brother tell you this?"

"Oh, after we'd gone upstairs. The men came up only a little later, and Johnny came to me, and I saw

at once that he was worried. Somehow I can always
see these things. So I asked what was wrong. He
didn't want to tell me, but I insisted and got it out of
him. He said finally that he'd opened the library door,
not knowing even that Dennis had come back, and
that there was Dennis holding Daphne in his arms
and that Dennis was saying—oh, I don't know what
exactly; a lot of love-making, I suppose." Her eyes
snapped once viciously at Dennis and went back to
the detective. "Anyway, that he said, 'We'll meet at
the springhouse, then, at eleven-thirty. We'll go away
together' and that she needn't marry Ben, that he
wouldn't let her—all that. Johnny was very upset,
didn't know what to do, and just closed the door
quietly and went away. Of course, I was horrified. I
said, 'But you ought to stop it, Johnny. This is dreadful. All the wedding presents have come. They can't
elope.' He said he knew he ought to. But he wouldn't
go and just sat there and said finally that he wished
he had the force that Ben had. And of course I saw
that the thing to do was to go to Ben. So I did. Right
away."

"That was about what time?"

"I'm sure I don't know," said Gertrude helpfully.
"But Ben hadn't started to undress yet. I told him
and, as I told you, he was really quite enraged and
just flung himself past me and down the stairs. I decided perhaps it was best and went back to my room."

"Was Johnny there waiting for you?"

"Yes," said Gertrude. "Sitting there looking sort
of sick and chewing his mustache. Johnny's always
been a baby about things. I told him what I'd done

and that Ben had gone out to the springhouse. He was very upset—I think, really, he'd had too much to drink, and he's never had a head for liquor. Anyway, he walked up and down in my room for an hour or so."

"An hour?"

"Well, he didn't leave till after the clock struck twelve-thirty. I remember that. We kept talking. I thought I had taken the wisest course, and I thought things would be perfectly all right. Ben would meet them, bring Daphne back and kick Dennis out. Which I thought he richly deserved. Johnny kept saying he ought to go down, he didn't want Daphne to be worried. I kept telling him not to go—that it was best to let them settle things themselves. Of course," said Gertrude, "I never thought of Dennis' murdering Ben. But I must say it didn't seem a bad idea."

"Mother!" said Rowley. "You'll talk yourself into the electric chair yet."

"Oh no, I won't," said Gertrude. "I have an alibi. Johnny was there with me the whole time Ben was being murdered. Ben went down the stairway, and I went straight into my room, and Johnny was there and we talked at least an hour. I figured it out later. I didn't tell you," she said blandly to Jacob Wait, quite forgetting her rage in the satisfaction of taking the center of the stage, "because I'm naturally close-mouthed about things. Like my father."

"You didn't tell because you'd thought of a way to use what you knew," said Wait. "You may have an alibi, Mrs Shore, but you have deliberately obstructed the progress of the law, and I'm not sure you are not in the position of an accessory after the fact."

"A what?" said Gertrude.

Wait turned to Rowley. He said, "All right, now, Shore. Let's hear your story."

"You've heard it," began Rowley.

"I mean the real one. You came to the spring-house—helped Haviland move the body—let's have it in your own words."

"Oh," said Rowley, giving Daphne an ugly look, "so they've told! Well, did they tell that I found them actually leaning over the body of the man they'd just killed?"

"Yes," said Wait. "Why did you go to the spring-house?"

"To investigate the shot."

"What time was that?"

"I don't know exactly."

"Miss Haviland, you say it was close to twelve when you let yourself out the front door?"

"Yes."

"You would have heard the shot if it had been fired when you were outside?"

"Yes. I think so."

"Then, say, it was a little before twelve. You, Mrs Shore, sent Brewer to the springhouse at about——"

"*Sent* him to the springhouse!" cried Gertrude. "I did not. I merely told him——"

"You say he went downstairs a little before eleven-thirty?"

"I didn't say it," said Gertrude. "But I suppose it was about that time."

"It must have been about a quarter after twelve, even a little later, when you arrived at the spring-house, Shore. What were you doing in the mean-time?"

Rowley hesitated. He rubbed a hand over the bruise on his chin, looked at the rug at his feet thoughtfully and finally said, "I thought my father had done it."

"Why?"

"Because he said he was going to see Ben. Be-cause——"

"Don't say anything, Rowley," said his mother shrilly. "Be careful."

"Well," said Rowley sullenly, "it looks as if I'll be better off to tell the truth. I didn't kill Ben."

"You mean you are going to retract your story alto-gether?"

"Yes," said Rowley calmly. "Up to the point where I found Daphne and Dennis there in the springhouse. Yes."

And retract he did. With the utmost coolness.

The trouble was, it offered no loophole.

His father had been in his room when he came up-stairs after dinner, he told Wait. That was true. It was also true that he had said he had come to see Ben. He, Rowley, had tried to dissuade him, but Archie had laughed and said he had business with Ben.

"What kind of business?" asked Wait.

Rowley didn't know. But Archie had seemed pretty certain of himself and sort of—well, said Rowley, excited. He did say, added Rowley coolly, that he expected to have all the money he needed very soon.

"I got the impression that he had something on Ben," observed Rowley. "But he was worried, too. He told me things would be all right and went away. I offered to go downstairs with him—I wanted to see that he got out of the house without causing any trouble. But he wouldn't let me. He went away——"

"When?"

"Oh, as soon as he thought everybody had got safely out of the way—about eleven——" Rowley stopped as if it had begun to have a sinister sound, but said it, "Eleven-thirty. Perhaps ten minutes earlier. I don't just know."

"You didn't see him at all?" said Wait, turning to Gertrude.

She bridled. "Certainly not."

He went back to Rowley. "Then what?"

Well then, said Rowley, he had been sort of worried about it. Kept thinking of it and wondering what his father meant and if he would actually try to see Ben after all.

"Did he go to Brewer's room when he left your room?"

"No. I watched him go to the stairway. Anyway, Mother would have seen him if he'd gone to Ben's room."

"Do you think he had given up his plan to see Brewer?"

"I don't know. I thought so when he left, because he didn't stop at Ben's door, but instead went downstairs and I supposed out of the house. But after what happened I wasn't sure."

"Go on."

"Well, finally, I decided it was nothing I could help. The room was thick with smoke, and I put up a window and leaned out."

"Did you hear the shot?"

"Yes," said Rowley.

Wait's eyes glowed. His voice was suddenly rich and deep and vibrant. Yet he was angry, too; an anger which mingled in the strangest way with the pulse of excitement that swept hotly along his veins. But people never told; not when they knew themselves in danger. Not unless they were made to tell.

"What time was it?"

"I don't know. But it was before twelve. I know that. I didn't go down at once. I waited and listened. I—well, I thought my father had met Ben and———" He stopped and shrugged. "You can understand I wouldn't care to get mixed up in it."

"Didn't you want to know if———"

"If my father 'd been shot?" A curious kind of glaze came over Rowley's eyes. "Oh—yes. That is, I wondered what had happened. But my father was never exactly a credit to the family. Oh, of course, I finally decided I'd better go down, and did, and went to the springhouse because———"

"Why?"

"Because the shot seemed to come from that direction. And that's all. I saw nobody along the way. There was a light inside the springhouse, and Dennis and Daphne were there. I didn't know who'd killed Ben, but I did know that my father had said he was to see him———"

"So you——"

"So I thought we'd better cover things up if possible. I never liked Ben and didn't much care who killed him. But, after all, if my father had killed him——" He stopped and shrugged. "It would have been a mess," observed Rowley with a certain detachment.

"So when he came back you subscribed to his story?"

"Oh yes. It was a good story. He told it at the dinner table before I'd had a chance to talk to him alone, but also before your—equerries had got hold of me and questioned me."

Schmidt was heard to mutter resentfully at this point, and Wait said, "That's your third story, Shore. Why should we believe it?"

"I don't care whether you do or not," said Rowley. "But I didn't kill Ben."

"You had the chance to do it."

"You forget the—second murder," said Rowley. "There wasn't much love lost between my father and me, but I wouldn't murder him."

Father and son, thought Jacob Wait broodingly. He had a strong, instinctive regard for a blood tie; he gave it meaning and weight. Particularly the tie between a father and a son. Well, here it had no such weight. He need not allow for it, but it was with a deep reluctance that he put it aside. Father and son: a phrase from the Old Testament stirred deep down in his mind, ". . . his blood be upon him," and was replaced by another command about murder. He said abruptly to Braley, "You've searched his room?"

"Yes, sir."

"You didn't find them?"

"No, sir. I'd have told you at once——"

"Yes, I know. Where's Haviland?"

"Kellogg went to get him. Shall I go——"

"Yes. No. Wait." He walked to the door and turned there and looked deliberately at them—shifting his somber dark eyes from one to the other as if considering them, objectively and soberly. Weighing what they had said and had failed to say and had been driven to say. Fitting them into a new set of circumstances as he would fit chessmen into a new combination. And considering the next move in exactly the same way. Except that he didn't hate chessmen.

It was one of those moments which seem to pluck themselves out of time and space and remain suspended, unrelated to any dimension and thus mysterious and obscurely terrifying.

Gertrude's green silk rustled a little, and her florid face had gone pasty and flat. The regular little thud and beat of the melting snow falling on the window sill became louder and took on significance. As if it had a fateful and ominous meaning.

Ghostly fingers beating at a window sill.

And all around the house those invisible fingers beat their uneasy tattoo. Around the house and along a driveway where, by that time, the trees along it veiled themselves in mist and darkness. And beat, too, insistently around the shadowed springhouse where a man had died.

Policemen, wading ankle deep in slush, looked for

what they didn't expect to find. Some mysterious word went around to the hovering group of newspaper men. Two or three at a time, smoking and splattering through the slush, they went across the drive and got themselves into cars and went into the village, slithering and skidding, with headlights making eerie lanes of light through the wet dark, and not talking much. Only one or two made telephone calls to city editors. The rest of them straggled into Dutch John's and sat on high stools before the counter drinking hot coffee and listening to the blare of a radio and cursing the weather, the thaw, the case, themselves.

But none of them went into town. For they were due for a break, and they knew it, as you know when a storm is about to break. And Dutch John, secretly pleased, was taking bets. Would the thing break in time for the late edition of the evening papers? Or would it hold off until the early editions of the morning papers?

And back in the old house, sprawling among heavy, drooping shadows that were trees, they waited, there in the library, for what Wait intended to do.

The ghostly fingers beat drearily upon the sill. Gertrude moved, and her silk rustled thinly again.

Dennis put his hand upon Daphne's wrist; she was so little, sitting in the armchair beside him; so tired and white; so dazed with disaster. He'd have given anything in the world to keep her out of the thing— anything? he thought. Well, it might come to that. For he couldn't let her stand trial. He couldn't let her be dragged through all the horror and ugliness and hideous suspense of it. He began to go over in his mind the things he must tell the lawyers; conjecturing up possible ways and means. Johnny had been right, he thought suddenly, to suggest confessing. He looked down at Daphne's brown hair, and she looked up at him, her eyes oddly blank, as if she didn't see him. But she did, for she tried to smile, a small, tremulous attempt. How long ago was it that they had stood on the hearthrug—not five feet from where he stood now? Daphne in his arms. Promising anything he wanted her to promise. With the fire making glancing, mellow lights against the soft dusk, and in the corner the glimmer of silver and crystal —the wedding gifts. Winking sardonically. As if they knew how dreadfully those plans were to go awry.

Wait brought his wrist up and looked at the watch on it. "Do any of you have anything at all to add?"

It was chance that his eyes lingered on Gertrude— chance or the fact that she was flourishing her handkerchief again, dispelling clouds of scent.

"Uh," said Gertrude on a short breath. "Why— why, no! Certainly not. Nothing at all. I've told everything I know. And I have an alibi. Don't forget that, Mr Wait. And as for Rowley, he wouldn't have killed Archie. That's nonsense. If you would just stick to business, Mr Wait, and not go off on tangents, you might get on a bit faster. After all, you know, it's not pleasant—murders and hammers and —and even my nail polish gone. Everything in the house out of order. I think it's——"

"What's gone?"

"—preposterous," said Gertrude, refusing to be caught up so shortly. "Preposterous. What are the police for if not——"

"What did you say about nail polish?"

"Dear me," said Gertrude. "There's nothing so important about nail polish—just a little bottle of enamel——"

"Keep the girl and young Haviland under arrest," said Wait and walked out of the room.

There was, except for the murmur of the thaw, complete and utter silence following Wait's departure. Dennis stared at the empty doorway. Keys—a bottle of nail polish. Keys—there had been no keys in Ben's pockets—was that it? Was that why Wait had questioned them at length about what could have fallen or slipped or been taken from Ben's pockets?

But there was nothing that Wait couldn't have unlocked if he so pleased. Nothing except, perhaps, a safe-deposit box. And even that could be opened—if you were, as Wait could be, armed with proper credentials to unwind a bit of necessary red tape.

And nail polish. . . .

It was just then that a shadow filled the doorway, and Wait said, in a rich, deep voice, "Will you come with me, please, Mrs Shore? You, too, Shore."

"The car's at the door, sir," said Braley quickly before the detective could vanish again. "Shall I take Miss Haviland and Dennis Haviland to the station?"

Light flashed on something he held in his hand, and Daphne's gaze was suddenly riveted on it. It was a revolver, very big and clumsy, yet somehow he'd got it from its leather holster into his hand without any of them being aware of it. And it was inexpressibly real.

She didn't know what Wait said, for Gertrude's green silk was swishing angrily across the floor. And another policeman—a new one—had come into the room.

And Dennis had taken his hand away from her and was looking in the queerest way at the palm of it. As if he'd never seen it before.

"Oh, God," said Dennis and turned wildly to the policeman. "You've got to let me go," he said. *"Now——"*

CHAPTER 21

THEY wouldn't let him go, and Wait did not return, although there were, during the hour or so that followed, several murmured conferences at the door between Braley and someone Dennis could not see, of which Dennis caught only a few totally unrevealing words.

Except for those few interruptions, the policemen hardly moved and kept them there, evidently at Wait's order. They didn't know why. They didn't know whether or not Wait had considered their story of sufficient circumstance and weight to induce, at least, further investigation. And they couldn't talk—not with the two policemen there in the room, watching, listening.

There was no use talking, anyway, thought Daphne once, listening to the heavy murmur of the thaw in a kind of spell, as if she were drugged with weariness. They had done everything they could: there was nothing more to do. Even her hands felt heavy and without impulse.

Dennis came to her once or twice and stood beside her, so near she could have touched him, and she was gratefully conscious of his presence.

But Dennis was uneasy, restless, smoking rapidly one cigarette after another. Obsessed by a notion; revolving it; testing it; rejecting it. Then adopting it again because their need was so great. Once Daphne saw him staring at the palm of his hand again, opening and closing his hand, frowning, doubtful.

Time passed, and still they waited and did not know why. It must have been after eight when, after another of those whispered conferences at the door and without a word of explanation, they were taken through deserted halls and up the stairway where the third step creaked and into the old playroom, where, still without explanation, they were left.

"I'll send you something to eat," said Braley shortly. "Orders are for you to stay here."

He went away, the second policeman accompanying him, and a few minutes later Laing himself brought up a tray of sandwiches and coffee. He looked old and tired and could tell them nothing except that things were very quiet around the house.

"Surely the police haven't gone," cried Dennis.

"Oh no, sir," said Laing. "Though a police car left here some time ago. Left in a hurry. Can I do something for Miss Daphne?"

But there was nothing he could do, and he went away.

"I suppose," said Dennis, attacking the sandwiches, "we may as well make the best of it. Come along, Daph; eat something." He poured coffee for her and took it to her and knelt beside her suddenly and put his face against her hand. "Oh, my dear," he said, "it's all my fault. But I'll get you out of it. Somehow."

The withdrawal of the police was a relief, even if, as Dennis believed, they were on guard in the hall. Even if there was no possible way for them to escape —and the effort alone would be damning evidence against them.

But Dennis would not talk much. He paced up and down the worn old rug, smoking, frowning, thinking.

"We'll get a lawyer in the morning," he said once. 'And again, "Try to rest, my dear. Put your head back and see if you can't sleep a little." He paused behind her chair and smoothed her hair back from her face. He looked taut and white, and his eyes were deeply withdrawn and remote under those peaked black eyebrows. "I love you," he said unsteadily, shaken with love and with fear for her and for the thing his love had brought upon her. He must get her out of the sordid, filthy slime of the thing: he must save her from something else which he didn't dare, just then, to think about.

All the blame for the thing was his: all the blunders, all the stupidity.

It was an inexpressibly bitter and cruel thought.

He turned abruptly away.

"You're cold," he said. "I'll stir up the fire."

She leaned back in the chair and closed her eyes, letting that drugged feeling of weariness and lassitude possess her. She was only dimly conscious that he remained for a long time there at the mantel, staring rather oddly and intently at the old, battered coal scuttle with two limp cotton gloves for handling coal hanging across it.

Nobody came near the room. Only once did they hear any sound from below, and that was when the heavy front door closed with a dull, faraway thud.

The house had grown as silent as if it were deserted and forgotten in the moist darkness. Along the window sills those ghostly, chill fingers still beat steadily. Outside in the grounds the night was murmurous with the thaw and very dark.

It was late when there were footsteps along the hall and someone opened the door and came into the room. It was Johnny Haviland, and he stopped when he saw them and blinked and said, "What's all this? They say you are under arrest. Good God, why?"

"There's evidence enough," said Dennis grimly and told him briefly while Johnny stared, chewed his mustache, and went to hover over the fire. He looked cold and said he'd been out on the grounds.

"It's damn wet and cold. Police seem to have stopped everything. Wait's nowhere to be seen. One of the policemen came for me awhile ago in a tearing hurry, said Wait wanted me; when we got to the house, Wait didn't want me at all. Changed his mind or something. I said, 'Any objections to my taking a walk?' He said none at all, that an arrest had been made. But why aren't you under guard if you're arrested? There's not a policeman in sight."

"Fine chance we'd have of getting away!" said Dennis.

"Well," said Johnny, rubbing his hands over the fire, "you see, it would have been a good thing if you had let me confess. Would have been much better all round."

"It would have been all right for you to confess to the murder of Ben," said Dennis, leaning against the mantel. "Gertrude gave you an alibi for the time Ben was killed."

"Oh yes. Yes, of course," said Johnny. "I counted on that."

"You——"

"Certainly. I counted on it. If worst came to worst, that is. But I wasn't going to let Wait know that you and Daphne were at the springhouse or that Ben knew of it. Good God, of course not. Certainly not. If I didn't have to in self-defense. You don't know how bitterly I've regretted telling Gertrude. You don't know—— God, it's cold."

He was hovering closely over the fire. Daphne, still in the clutches of that strange lassitude, had leaned back again, her head on the cushions behind her, her eyes closed. There was nothing Johnny could do. Nothing anybody could do. The case was too strong.

Their voices hummed quietly and distantly, with now and then a word or phrase emerging. Lawyers—money—evidence—Archie—tongs—nail polish . . .

"What about nail polish?"

"It's only an idea."

The voices merged again, blurring together until she heard Dennis say clearly:

". . . a nasty trick of pinching one's hand."

"*Hand!*"

"Why, yes. I was thinking that if so slight a pres-

sure as one needed to grip a piece of coal made the
handle pinch as it did, then so heavy a grasp as would
be needed to—to kill a man must have left a mark of
some kind on the murderer's hand."

"A—— Oh, come, Dennis, that's fantastic."

"And you see, the nail polish acts a good deal as
collodion might act. It's a kind of lacquer or something, isn't it, Daphne? . . . *Daphne!*"

She brought herself back from a tremendous distance.

"Nail polish, Daphne. What's it made of?"

"I—— Why, I don't know, Dennis. Lacquer, I
think. Something that evaporates quickly——"

"My idea, you see," said Dennis. "Oh, it may
sound farfetched, but it struck me all at once, and I
think it struck Wait, too. My idea is that whoever
used the tongs and killed Archie had a badly pinched
or perhaps cut hand. And that the murderer may
have thought the nail polish would pull the edges of
the cut together. Would it do that, Daph?"

"Yes."

"And also serve to disguise the cut. It might not
have worked—but the whole point is, the murderer
might have thought it would work. Anyway, I'm sure
there would be a cut. I've known those tongs long
and well, and the damn things have given me many
a pinch."

"Oh, Dennis," said Johnny deprecatingly, "it's
such a—such a slim chance. I hate to discourage you,
but——"

"Yes. I suppose it is slim. But we are in a position

to grasp at slim chances. After all, you know, Johnny, it's—it's our lives at stake. Murder——"

Johnny fidgeted.

"Something will happen to help you," he said. "I wouldn't worry too much. No need to talk of it so desperately."

It was like Johnny.

"I've got to *make* something happen," said Dennis. He was leaning on the mantel, staring down at the place where the tongs usually stood against the coal scuttle. Staring at the cotton gloves hanging limply across the coal scuttle. Daphne's eyelids drooped and then flew open. For Dennis said in the strangest voice, "There were no fingerprints on the tongs."

"Uh!" said Johnny in a startled way. "Fingerprints! What do you mean? Certainly there were no fingerprints."

"No fingerprints," repeated Dennis and stared down at the coal scuttle. Daphne was all at once rigid, except for her heart, which for no tangible reason was leaping and fluttering in her throat.

It was very still. So still that Johnny, who never liked silences, began to wriggle and murmur something about the dampness and chill, the slush outside.

The windows, black and glittering, reflected them knowingly. Reflected Daphne's shining hair and the scarlet scarf she wore. Reflected Dennis' long, easy figure, so curiously still. So alert in its stillness. As if —which was absurd—as if he were stalking something.

"Funny," Johnny was saying all at once. "What's

happened to everybody? First time since the murder
the house hasn't been lousy with policemen. Where
do you suppose they are?"

Dennis still said nothing. And still did not move,
and there was no way for Daphne to know, as she
did know, that every nerve in his long, lean body was
strung tight and tense.

Johnny stopped rubbing his hands together and
looked at Dennis, his blue eyes very bright. Looked
and bobbed suddenly to his feet.

"You didn't fix the fire," he said. "You
didn't——" and slid across the few feet intervening
and clutched something and dropped it in the fire.

Dropped it in the fire, and Dennis sprang upon
him too late and snatched the flaming cotton gloves
out of the fire, and Johnny was struggling with him
while Dennis tried to push him back and to stamp
out the fire from the flaming gloves on the hearthrug. He flung Johnny away, but Johnny returned to
clutch again at Dennis. Daphne thought she
screamed, but she couldn't have, for no one came.
The struggling bodies of the two men made a confused, changing blur against the red fire. Nightmarish in its silence. All at once it stopped; Johnny was
panting, and everything in the whole world was terribly, horribly awry. For Dennis was saying, ". . .
there's blood on them. Blood on them."

And Johnny said pantingly, "You're too late.
They're burned. Burned. The only evidence——"

"The evidence that could have saved us. Your
daughter."

"Not my daughter," said Johnny, whispering

stertorously, and his eyes darting brightly here and
there. "And they'll let her off, anyway. She's pretty.
They never execute a pretty woman. She has more
chance than I would have."

The queer thing was that even then he was handsome and amiable, except that his eyes were so bright
and glassy.

"Wait, Johnny. Tell us how you did it. You were
so clever. You——"

Johnny gave an odd little giggle.

"You're trying to get me to talk. Well, I won't.
But I didn't kill Ben, and nobody can say I did."

"You're sending us to death in your place, John
Haviland. You can't do that. I'll——"

"You can't threaten me, Dennis. I'm perfectly
safe." He did not even look at Daphne. "You can't
prove any of this."

Dennis took a step forward, and Johnny humped
back toward the door, but Dennis did not follow
him; he bent instead to pick up the gloves—gloves
which fell in charred fragments under his touch.

"I'm perfectly safe," said Johnny again. "And I'm
going away." Except for his bright eyes and his
voice, which had grown high-pitched and feverish,
he looked as unruffled and bland as if he had an-
nounced a pleasure trip. "I've money. I've a little left
from it. Put away where nobody could find it. You'll
tell them; you'll try to set them on my trail, but I've
got it planned. I'll——" He stopped suddenly and
blinked. "But I don't need to leave at all, do I? That
would make them think I was guilty. You'll tell, but
you can't prove it, and I have an alibi. I have——"

The door opened so quietly that they did not hear it; they were only suddenly aware of its opening and that Wait was standing there near Johnny. Standing there and saying, "Come along, Haviland."

"You can't—I didn't——"

"We've found the keys. You led us to them. Come along."

"Father!" cried Daphne, remembering suddenly only the false face he'd showed her; she ran to Johnny. "Father!"

He thrust her roughly away.

"They killed Ben," he cried to Wait. "Dennis. Daphne. I didn't."

Wait caught his hand. Turned it palm upward to the light, showing a deep red cut with shiny, puckered edges from the lacquer which only partially concealed it. Johnny writhed and struggled, but Wait held him. Other men were in the room, too. Somebody had the gloves which had been burned. No—it was another pair of gloves, unburned; loose cotton gloves, coal-stained, pulled inside out. And there was a dark brown stain on the inside—a stain which they were fitting over the cut on Johnny's palm.

Out of the confusion came Wait's voice, suddenly rich and deep, "Give a man rope enough," he said, "and he'll hang himself. You've done it, Haviland."

"It's a trap," screamed Johnny, his eyes glittering. "It's a trap!"

"The trap," said Wait, "was when we let you show us tonight where the keys had been lost. We found them after you gave up."

Daphne was stifling—the room was sliding away

from her into darkness. "Come, Daph," said Dennis and took her away. So she could not hear—so she could not see . . .

They met Amelia in the hall, who went past them as if she did not see them and into the playroom. Rowley came, too, and Gertrude huddled in the hall, listening and trembling.

But Daphne did not hear.

"You are under arrest, Haviland. Charged with murder——"

"I didn't kill Ben. I have an alibi. I——"

"*Johnny!*" said Amelia and turned to Wait. "Tell me. Why are you arresting my brother?"

Wait looked at her thoughtfully. "Very well," he said. "A fund—an emergency fund—a secret contingency fund—was left by your father. Did you know of it?"

She thought for a moment and said, "No," clearly.

"He refers to it in his will, but in so general a way that it would have significance only to someone who knew or guessed of the fund."

"Where, in the will, Mr Wait?"

Wait quoted it quickly and accurately, as if he were reading it: " '. . . with the knowledge that in case of a future period of economic depression and financial need the said company and corporation is amply protected and duly provided for under the now existing agreements and provisions.' "

"Yes, I suppose it could mean that. I never thought of it, however; 'agreement,' yes, that might be interpreted to mean something definite and specific. Did you find such a fund, Mr Wait?"

"I found the record of it, but the fund no longer exists."

"No longer——"

"There is no fund," said Wait. "This evening, late, we found something we'd been looking for for some time. Since, in fact, a visit to the Loop office of the Haviland Bridge Company. Keys," said Wait, "that ought to have been in Brewer's pockets—along with the other things you expect to find in a man's pockets which were all there when the body was found. But no keys. And no keys could be found here or at his apartment. We found the keys tonight, sent a man into town with them, who telephoned to us after he had roused Brewer's senior secretary, who recognized one of the keys as possibly belonging to one of the small locked boxes in the company safe. There are a number of such boxes; Brewer himself —and your father before him, Miss Amelia—kept a record of the boxes, and one was for various confidential matters which passed on, when old Mr Haviland died, to the incoming president and manager. It wasn't exactly a secret, this box; still it was nothing even the various secretaries knew much about. Their duty was to put files and records into the big safe; to see it was locked at night and unlocked in the morning. Not to examine certain small boxes. In short," said Wait abruptly, "one of Brewer's keys unlocked one of these small boxes. In it was found a signed receipt for this fund which had been placed in another bank and under John Haviland's name. Old Mr Haviland's idea seems to have been to keep the fund a secret in order to prevent its use unless the company was in real and desperate need. And he trusted his son."

"It sounds very like my father. But I knew nothing of it."

"The fund is gone," said Wait. "And Ben Brewer demanded its return." He paused. Johnny did not move or speak. Wait went on, addressing Amelia: "Brewer threatened exposure——"

"I don't think he would have carried out such a threat, married to Daphne," said Amelia quickly.

"John Haviland must have thought that, too. But Brewer told her he would not be influenced by her. Probably he thought she knew of the missing fund."

"How much money was this? What happened to it? How was it invested? Where——"

"It was in bonds, originally. Bearer bonds. It's gone, though; doesn't exist. And couldn't be replaced without exposure, so Ben was murdered. Ben was murdered by one of three people."

"Who? Have you proof?"

"There's evidence on the key ring. Evidence for a jury, which needs, to be just, material evidence. Evidence for me and for the coroner and for the grand jury, who are not given by God any assurance that our own reading of the heart and guilty soul of a murderer is right. Material evidence. Where's the key ring, Schmidt? . . . Thank you."

It was a pigskin case, which unfolded. A row of keys dangled from a bright metal bar and made a small, hoarse clatter. And there was a dark smudge on the pigskin case.

"A fingerprint here," said Wait, pointing to the

metal bar. "A smudge of blood here. Soaked by the snow and slush, but blood, indicating it was taken from Brewer after the murder."

"Where did you find it?" said Amelia in a whisper.

"Behind the firs along the path to the springhouse. It slipped, I suppose, from the murderer's grasp when he was trying to descend a very slippery little decline—because someone—Daphne Haviland—was climbing the path, and the murderer heard footsteps and turned away to avoid her. He slipped, perhaps —perhaps flung out a hand to grasp at a low-hanging bow of fir—at any rate, he must have dropped the key case and could not find it in the snow. Was obliged at last to give up and—and return to the house without it."

"Whose fingerprint?"

"Archie Shore's."

"But Archie—Archie was killed!"

"Oh yes. Archie was killed. John Haviland killed him."

"Do you have proof?" said Amelia again, with stiff, purple lips.

Wait looked at the cotton gloves—the gloves for which he had substituted other gloves—now burned —to bait another trap; the gloves which had left no fingerprints on the tongs; the gloves which had a bloodstain on the inside corresponding to the position of the cut on Johnny's palm; the gloves Johnny had returned to the coal scuttle after Archie's murder and under their very eyes. He ought to have seen that, thought Wait; but he didn't. When Dennis had

put the coals on the fire that night there had been no
gloves; he had used his bare hands. And Johnny a
little later . . . He turned to Johnny.

"You killed Archie Shore because, when he killed
Brewer at your bidding——"

"No. No. That was Archie's doing. I didn't tell
him to do that. I didn't know he was going to kill
Ben. He promised to silence him. To——" The
voice broke and stopped, as if suddenly aware of the
things it was saying.

"Come, now, Haviland. We know you killed
Shore. We know your motive. Tell us just how and
why Brewer died."

"No. I mean, I don't know."

"You mean you won't tell. Shall we guess? And
prove our guess?"

"You can't."

"Oh, can't we! Listen: Archie came to you and
had no money and wanted some."

"No."

"You said you had none. He said, 'What about
this fund that was left in your care?' Archie had a
position in the company at the time the fund was set
aside in your care; somehow he knew of it. You said,
'There is no fund.' "

"No. No."

"He said, 'There must be some of it left. No matter what you've done, there's some left.' You told
him Brewer knew of it. You knew Archie Shore was
a thoroughgoing scoundrel; you knew if anybody
could get that receipt away from Brewer, could make
him let up on you, it was Archie."

"No."

"Archie, say, was to dig up something against Brewer; something he could hold over him. You didn't propose to look too closely into the manner and means Archie Shore was to use. You preferred not to. All you wanted was the result."

"This is all guesswork. You can't prove any of it."

"So Archie Shore set about the job. He thought you still had money; you let him think so and promised him money if he managed this affair with Brewer. And Archie failed, perhaps, to find any weapon he could use against Brewer—any threat, that is, for he resorted to another weapon. A revolver. You were to see that Brewer got to the springhouse to meet Archie, as he had planned, away from the house. You chanced upon the means of sending Brewer there. And instead of saying Dennis Haviland and the girl were to meet about midnight— when the house was still, they said—you told Gertrude definitely they were to meet at eleven-thirty. Because you hoped Archie would have finished with Brewer before they came."

"Not murder. Not murder."

"Archie killed Brewer. Because, perhaps, Brewer defied him. Because there was by chance another revolver in the springhouse, and Archie must have seen it and at the same time a way to throw any particle of blame from himself. He probably had his own revolver, which we later found in his room, but if so he did not need it. But after that murder Archie had you at his mercy. He told you so openly. He knew what you had done. He had keys to the private box.

He could wait his own time to secure the record of the fund that was entrusted to you. He'd lost the keys, but knew approximately where they were to be found, when he dared look for them. He must have told you. You searched for them tonight when the thaw came—and we watched, hidden, while you searched. And after you'd returned to the house, we found them because you showed us the way."

"You can't prove it. I admit nothing."

"You knew you had to kill Archie, for you were afraid to threaten Archie Shore in turn, because he was stronger than you; because he laughed at you."

"You can't prove any of this. This is all supposition."

"We can prove it all," said Wait. He had hoped for a confession, but he didn't really need it. It took time and pressure to secure confessions; people never confessed wholly just at first. It might even mean a long court battle.

"You murdered Shore. And you are morally responsible for the murder of Brewer, though unfortunately we can't charge you with it. Good God, man, we can prove all the facts—the record of the fund, the way you used it——"

"How was it used?" said Amelia.

"Stock market," Wait said shortly.

"Trying to make the fund bigger," said Amelia bleakly. "Trying to build a fortune for himself. Oh, Johnny, Johnny, if you hadn't been born such a coward—and such a selfish fool!" said Amelia bitterly.

In the quiet dining room beneath old Rowley

Haviland's portrait Dennis held Daphne tight in his arms. He didn't say any of the things he might with truth have said. Things they had all known but that Daphne had not admitted except perhaps to herself. That Johnny 'd been kind only when it cost him nothing. Because it was easy for him. That he'd used that facile charm to avoid anything that pressed upon him.

And that at the last—well, he would make her forget.

But Johnny, he thought once, holding her tight against him, Johnny would somehow manage to evade a trial as he had always evaded unpleasantness. He would deny everything. Funny, how crafty he was under that mild amiability. He'd sent Ben to the springhouse so neatly. Had provided himself with an alibi so deftly. Had he done so because in his heart he expected Archie to murder Ben?

He thought of Gertrude, too; had her accusations of himself and Daphne been pretense—because her knowledge was to be useful to her? She'd always feared Amelia, because Amelia was stronger than she, because Amelia feared nothing herself. Had Gertrude, actually, below all that storm of threats directed at Daphne and at himself—had she actually thought that Amelia had killed Ben?

Amelia opened the door and came in. "We'll have to go through it all, Dennis. Will you stand by the company? We shall need you."

Again involuntarily he looked up at the portrait. Met Rowley Haviland's eyes. A great company, its trade-mark all over the world. Founded, maintained, carried on by Havilands—there was no possible indecision.

"Yes, Aunt Amelia."

She was looking at the portrait, too. "Things like this happen," she said stiffly. "It's life—frailty, strength, vanity. Weakness, Dennis."

"He'll never stand trial," said Dennis. (And he was right, but in an unexpected way, for Johnny Haviland died of pneumonia before the week was out.)

Daphne stirred and lifted her face. Later, she thought, she would feel. Now she was inexpressibly thankful for the warmth and tenderness and strength of the arms that held her.

Dennis looked down, searching her eyes deeply, finding below the shadow of tragedy and pain the thing he sought.

"I'll come back," he said to Amelia. "But we're going away first. Together—Daphne and I—until we are ready to come back."

THE END